A CHRISTMAS KISS

"You remember, don't you?" Megan said, running a finger over the edge of a table where she stood a few steps from Neal.

"Yes. Wyndom House near London the Christmas of 1810. How old were you?"

"Sixteen."

"Gad, I was twenty-six. Had your father come upon us, he would have horsewhipped me, and deservedly so."

"You did not do anything so grievous as to warrant such a harsh punishment," Megan said. "Besides, I enjoyed it."

Their eyes met and held. Megan could hear his quickened breath, joining her own. He still stood directly beneath the mistletoe. Megan sensed he wanted to kiss her. And she wanted to kiss him more than she had ever wanted anything. She stepped to his side, lifted her head, and offered her mouth to him.

Neal caressed her flushed cheeks with his fingertips. The curve of her lips was deliciously sensual. This was not the wide-eyed schoolgirl of their first meeting, but a desirable woman.

He cupped her face in his hands and brought his lips over hers. She melted against him and responded to the heat of his mouth on hers. Her mouth opened to his own, and her hands ran through the thick hair that curled at his coat collar. The simmering passion intensified, and for a long time, neither could stop kissing the other . . .

—from "Beneath the Mistletoe" by Alice Holden

BOOK YOUR PLACE ON OUR WEBSITE AND MAKE THE READING CONNECTION!

We've created a customized website just for our very special readers, where you can get the inside scoop on everything that's going on with Zebra, Pinnacle and Kensington books.

When you come online, you'll have the exciting opportunity to:

- View covers of upcoming books
- Read sample chapters
- Learn about our future publishing schedule (listed by publication month *and author*)
- Find out when your favorite authors will be visiting a city near you
- Search for and order backlist books from our online catalog
- Check out author bios and background information
- Send e-mail to your favorite authors
- Meet the Kensington staff online
- Join us in weekly chats with authors, readers and other guests
- Get writing guidelines
- AND MUCH MORE!

Visit our website at
http://www.zebrabooks.com

UNDERNEATH THE MISTLETOE

**Monique Ellis
Paula Tanner Girard
Alice Holden**

Zebra Books
Kensington Publishing Corp.

http://www.zebrabooks.com

ZEBRA BOOKS are published by

Kensington Publishing Corp.
850 Third Avenue
New York, NY 10022

First Printing: December, 1998
10 9 8 7 6 5 4 3 2 1

Printed in the United States of America

CONTENTS

THE YEAR FATHER CHRISTMAS CAME CALLING

Monique Ellis

One:

Travelers

"They're here!"

Twenty-two-year-old Sarah Forte set the cup of goat's milk aside, smiling as she snugged the infant more securely in the crook of her arm.

"Of course they are. Martha and Mrs. Terwilliger haven't failed us yet. For them to do so would imply an impediment of astonishing proportions—perhaps Bonaparte slipping his chains again, and Lord Wellington deciding they were precisely the ones to organize his capture."

The children greeted her sally with delighted laughter. All was right with their world now. Christmas would come, even if it was a practical one having more to do with boots and scarves than toys and sweetmeats.

"Tim, please light the parlor fire. Charlie, if you'd greet our guests and see to their wraps? Patsy, straighten Bitsy's apron, wipe the soot from her nose, take Maria's basket in, and tell Mrs. Terwilliger I'll be just a moment."

The four pelted from the kitchen, for once acting like normal children. Even twelve-year-old Patsy was glowing—a welcome relief, for the girl had sunk into despair when the customary date of Gamonea Terwilliger's visit had passed.

Sarah spread a scrap of blanket on the table to change the infant's damp napkin. It whimpered, eyes lusterless. Too pale, too thin, too fretful. Well, she'd make it thrive. This wasn't the first stray of which she'd at first despaired; but of them all they had lost only Clara, and that had been to consumption so advanced that all her mother's skilled nursing could not suffice.

She banished the thought. If her mother hadn't counted the cost of sheltering Clara, then she mustn't either. Still, it had been a long twelve months since Mrs. Terwilliger and her abigail last stopped on their way north to visit friends during the holidays. There had been times when Sarah wondered where she'd find the fortitude to face another dawn, or another skirmish with the vicar who had replaced her father nine years before. Uncaring absentee landlords were curses to more than their tenants.

"Sarah, we're so sorry."

She turned at the halting words, attempting a smile that faded at the sight of Gamonea Terwilliger's expression. Behind her, Martha's customarily twinkling deep blue eyes brimmed with tears.

"Patsy told us," Martha quavered. "We were so very fond of your mother, both of us. How you must miss her."

Then their arms were around Sarah. She shuddered, determined she wouldn't spoil this yearly treat with open mourning. Life was to the living—especially to the young, and especially at this season.

"Mama is beyond pain and sorrow," she said. "That's what matters."

The strapping widow patted Sarah's shoulder, then stepped back, settling her myriad shawls as she examined the young woman through deep-set dark eyes.

"Janet was already dying when we stopped last Christmas, wasn't she," she said without a trace of doubt in her husky voice. "And hid it as best she could. We've wondered and worried all year, haven't we, Martha."

Martha nodded, bright ginger curls bobbing beneath her cap, as she took over for Sarah and secured the infant's napkin, pulled down its threadbare dress and wrapped the mite in its shawl, then picked it up with the look of one who needed to receive comfort as much as give it.

"And of course now you're trying to go on as if nothing's changed, and bearing all the burdens alone." Mrs. Terwilliger paused, then patted her abigail's plump shoulder, murmuring, "Time for brave faces, my dear. We'll mourn later."

Martha gave herself a shake and nodded. "And who have we here?" she cooed, settling the tiny head beneath her well-padded chin and patting the infant's back. "Such silky hair. Such big eyes. And such a delicate bubble! Isn't she a darling? Can't have more than a week or two to her credit."

"Have a care it doesn't bring up more than a bubble," said Mrs. Terwilliger. "Babes're fine and well if one enjoys mewling and noxious odors. Otherwise they're nothing but a bother. It's the lads I'm concerned about. Sprouting, and without enough yardage to their togs—or food for their bellies, I'll warrant. Well, the things we've brought'll help with those problems for a bit."

She stroked the infant's cheek, then leaped back at its thin wail. "Never was much good with the infantry until they were out of leading strings," she apologized. "How'd you acquire this one, Sarah?"

"Left on the doorstep a week ago." Sarah went to the dresser where she'd hidden a precious packet of tea and a small pot of gooseberry preserves. "The vicar wants me to send her to the foundling home in Chilford, but there's too much illness there. I've been giving her goat's milk. For all the squire's wife told me that's best when there's no wet nurse, she doesn't seem to care for it."

"Pity." Mrs. Terwilliger roamed the kitchen, poking in cupboards and prying in the larder, as had been her custom since she had appeared at their door covered with snow five years previously, seeking shelter following a carriage accident in a bitter storm. "You may well lose this one, just as you lost that girl two years ago. Pretty thing, had consumption. No hope for her, either."

"There's always hope. I couldn't go on if I didn't believe that."

The widow turned, assessing Sarah's appearance with a care that would've been the height of impertinence had the woman's dark eyes not been so filled with concern. Sarah flushed, and busied herself with preparations for their simple holiday tea.

"And how are you faring, my dear? Yourself, I mean. It wasn't easy before. Must be close to impossible with your mother gone. It seems to me there're more patches to that gown, and you've a careworn air I don't like."

"We manage. Patsy's a wonderful help."

"Naturally. She always has been, but soon you'll be placing her in service. Then you'll be in worse case than ever. Still only lectures and sermons from your vicar, I suppose, and not a scrap of assistance. That scoundrel deserves to have his cork drawn."

"I do have a basket of things from the charity box."

"Which Mr. Snead left for us to mend so he could give 'em to others," Patsy snapped from the doorway where she'd been listening unnoticed, several parcels in her arms. "Don't try to pretend different, Miss Sarah."

"Patsy, your manners," Sarah murmured.

The young girl put the parcels on the table, fetched a tray, and slammed it beside the parcels. "And he's chased Miss Sarah from her position at the parish school. It's true, Mrs. Terwilliger. Just ask if it's not."

"Well, Sarah?"

"We did the charity mending when Papa was alive. I've merely continued the custom at Mr. Snead's request as he has no wife to see to it."

"And you with greater need than any in the parish, taking in every ragamuffin who appears at your door? Scoundrel is too generous a term for that blackguard," Mrs. Terwilliger growled, then subsided at Martha's cautioning glance. "And your position at the school?"

"I requested a leave of absence when Mama was too ill for Patsy to see to alone, and another was hired in my place. It would be unfair to expect—"

"Fustian!"

"The little ones're being good about waiting," Patsy said

in the sudden silence, "but maybe you should talk about this later if you want 'em on their best behavior. Tim and Bitsy've only been with us going on a year. That isn't enough to've broken 'em of all their bad habits."

"There's nothing to discuss." Sarah retrieved the steeping pot from the hob and placed it on the tray as Patsy unwrapped the first of the widow's parcels, gasping over a seed cake and candied fruits. "I'll never abandon Papa's custom of taking in those who need assistance." She picked up the tray and nodded for the others to precede her. "We have a snug roof over our heads, thanks to the squire. The garden produces well most summers, and there's deadfall in the woods to keep us warm."

"It won't do," Mrs. Terwilliger muttered. "You want a husband, my dear."

"Who would have the dowerless daughter of a country vicar better known for his generous spirit than his deep pockets— except as an unpaid servant?" Sarah's smile was unforced. "I've always known I'd be a spinster, and am only too thankful I've no need to answer to some self-important fool for my every action."

The Blue Boar was filled with holiday travelers, the taproom ringing with song, laughter, and conversation. Edwin Pallister had expected that, and reserved the inn's best accommodations. Unfortunately, the twenty-eight-year-old viscount hadn't bargained on his sense of compunction, or an elderly gentleman who had contracted a chill while waiting for assistance with a broken axle and was thus forced to stop at the first inn that offered.

"Of course he can have my bed, poor fellow," Pallister said as his valet protested at his side. "Send up a bowl of your best punch with my compliments. Put plenty of lemon in it. Best thing I know of to ward off the ague. I'd be grateful if you'd call me plain Mr. Pallister, though. I've no desire to be stared at as if I were a two-headed toad. Is it a bargain, Mrs. Bowes?"

"But there's the crest on your carriage. Someone's sure to—"

"If worse comes to worst, say I'm delivering his lordship's Christmas gifts while he makes merry elsewhere."

He glanced around the taproom. Every table was taken.

"We might consider pressing on, my lord."

The expression on Cray's face would've had Pallister chuckling under better circumstances. Just so might the scrawny fellow regard an ill-cut waistcoat.

"There's nothing but hedgerow taverns between here and Chilford with the exception of the Drum in Chively, and nothing will induce me to stop there. Food's abominable. Besides, they're probably full up as well. You have your choice of taproom, kitchen, or stable, Cray. For myself, I'll risk the taproom."

Only two tables had space. At one a couple who had imbibed perhaps a trifle more than was consistent with decorum struggled to restrain a pair of boisterous children. As he watched, the boy's elbow connected with his father's tankard. The ensuing shrieks could be heard in the hall. Pallister shuddered.

At the other a well-looking man with a grizzled black crop and his plumpish female companion were deep in conversation as they consumed the pork pie and roast duck before them, their expressions troubled. That was better. The man's head lifted. Deep-set dark eyes assessed Pallister as keenly as he'd been assessing the fellow. Fair enough. After a moment the man gave a polite nod and returned to his dinner and his discussion.

"I'll admit to being a trifle peckish and more than a trifle chilled, Mrs. Bowes. If you'll inquire of that fellow in the green coat if he'd object to our company, I'd be most appreciative."

"That'd be William Fitzmorris. Irish." At a signal from his wife, Bowes scurried over to Fitzmorris, oozing persuasion. "See him about this time each year, just like yourself, my lo-*sir*. Actor, does special engagements. Woman's his wife. Never has much to say for herself, but pleasant enough. On their way to York for the holidays."

"Irish?" Cray sniffed. "I believe I'll accept the hospitality of your kitchen, Mrs. Bowes."

"What, above their company, Cray? They appear perfectly respectable."

"No Irishman was ever respectable, my lord, nor any actor, either."

Fitzmorris was studying him again, brows raised. Pallister gave the man a courteous nod. The journeyman actor cocked his head, lips moving. Mrs. Fitzmorris glanced over her shoulder. She smiled. Fitzmorris beamed.

"You're far too particular. Dining with an actor's sure to prove amusing"—Pallister grinned—"perhaps even educational."

"I've no desire for education of that sort. Neither should you, begging your pardon, my lord."

Pallister shrugged. If the high-in-the-instep valet he'd inherited from his father along with fortune and estates preferred a noisy kitchen to a merry taproom and a doubtless entertaining rogue, so be it.

Payton Bowes was nodding in his direction, one of the serving girls scurrying up with cutlery, another with a heavily laden tray.

"Buck up, old fellow," Pallister said, clapping Cray on the shoulder. "Dining with an actor'll hardly ruin me."

He settled his cuffs and strode across the room. If chance was going to turn the tedious trip from London to Monkton into an adventure, let it be a merry one. He was sick of Cray's sour looks and complaints.

William Fitzmorris proved every bit as entertaining as Pallister hoped. Roguish, possessing a felicity of expression that owed much, the fellow claimed, to a devotion to some minor Irish poet, as a raconteur he was a nonpareil, playing a hundred parts in turn. Within minutes Pallister felt as if they had been acquainted for years, and the very best of friends for most of them. As the hours passed, the splendid fellow held the company entranced as first one and then another turned to listen. Even the children hushed, eyes round, mouths open. Fitzmorris told tales of wonder and terror. He told jokes. He performed conjurer's tricks and sleights-of-hand that left even Pallister mystified.

When their conversation turned personal as sleepy travelers

straggled off to seek their beds, it seemed natural to confess he wasn't a simple mister, and was on his way to join his mother, sister, and brother-in-law in a carriage so crammed with gifts there was barely room for his man inside, and he was forced to ride on the box.

"No nieces or nephews, my lord?" Fitzmorris refilled Pallister's cup from the bowl of punch they had been sharing. "Must be a dreadful sorrow to 'em."

"Hardly." Pallister grinned, sipping his punch, as an army of serving girls swabbed tables and straightened chairs and benches. "There're five, actually—stepping stones from ten down to a few months. Scamps, every last one, but good-hearted. Not an empty attic in the lot. Course Richard Monkton's a downy one, for all he doesn't give the appearance of it. My sister's never lacked in that department, either."

"Not a lonely house, then." Fitzmorris was tilting his chair against the wall now, face hidden in the shadows. "Pity, though—you and your good lady not having a few of your own. Spoil your nieces and nephews dreadfully, I suppose, in consequence?"

"It's always a pleasure to play Father Christmas, but I've avoided parson's mousetrap so far. Can't bear the goose caps one generally encounters among the *ton*. For all she'd like to see me wed, my mother agrees. My sister was the only woman of sense in her come-out year. There hasn't been her like since."

"Self-consequential, though, I suppose," the Irishman sighed, refilling Pallister's cup. "Works her servants to the bone, and keeps her husband under the cat's paw. That sort always does, more's the pity. And forever hanging on your sleeve for essentials and begging fripperies for herself, I've no doubt, given all those children."

"Richard and Annabelle, hang on my sleeve?" Pallister broke into full-throated laughter. "Richard could buy and sell most of us and never miss a groat. As for Annabelle, she dotes on him, just as he dotes on her. Oh, they brangle on occasion. What couple doesn't? But neither rules the roost. And your own family?"

"We have none," Fitzmorris sighed, dark eyes clouding,

"unless you count a few courtesy nieces and nephews scattered about."

"Our only daughter died young," Mrs. Fitzmorris explained.

"I'm sorry." Trust him to put his foot in it—him, and more cups of punch than were good for him.

"Ah well, it was a long time ago, and many miles from here. Another lifetime, it seems." Mrs. Fitzmorris shook herself, then smiled. "As William says, we've the odd courtesy niece and nephew, and a chance to do a bit of good now and then while seeing to ourselves. That's not to be despised."

"No, it isn't. You're originally from Ireland?"

"That, too, was a lifetime ago," Fitzmorris rumbled in a tone that put *finis* to the topic. He stood and stretched, then patted his wife's plump shoulder. "Time for us to retire, my dear, as we must make an early start." He turned to Pallister as she gathered reticule and shawls, ginger curls bobbing. "It's been an honor and a pleasure, my lord."

"The pleasure and honor've been mine." Pallister rose and extended his hand. "May your courtesy nieces and nephews bring you joy, and sunlight gild your path."

"Now there's a blessing worthy of an Irishman." Fitzmorris gave Pallister's hand a hearty shake. "You're not a bad sort, my lord, though I wondered when you arrived with that scrawny badger. Keep you well, for I doubt we'll be passing this way again to wish you so."

"And the most joyous of Christmases, my lord," Mrs. Fitzmorris added with a twinkle in her deep blue eyes. "I've a notion it may be."

Edwin Pallister shifted on the settle, chilled to the bone. His greatcoat had fallen to the floor, the taproom fire long since gone out. The result was a stiff neck of gargantuan proportions. He groaned, wondering what had woken him, then retrieved his greatcoat and weighed the effort required to rise and make up the fire compared to the benefits. Both, he decided as he drifted off, would've been infinite. Where had he gotten such a head? Not even all he'd drunk accounted for it.

How many hours passed before he roused the second time he had no notion. This time there was no question of the reason.

He struggled to sit, blinked, and glanced around the taproom. Dawn had yet to poke thin fingers past the shutters. The hearth was cold, the garlands of holly and yew decorating the mantel more menacing than festive.

"Damnation," he muttered.

An icy taproom. A hard bench. He must've taken leave of his senses when he ceded his bedchamber, just as Cray had grumbled while settling himself for the night.

Pallister slung his greatcoat across his shoulders and pulled on his top boots, ignoring the opposite settle on which Cray still feigned sleep. It might, the viscount decided as he stumbled in the direction of the shrieks, have been amusing were it not so deuced uncomfortable.

Peg Bowes stood in the middle of the kitchen, hair straggling from beneath her nightcap. The inside staff huddled by the door to the larder and storerooms, their wails more subdued than their employer's, as was fitting. Bowes stormed in. He looked at his wife. He looked at Pallister. He shrugged. Then he seized a pan and banged it on the table.

"It's not just the larder," he announced in the sudden silence. "Their carriage's gone, and yours emptied, my lord. Seems Fitzmorris provided the lads with a bottle in honor of the season. Not a drop left, and themselves with heads to be pitied."

Mrs. Bowes collapsed on a bench, keening as she rocked back and forth.

"Isn't bad as it might be." Bowes placed a heavy hand on her shoulder. "They left a ham and apples and flour. I've sent one of the lads for eggs and butter. Breakfast's no problem if you'll stir your stumps. Then we'll consider what to do next."

A low moan of, "All my famous mince pies gone," greeted his words.

"Only two of 'em." Bowes pointed at the kitchen workers. "Build up the fires. Bring out what's left, and start using your heads 'stead of your lungs. I'll not have it said the Blue Boar couldn't overcome a minor inconvenience."

"Minor inconvenience?" his rib wailed. "I'll show you minor inconvenience!"

Bowes pulled his wife to her feet and bustled her toward the back stairs. "Hop to it," he snapped over his shoulder. "I expect bread rising when we return."

Pallister shook his head to clear it—a major error. Stifling a groan, he backed into the taproom and fumbled for his purse.

"And so much for respectable Irishmen, my lord," Cray said, voice like nails on slate, "and being entertained by actors."

"Stubble it. Not one word, or you'll be seeking a new position. I mean it this time."

"Unlikely, my lord. You could never replace me."

"With ease and joy."

He groped through his pockets. Nothing. Well, not entirely nothing. There was a crisply folded piece of paper in his waistcoat where there hadn't been one before. How the devil had the light-fingered Irishman managed that?

Pallister pulled out the note, strode over to the windows, flung open a shutter, and slit the seal. There was barely enough light for him to make out the convoluted script.

"My lord—" the damnable thing began. *"With apologies for any inconvenience, we've put your purse and goods to better use than you could have without our assistance. Please inform Mrs. Bowes the same is true of her larder.*

"If you wish to confirm this, travel toward Chively and stop at the cottage with a green door just to the south of the village. I commend its denizens to your charitable instincts and warm heart, knowing you will fail neither them nor us.

"Your humble servant, William T. Fitzmorris, Esq."

Pallister raised his head and roared. Words would come later. For now, noise sufficed.

His mother had chosen the sable trimming for her cloak and toque herself. It had taken him weeks to find perfectly matching pelts for the muff she wasn't expecting.

Freddy's rocking horse was a masterpiece of the art.

Margaret's and Catherine's dolls had come from Paris. The pearls clasped about their elegant necks were real.

Thomas's miniature steam engine was precisely to scale, and

it functioned. He'd even brought along some coal, knowing Thomas would appreciate the joke.

Annabelle's porcelain chocolate set had been designed for her particularly. It had taken months of listening and more months of searching to collect the contents of his carriage. As always, each gift bore a message of love.

He roared again and smashed his fist against the wall, in perfect accord with Mrs. Bowes, and not caring whom he woke. At last the words came.

"I will find the thieving blackguards," he ground out, nursing sore knuckles, "and I will kill them. Slowly. Cray, inform the kitchen I'll have what's to hand immediately, and the stableboys I'll be wanting their best hack in five minutes."

"Not in the coat and shirt you've slept in, my lord. A gentleman is known by his—"

"And with the stubble on my chin. At the moment I'm not a gentleman. I'm merely the dupe of the cleverest pair of rogues I've ever encountered. Step lively, or take yourself back to London—I don't care which."

"I will not have a gentleman in my care presenting such an appearance," Cray bristled, reaching for Pallister's greatcoat. "I'd never survive the shame, my lord."

He didn't know if it was his pounding head, or whether it was simply that enough had finally become enough. Pallister managed a good-humored smile as he drew back.

"You've never approved of me," he said. "You probably never approved of my father. Perhaps it won't surprise you to know neither of us ever particularly approved of you either, Cray. The time has come for a parting of the ways."

"You can't attend a Christmas houseparty without me," Cray sniffed. "Who would ensure your neckcloths were properly starched and ironed, my lord, or hand them to you and inform you when you'd achieved an acceptable result?"

"I'll hang my neckcloths on the back of a chair, and judge for myself whether I'm *point-device*. Good Lord, Cray—it's only a simple family party."

"There is no such thing," Cray intoned, nose in the air, "as a simple family party."

"That's where we differ. Did Fitzmorris empty your pockets as well?"

"Naturally not, my lord."

"Then you've the wherewithal to get yourself to London. Present my man of business an accounting. He'll reimburse you."

"You'll regret this, my lord," Cray muttered.

"Not likely."

Pallister spun on his heel and headed for the kitchen. That easily he was done with the self-consequential gadfly.

And then he laughed. Little as he intended it, Fitzmorris had done him an immense favor. Finally—an incident that made it possible to rid himself of a nuisance who had too often confused the positions of master and servant.

"But Father Christmas signed the letter," Bitsy protested, lower lip quivering.

Patsy placed a comforting arm around the six-year-old's shoulders. "There's no such thing as Father Chri—"

"Customarily Father Christmas doesn't mistake the houses where he leaves gifts," Sarah interrupted, "but this time I'm afraid he has. What could we possibly want with snuff or an elegant lady's gown?"

"You could sell everything, just like you did Mother Forte's pearls," Patsy suggested. "Then you could buy Mother Forte's pearls back from Squire Hadley."

"But I never—"

"We all know you did, so there's no sense pretending you didn't. I heard Mrs. Hadley scolding the vicar about it when I was fetching the baby's milk yesterday. Right in front of the church, they were. Mrs. Hadley told him you should have your position back. She even shook her fist at him."

"Oh, dear," Sarah murmured.

"Then Mr. Snead said Mother Forte's pearls'd made you vain and prideful, just like Mother Forte." Patsy's voice was flat. "He said it was a good thing you had to sell 'em. He said it'd be even better if you gave him the unclean proceeds—

that's what he called 'em, 'unclean.' He said it might be the saving of your sinful soul.''

Sarah clenched her jaws, arms tightening about Maria as she reproved herself for unseemly thoughts regarding Chively's current vicar. The infant whimpered. She sighed, loosened her grip and soothed the mite with murmured nonsense, gazing out the frost-forested window as dawn broke.

Heaven alone knew where strangers had learned of her odd household. Perhaps *ton* bucks on their way to visit friends, in their cups and determined to cut a caper? Gossip at the Drum, then, though why even the cruelest would find amusement in worsening her already precarious situation was beyond understanding.

"He said if you'd give us up, that'd be a good thing, too," Patsy droned behind her. "He said as how there was maybe some excuse when Mother Forte was alive on account of your father always took in strangers at Christmas, but now Mother Forte's dead it's a crime against God and man. Told her you can have your position back soon as the squire puts us in the workhouse.''

"I'd dearly love to see the squire try," Sarah muttered, resuming her pacing.

"Squire'd never! Isn't a soul in Chively likes Mr. Snead.''

"You shouldn't say such things, Patsy, or even think them," Sarah reproved, but her heart wasn't in it.

"I'm not sure it was Father Christmas.'' Nine-year-old Charlie glanced about from where the children sat, hands folded in their laps to keep them from temptation. "There's an awful lot.''

Indeed there was.

Sarah pulled her shawl higher, resettled tiny Maria on her shoulder, then paused by the table where luxuries unpacked from several hampers were piled. On top of a wheel of cheese lay a letter signed "Father Christmas," beside it a stack of bank notes. As if all this were not enough, an elaborate rocking horse stood by the fireplace. They had stacked the profusion of boxes tied with bright ribbons against the far wall.

Only two had been opened before Sarah called a halt to the

children's exuberance in the small hours. A gold snuff box set with pearls and sapphires and an enameled jar of snuff were on the mantel between sprigs of holly the children had gathered to decorate the parlor for Mrs. Terwilliger's visit. A lady's maroon velvet cloak with sable trim, a matching muff and toque, and a gown of deep rose merino had been returned to their nest of silver tissue.

Sarah averted her eyes. The contrast between the elegant garments and her much-mended gown of brown stuff and patched gray apron couldn't have been more startling, or more tempting. Maybe Mr. Snead had the right of it. Maybe she was vain—a lowering thought.

"Couldn't we at least have the pork pie for breakfast?" Charlie pleaded. "It's only half a one."

"And maybe ride the rocking horse?" Bitsy's eight-year-old brother chimed in.

"No, Tim. There's been a terrible mistake. Even you know that."

"I suppose so," he mumbled.

"We have to find the person to whom all this belongs. Just think how disappointed his poor children will be if Father Christmas fails them."

"Bet they aren't that poor," Charlie said, then hung his head. "I'm sorry," he whispered.

"You could never enjoy these things knowing they aren't yours."

"But Father Christmas's note," Bitsy pleaded. "He used our names. He even used yours, Miss Sarah."

"This particular Father Christmas doesn't exist, no matter what the note says." Sarah turned from the table, doing her best to ignore the bank notes. "It shouldn't take long to discover the owner. The hue and cry he'll raise'll make a fox hunt seem a lullaby. The only puzzle is why thieves considered this a safe place for their booty."

"I don't think we'd feel all that guilty. I know I wouldn't," Patsy said, then flushed at Sarah's reproving glance. "Being warm and full wouldn't be such a bad thing for once," she insisted. "I doubt God'd mind. He knows about being hungry."

"None of us is ever asked to bear more than we can."

"You're sure? Because I think you are. Mrs. Hadley said so to Mr. Snead yesterday, and then she said—"

For the second time that morning there was furious pounding at the door. The first had roused them from sleep, and been followed by the clatter of a carriage and team disappearing to the north. This time there was only pounding.

Sarah hushed Maria's wails, certain who had arrived on her doorstep, if not of his actual identity: the unwilling Father Christmas who owned the hoard they had moved from stoop to parlor by the light of the stars.

Pallister honored the slattern who came to the door with a hard-eyed glare. He'd been afraid he might have the wrong place. Fortunately—or unfortunately—he didn't.

Dull yellow hair straggling about pasty features, threadbare gown consisting of more patches than whole cloth, a whimpering babe in her arms and four more in stairsteps clutching her skirts—well, what had he expected?

"Good morning," she said.

"Is it? For me, perhaps. For you? I doubt it. Transportation's customary for a loaf of bread. I wonder what you and your confederates've earned by this night's business. Why the devil," he muttered as he brushed past her without waiting to be invited, "can't the lower orders control their concupiscence, or at least report to workhouses established for their benefit rather than turning beggar and thief?"

"I beg your pardon?" she said, closing the door against the frigid dawn.

"As well you might." He glanced around the flagstoned entry, scowling. No smell of food. No heat. No light. Dear God, what an imbroglio. "Well, where is it all? Don't bother to deny you have my property, because I know you do."

She pointed wordlessly to a doorway at the front of the cramped cottage.

"Transportation?" one of the brats whimpered.

"I doubt the gentleman is seriously considering such a

thing," the drab murmured. "If he is, we'll soon disabuse him of the notion."

"Don't count on it."

He strode into what must be the parlor. It was part and parcel with the woman and her brats: undersized, shabby, and colorless. The sprigs of holly on the mantel gave him a turn. Apparently even the lowest held a celebration at the Christmas season, and spruced their sties in honor of it.

"I suggest you summon your husband from wherever he's nursing his doubtless sore head," he said more mildly, turning to face her. "He has a deal of explaining to do—not that I'll believe a word from his lying mouth."

"I have no husband, sir."

His brows soared. The mewling babe on the woman's shoulder had survived this vale of tears less than a fortnight if Annabelle's were anything to judge by, its mother too frail and slight, and far too young, for such an extended string. Well, she was needy enough, he'd grant Fitzmorris that.

"Your fellow thieves, then—where are they?" he snapped, enraged by customs that forced the woman to ply her trade. No doubt a case of like mother, like daughter, the tradition to be carried on by this latest litter in an endless string from the beginning of time to the end of it. "Taken to their heels, leaving you to bear the brunt?"

"You'll have to make do with me, I'm afraid." She followed him into the parlor, her pack trailing after. "Charlie, please see to the gentleman's mount. He appears to've forgotten it in his haste to be reunited with his property."

"I don't like the looks of him," the bigger of the ferret-faced runts snarled. "Didn't even shave hisself or brush his coat afore he come the way a toff would, and his boots is a disgrace."

The slut's smile was another surprise—warm, and filled with humor. "A little courtesy please, Charlie," she said, throwing Pallister a cautioning look that put him in mind of narrow school benches and aching knuckles. "You know indulging in personalities isn't permitted."

"May talk like a swell, but there ain't no swell I ever heard of'd go about like that," the boy grumbled. "Probably isn't none of this is his."

"We have no more notion of this gentleman's circumstances than he does of ours. That he leaps to erroneous conclusions is no reason to emulate him."

The sly glance she sent Pallister had him choking. This encounter was developing all the characteristics of a low-bred farce. Next they would be holding him for ransom.

"Perhaps he's met with more disasters than having his property vanish in the middle of the night," she continued. "Besides, wouldn't you be a trifle put out if someone absconded with our woodpile?"

"There's a mort of difference. We had to find most of it and drag it home. Cove didn't lift a finger to get all them things, just opened his purse." The boy threw Pallister a glare that promised swift retribution should he take a step toward the tatterdemalion female or her brood.

"I'll be perfectly safe for a moment or two, Charlie," she insisted, rubbing the infant's back. "A touch of proper diction wouldn't be amiss, though."

The boy colored and stammered out an excuse regarding being driven beyond what he could bear. It was all Pallister could do to snort rather than breaking into the derisive laughter that tempted him.

"You know horses mustn't be left in the cold," the woman nattered. "I doubt this gentleman intends to take a whip to me just yet. He needs to ascertain everything's here, and make arrangements to cart it away. Besides, gentlemen delegate such fatiguing duties to others—even gentlemen who neither present the appearance of a gentleman nor speak in a gentlemanly manner."

The little vixen! Pallister's lips twitched at the look she gave him. Amusement brimmed in her eyes, for all concern lurked in their blue depths—as well it might. Well, he wasn't going to be taken in. She'd pay for what she'd done. So would they all.

"You don't go near Miss Sarah, you understand?" the lad

said, turning to face Pallister, hands balled into fists. "You do, and I'll draw your cork."

"Miss Sarah? Yes, I can see why little bas-beggars such as yourselves would call their mother that."

He stalked about the parlor, muttering at a chip on Freddy's horse, at his mother's new ensemble lying exposed to grubby fingers and prying eyes, at Monkton's jar of snuff and box on the mantel. The provender from the Blue Boar, displayed on a table, had his stomach growling. Damn, but this was an impossible situation. He was merely hungry. These thieving paupers had the look of skirting starvation by inches.

He spun as a small hand gripped his elbow.

"Patsy," the drudge said, "don't importune the gentleman. Perhaps you'd best fetch the vicar."

"And perhaps I'd best not."

"Well?" Pallister growled.

The look the saucy bit of muslin in training threw her mother was intriguingly adult. There was little of the child to any of these waifs. That was to be expected—though, unlike their faded mother, when perturbed their diction slipped past farm-yard and workhouse into the stews. What the devil had he stumbled on?

"Me and you've got to talk," the girl called Patsy hissed. "Now. Outside, where Miss Sarah can't hear. If she don't catch your drift, I do. You got it all wrong."

"And precisely what've I got wrong?"

"Outside," she insisted, tugging on his sleeve, "or I won't answer for Charlie. He's that put out with you. Got every right, too."

Pallister glanced about him. Nothing would grow legs or sprout wings.

"You stay away from that rocking horse," he snapped at the smaller boy. "It's not intended for the likes of you."

"I'm going to show himself where to put his horse." Patsy pulled Pallister toward the doorway as if accustomed to taking charge. No surprise, he decided. With her mother perpetually increasing and giving birth, someone had to seize the reins. "No need for Charlie to freeze. Then I'll fetch Mr. Snead.

Charlie, build up the kitchen fire and set the kettle to boil. Bitsy, change the linens in the baby's basket. Tim, fetch its milk from the keeper and put it to warm. Sounds like it's hungry again.''

Patsy retrieved a cloak from one of the pegs by the door. Then they were across the stoop, down the steps and on the path leading to the lane. He glanced back at the cottage hunkering among the bare-branched trees. The woman was at the window, the babe still nestled against her shoulder, watching them. He pretended not to notice.

''Miss Sarah ain't our mother.'' The girl glared at him, shivering as she clutched the cloak around her and stamped her feet in the crusted snow, her breath clouding in the frigid air. ''Her father was vicar here. That was afore me. I was six when Mother Forte took me in. My pa'd gone off. When my ma died I took to the road, begging at fairs. Miss Sarah'll probably find me a post come January.

''Charlie's been here two years. He'd been traveling with a sod what claimed to be a tinker and beat him black and blue when he wouldn't break into houses.

''We found Bitsy and Tim in a ditch. Tim was a climbing boy what bolted. He took Bitsy with him on account of their pa was going to sell her into a house.

''Somebody left the baby a week ago. Miss Sarah sold the squire Mother Forte's pearls to buy goat milk. Squire wanted to give her the money, but she told him she wasn't reduced to begging yet. Baby ain't thriving and'll likely die, which is probably a good thing, but Miss Sarah won't give up.''

''Dear God,'' he muttered, staring at his boots.

''Mother Forte, what was Miss Sarah's mother and the vicar's widow, has been dead these eleven months,'' the girl stormed on. ''Wouldn't be, 'cept they took in Clara what had consumption, and both of 'em died of it. Miss Sarah won't send us to the workhouse no matter what the vicar says or does, and he's said an' done a lot. Now, you got any other notions need dispelling, or can I go fetch him like Miss Sarah wants?''

''I suppose you've never heard of a gentleman called William Fitzmorris?''

"Only gentleman I know's Squire Hadley, an' that includes you and the vicar."

"I'm not as bad as you think," Pallister sighed. "Truly I'm not."

"Then prove it."

"I suspect I'm about to try. You've truly never encountered William Fitzmorris? Of course that might not be his name. Moderate height, considerable girth, grizzled hair in a crop. Colorful sort, full of tricks and tales. He could charm the oats from a starving horse. Irish, claims he's an actor. Wife's a quiet thing except when she talks of their child that died—which may be a fiction, of course. A plumpish woman, lots of curls."

"No one in these parts like that. You'll not summon the constable?"

"Summon a constable? If all is as you claim? I'd deserve to be bundled off to Bedlam were I fool enough to even consider it."

Patsy cocked her head, eyes narrowed in the growing light.

"You've no need to fear me so long as you're telling the truth, Patsy," he said. "Quite the opposite. My name's Edwin Pallister. I'm excessively trustworthy, and have considerable resources at my disposal—though I'd rather you not mention that to the others just yet. Fitzmorris realized it, though. More to the point, I suspect he knew precisely what he was about when he left my property in your safekeeping."

She hadn't heard a word of their exchange. Mouths had moved. Expressions altered. Then the arrogant stranger was holding out his hand. After a moment Patsy placed hers in it, nodded, pointed to the rear of the cottage, then scurried down the lane. He turned, looking directly at Sarah. Her breath caught in her throat as she blushed and backed away from the window, furious she'd permitted herself to be caught spying.

"You want I should bar the door?" Charlie said, edging toward the entry.

"To what purpose? He'd only break it down or return with Constable Morris, whichever suited his fancy." After a few minutes there was a courteous knock rather than furious pounding. "Let the gentleman in," Sarah said.

He appeared in the parlor doorway, silent in his many-caped greatcoat. If he'd been imposing in his fury, this mildness unnerved her far more. He could be a real danger—to the children as well as herself. The why of that she'd examine later. For now she'd defend them as best she could.

He smiled. Features that had been merely attractive became something that caused her heart to leap.

"Edwin Pallister at your service, Miss Forte," he said.

He bowed as if she were a duchess.

"Mr. Pallister." She curtseyed as if he were a king, clinging to Maria.

Then he picked Tim up and placed him on the horse. "Go ahead, rock," he ordered. "It's all right. Explore the entire world while you're at it. I understand there're glorious castles in Spain, and the mountains of Cathay're beyond compare."

"Tim, get down. Charlie, help him," she said.

"What, a spoilsport?" Edwin Pallister turned to face her, tone still mild for all his dark eyes taunted. "I'd never've suspected that of you."

"It's preferable not to become accustomed to luxuries beyond one's means."

"Spoken like a true ascetic."

"Tim already has a horse."

"Not like this'un." Charlie, after a glance at the stranger, put the reins in Tim's hands and closed them over the grips. "Hold on." He gave the horse's rump a push, then turned to Mr. Pallister. "His is a branch with a knob on the end. He can't ride it. He has to pretend."

"This one stays here. I'll find another for Freddy. End of discussion. Now, I wonder what we can find here for you," he said, turning to Bitsy. "Shall we look? Mrs. Fitzmorris must've showed you which package was yours before she left."

Sarah held her breath as he knelt and extended his hand. The moppet darted behind her, then peeped past her skirts, eyes wide.

"Who's Mrs. Fitzmorris?" Charlie asked.

"Mr. Fitzmorris's wife, of course." Mr. Pallister's smile hinted at a hunting wolf. "They know them both at the Blue Boar. Pass through at this time each year."

"I'm afraid we're unacquainted with anyone by that name," Sarah said.

"You're certain? Because that's who left all this. Of course you may know them by another name." He rose then, towering over her. "Irish actor, not overly tall, wears his hair in a crop. Wonderful raconteur, adept at sleight-of-hand and other tricks. Entertained the taproom last night."

"Coo-ee," Charlie whistled. "Wish we did."

"And she's a quiet, motherly sort."

"I'm sorry, but no. The only persons who'd even begin to fit your description are Squire Hadley and his wife, and they're too well known to pass themselves off as anyone but themselves."

" 'Sides, squire don't know the first thing about magic tricks," Charlie said.

"I don't like mysteries," Mr. Pallister snapped.

"Neither do I, but apparently we must endure this one."

"For a time, at least. I warn you however, Miss Forte: I'm determined to learn who they are. You may not be acquainted with them, but they're certainly acquainted with you." He extended his hand to Bitsy once more. "Now, young lady, shall we find a package that might contain something you'd like?"

"Oh, I don't think—"

Sarah flushed at the look he threw her.

"It's all right," he said. "My nieces and nephews lack for nothing. This lot lacks even the barest necessities. Humor me. I've a notion to play Father Christmas today."

Moments later Bitsy was kneeling on the floor, hands clasped behind her back, staring at the marvel. Even Sarah had to admit the doll was every moppet's dream, for all it wasn't the least use as a plaything.

"There are items of a more practical nature as well," Mr. Pallister murmured beside her. "Clothes, books, and such. We'll start, I believe, with what I'd intended for my mother. You could use a warm gown."

Sarah laughed. "You can't possibly mean that," she said, pointing to the mantua maker's box.

"I do, indeed."

"A sable muff for digging turnips? A fine merino gown for scrubbing floors? My dear sir, you've taken leave of your senses."

"At least you'd be warm."

"And the butt of scorn. Deservedly so. No, I'm fine as I am."

"What of the children?"

"A kind friend gave us some lengths of stuff, just as she does each year. They'll soon be better garbed than they have since last Christmas."

He was regarding her quizzically. After a moment he nodded. "There's one item, however, I believe you'd like. Oh, not for yourself. I wouldn't dream of it as you find cloak and gown beneath your touch. For this wee sprite."

He touched the worn cap tied beneath Maria's chin, then pulled a box from the stack in the corner and handed it to Sarah. "I'll take the babe, Miss Forte," he said. "A girl, isn't it? Yes, I know how to hold them. My sister insisted I learn."

Sarah watched as he adjusted the scrap of ancient coverlet in which Maria was wrapped, then nestled her amid the capes of his greatcoat.

"Warmer in here. You see I know what I'm about." He grinned. "Now, open it."

Her fingers trembled as she set the box on a stool and untied the green satin bow, trying not to snag it with her work-roughened hands.

"It may be a trifle big," he apologized. "Michael's a bit older, and very sturdy."

She lifted the lid, set it on the floor, unfolded the tissue, and gasped. The infant's gown was embroidered with butterflies and French knots from which daisy petals spread. Beneath was a shawl of finest wool, a band of daisies worked just above the deep fringe. A teething coral and silver rattle rested atop the whole.

"Oh," she whispered, not daring to touch. "Oh, how lovely. Fit for an angel."

"Patsy told me the baby hasn't been christened yet as your vicar refuses to perform the ceremony here, and you don't want to take her out in the cold. Perhaps it'll encourage her to get stronger, and then she can wear it for her christening come spring. All ladies love pretty things—even little ladies, my nieces inform me."

She nodded, unable to speak. What a whimsical turn of mind Mr. Pallister had. How delicately he put things. How easy it would be to sink into the web he was spinning without a thought to the consequences. And, how disastrous.

The box with its exquisite contents was gone, Maria in her arms.

"We'll wrap her in the shawl later so she'll have a notion what's expected," he said, "and give her the rattle to hold. Even the most delicate infant knows how to make a fist, and it strengthens them. Now, Charlie, let's find the woodpile, shall we? Patsy said the kitchen fire must be built up, and there's need of one in here as well."

"Not in the parlor." Sarah blushed at his raised brows. "There's not enough wood for both as we must make do with what deadfall the children can gather. It's been so cold almost nothing's left of what the squire sent over."

He retrieved a bank note from the stack on the table and thrust it at her.

"Fitzmorris retained a considerable fee for his services, but enough remains to ensure you shan't freeze. There'll be a fire in here as well. As for Father Christmas, I can't help but wonder where else he's spreading cheer at my expense—not that I grudge him his fun. I'm developing considerable respect for his acuity."

"And for precisely what sinful service is that blackguard paying you, Miss Forte?" Mr. Snead snarled from the parlor door.

"I'm sorry," she whispered to her accidental guest. "This may not be pleasant."

"Don't think a thing of it," Mr. Pallister murmured. "I'll settle him down soon enough."

Two:

Guests

"Good heavens, Neddy, where've you been?" Annabelle Monkton darted across the entry, arms outstretched. "Mama's beside herself. Couldn't you at least've sent word you were going to be delayed? We expected you for nuncheon, have put off dinner three times, and paced the floor every intervening minute!"

"I'm delighted to see you, too. You're positively blooming, Annabelle."

Edwin Pallister handed his hat and greatcoat to Webster as footmen trundled his trunks up the stairs, then seized his sister in his arms and whirled her across the floor.

"Careful, love," she giggled. "I've retained an extra stone or two since Michael's birth that I despair of shedding. Best set me down before you do yourself an injury."

He fetched them up beneath the cluster of mistletoe hanging from the largest chandelier, gave her plump cheek a kiss, and plucked a berry.

"You're radiant"—he grinned, stuffing it in his pocket—"so let's not hear another word about your *embonpoint*. It's infinitely fetching."

"All it 'fetches' is an endless stream of dressmakers, alas.

They're pleased, of course. Far more custom than they expected. So's the draper. Takes infinitely more to cover me these days.''

"But it covers you so elegantly.''

"While you,'' she reproved, drawing back and inspecting him from the top of his disheveled head to the tips of his dirty boots, "present a distinctly shabby appearance. Are you turning hermit? You look as if you've been rooting in woodpiles.''

"I have. No—later.'' He placed a forefinger on her lips.

"Is there a lady involved? There is, isn't there. I can see it in your eyes. Oh, Neddy,'' she sighed, "at last you've met someone you can tolerate for more than five minutes. How wonderful. Only a true lady could make you root in woodpiles.''

"Actually, it was an undersized scrap named Charlie. No— enough. There's nothing to tell. An inconvenience.'' He shrugged. "Will you accept a wild man complete with stubbled jaw, or shall I have a tray brought up? I could do with a bath, as I've spent a rather energetic day.''

"A tray? Dear heaven, no. Mama'd skin us both alive. You'll do just as you are if you run a brush through your hair.'' She glanced about the entry. "Where's Cray? I can't believe he permitted you to arrive in such a state.''

"He didn't. I've, ah, dispensed with his services. Permanently.''

Annabelle's bright blue eyes widened. Her mouth gaped. She consulted the watch pinned to her corsage.

"Let it be known throughout the Christian world,'' she said, "that John got it wrong. The Last Days began at precisely five-thirty on the evening of the seventeenth of December in the year of our Lord 1818—or slightly prior to that. I *knew* I heard trumpets yesterday, but Richard and Mama said it was only the children. Freddy'd found an old coach horn in the attic and was making the most dreadful noise. It sounded precisely as the end of the world should. Is Gabriel called Freddy by his friends, d'you think?''

She turned in a swirl of silken skirts. "Webster, tell Cook dinner can be served in half an hour, and send Gibbons up to lend my brother a hand. Just a good brushing—be sure you tell Gibbons that or dinner'll be ruined and Cook'll give notice.

That's a disaster I couldn't survive at this season. Far better an ill-tied neckcloth than no puddings. Oh—and select someone to see to his lordship while he's with us, please.''

"What, still riding roughshod over your household?" Pallister murmured as Webster vanished toward the back of the house. "Poor Richard! Is it any wonder I avoid parson's mousetrap given the example you two set?"

He left his sister laughing and took the stairs three at a time, wanting to revel in the sensation of well-being arriving at the manor always gave him. It wasn't just that the house was comfortable. The decorations in honor of the season—mistletoe in unlikely spots, yew and holly caught around banisters, pine boughs on mantels—even the whispered conferences were only symbols. It was as if the house itself were singing, though this time the melody held a touch of reproof.

He wanted to forget the cottage just to the south of Chively for this one evening. He couldn't. No matter where he glanced, something served to remind him of the pale young woman and her flock of abandoned waifs.

Pallister shivered, and turned down the corridor to the suite that was his whenever he visited.

He could order Pallinvale Court or the house in London spruced up for the holidays, but it wouldn't be the same. Both lacked a soul given his mother spent most of her time at the manor, claiming her daughter and grandchildren needed her. In actuality, he suspected she avoided London residence and country seat because she found them cold lacking his father's presence. Not surprising. He found them cold as well.

He set the problem aside as he strode through the empty sitting room and into the bedchamber. Gibbons was directing a pair of footmen in unpacking what had to be some of Monkton's neckcloths and his shaving gear on the dressing table. A copper can steamed on the hearth.

"Hallo, Gibbons," he said. "How've you been keeping yourself?"

"My lord." The fellow gave Pallister's appearance a practiced glance. "Oh, my—as bad as after a day's hunting, and only a quarter of an hour to rectify matters."

Pallister grinned and extended his arms scarecrow fashion. "Have at me," he said.

Dinner was a rollicking, en famille affair. Thomas, Margaret, Catherine, and Freddy arrived in the drawing room hard on Pallister's heels to join the adults—an honor accorded them the first night of his visits at his own insistence. This time, Pallister wished he hadn't begun the tradition.

He looked at their rosy faces and saw the woebegone eyes of Patsy, Charlie, Tim and Bitsy when he left the cottage after delaying his departure until there was doubt of his arriving at the manor before nightfall. His mother boasted of Michael's latest tricks, and he felt Maria's fragile form in his arms as he coaxed a few drops of milk past her lips. Monkton twitted Annabelle, and he heard Humphrey Snead sneering no viscount would stop at the cottage for any but the most nefarious reasons. The blockhead had actually accused him of being Maria's father, Miss Forte of somehow being her mother. Well, he'd disabused the nodcock of that notion swiftly enough.

"You've touched nothing on your plate, Edwin," Pallister's mother murmured beside him. "Are you unwell?"

He shook his head.

"What's wrong, then?"

"Preoccupied, I suppose."

"The children annoy you? You've cast them several black looks."

"No," he sighed, toying with his glass. "It's not their fault they've never experienced cold or hunger, and refuse food others would consider the greatest of treats. After all, they've never known anything different."

His gesture took in the fine silver and porcelain, the roaring fires at either end of the family dining parlor, the sideboard with its burden of tender meats and rich sauces, the pupton of hothouse fruits in the center of the table, the servants hovering at the ready.

"Neither have you, my dear."

"No, my education has been lacking as well."

"What's happened? Where've you been? What delayed you?"

"Good heavens, Mama—I can't possibly answer so many questions at once."

"When you were so late, I hoped you'd stopped by Greylock. Lady Grey hinted at a budding attachment to Suzanne."

"You require fresh informants." He raised a cautioning hand. "I danced attendance just as you requested, but only once. Before you ask, Miss Grey was undeniably the best of what I encountered this fall. At least there was neither duplicity nor meanness in her, and she bestowed her lisped confidences on any who would listen. Neither was there goodness, caring, or a scintilla of intelligence. There was, in fact, nothing but devotion to herself."

"Then what delayed you? It's barely three hours to the Blue Boar. Did you stop at Chiverton Park?"

"Why would I? Peminster's never there—though I'm going to have to speak to him about the scoundrel he has installed in Chively as vicar. No, I was made aware of an undersubscribed private charity," he said, nodding that his plate could be removed. "That about sums it up."

"And this undersubscribed charity put you in a foul temper?"

"An uncertain one, at least. Word of warning: All that's left of my foraging are a few things for Richard. The rest'll have to be replaced in Chilford."

"Whatever—"

"Enough, Mama," his brother-in-law interrupted with a sympathetic glance for Pallister. "You can grill Ned later regarding his semiannual hunt for a wife. What news from London? Annabelle wants to know—"

"Chits making their bows remain unrepentantly vapid. In consequence, I remain unrepentantly unbetrothed. Balls and routs remain a dead bore, most other entertainments ditto. Hoby remains the best boot maker, and I still prefer Weston's tailoring to Stultz's. In fact, everything remains more or less as usual. Don't tell me you expected change? The *ton* thrives on inertia."

"Dear heaven, what cynicism," his mother murmured as the children followed the exchange with wide eyes.

"Hardly, Mama—merely candor."

"No, there's a difference," his sister insisted. "Before you chuckled at the sameness. Now you're sneering at it, perhaps even at yourself."

"Are you sickening for something, Uncle Edwin?" Thomas regarded Pallister with concern. "When I'm sickening for something, Mama says I turn sour, and my eyes don't look right. Maybe Nurse should give you one of her fortifiers."

"How acute, Thomas," Pallister returned with a grin and a shudder, "though I doubt such a dramatic measure is necessary. A sound night's sleep should see me right with the world. It's merely I'm not in my first youth, and subject to being laid low by drawing water, chopping wood, cleaning grates, and building fires. You've a distinctly long head on those shoulders, though."

The boy flushed at the compliment, stuttering his thanks.

Lady Pallister's brows soared. "Is that what you've been about? Dear heaven!"

"For my sins."

"You must tell us. This promises to be entertaining."

"It's not. Now," he said, turning to Thomas, "how's school?"

He quizzed each niece and nephew. He became a wit in the Fitzmorris mold. He told tales. He made jokes. He proposed conundrums and riddles. It was a relief when Miss Breame arrived to take the children to bed, and Annabelle and his mother retired to oversee the process.

The covers were cleared. Jars of snuff, a canister of cigarillos, and decanters of brandy and port appeared. A look of understanding passed between the brothers-in-law as the last of the servants withdrew after building up the fires.

"In the suds?" Monkton poured himself a glass of port, then shoved the decanters within Pallister's reach.

"Not really, though I'm a bit short of the ready, and have my father's signet ring to ransom at the Blue Boar. I had to leave it as a pledge in lieu of paying my rather exorbitant shot on the spot. Mama didn't notice its absence tonight, but you may be sure she will tomorrow."

"Whatever you require, you need only ask.

"I appreciate it. Lacking your assistance, you'll be the only one with a token or two waiting for you Christmas morning, and I'll receive a drubbing from my mother that'll leave me a quivering schoolboy."

"What *have* you been about?" Monkton grinned.

"Playing Father Christmas. Let's leave it at that, shall we? It's an amusing tale in part, but until I know the end I'm unwilling to recount the beginning."

"Fair enough."

Monkton selected a cigarillo and lit it, then leaned back and waited. Pallister poured himself a glass of brandy, cradled it in his hands, swirled it, tested its aroma, and smiled.

"Good stuff," he said.

Monkton nodded, and waited.

"How well acquainted are you with your vicar?" Pallister said after a silence punctuated by the snap of logs on the twin hearths and the sough of the wind as it teased the corner of the building.

"You've met the Whitelys. She's a great favorite with Annabelle and the children. He's a considerable scholar more concerned with the spirit than the letter of God's word. Plays an excellent game of whist, too."

"How extensive is his acquaintance within his profession, would you say?"

"Wide. Those of his fellows I've met are as solid as he. Why?"

"And he's no gossip? Some are. I don't want a gossip."

"Then you're in luck."

Pallister nodded. "You've no objection if I call on him?"

"None at all, though I suspect it's not spiritual guidance you're seeking. Look here, old friend," Monkton said, leaning forward, "if there's any way in which I can assist or advise you—"

"Not yet, beyond filling my pockets and the use of a mount from your stable. If there is, I'll have no compunction turning to you. For the moment," Pallister said with a genuine grin, "holding my mother and sister at bay will suffice, if you'd be so kind?"

"I can see Annabelle placed her finger on the heart of the matter as usual. Yes, she told me her suspicions, and no, I won't ask. No one else's look-out until you want it to be. I'll even assure Annabelle she's all about in her head. With any luck she'll believe me so long as I don't make too great a point of it."

"He's in the woods again, watching."

Sarah Forte glanced up from the washtub. "Pretend you don't notice, Charlie. I won't have us become his lordship's latest entertainment."

She shivered and plunged her arms back in the water, trying not to consider the dark-haired nobleman or the probable reason for his repeated presence on the thickly wooded hill behind the cottage. And it was he, no question about that. Charlie had snuck through the trees two days before to confirm his identity—an adventure she hadn't had the heart to refuse the youthful would-be runner.

The sheets seemed heavier this morning, especially after a night spent pacing the floor with a fretful Maria nestled in her arms. Well, soon this last one would be on the line with the rest to freeze in the brisk wind, and she'd be able to retreat to the kitchen. At least his lordship couldn't see through solid walls. Better yet, neither could she.

"But why doesn't he come down? It's got to be cold up there."

"Never attempt to understand the aristocracy, Charlie." She sighed. "They're beyond comprehension. One has only to avoid them whenever possible, and hold one's tongue when it's not."

She kept her back to the tree-covered hill, the only indication Viscount Pallister's continued spying unnerved her. At least the children hadn't mentioned him when the vicar stopped by to pry and poke and carp—and appropriate funds, food, and goods.

She shuddered. It was difficult not to despise Humphrey

Snead. No, it was impossible—almost as impossible as it was to hold Lord Edwin Pallister in dislike, much as she knew that would be her safest course.

Distrust was another matter. No aristocrat spied on one such as she with any but reprehensible intentions.

"Maybe he's waiting to be invited."

She dragged the sheet from the water and plunged it back in. "Who, Charlie?"

"Lord Pallister."

"Then his lordship will have to wait until roses sprout from stones. Here—take this end while I wring out the rest. Whatever you do, don't let it trail on the ground."

She straightened, arching her back to ease the ache, then began to twist the water from the sodden linen, arms trembling with effort, fingers cramping in the cold.

"I insist you discipline that ill-regulated hussy," Mr. Snead squealed behind her.

Sarah whirled, slipped in the mud and tumbled to the ground, drenched and shivering, the wet sheet tangled around her shoulders, the emptied tub against her back. Charlie took to his heels up the hill at the sound of a roar that might've been a wild animal, but was more likely Lord Pallister.

"What are you doing here?" she gasped as she struggled to her feet. "You gave me such a turn. Now look what's happened."

"Come to collect the rocking horse and mannequin doll, and that infant's dress. Embroidered lawn isn't suitable for a nameless foundling."

"She wouldn't be nameless if only you'd christen her."

"I want them for Squire Hadley's grandchildren, but your oldest one chased me from the door with a poker."

"Good for Patsy," Sarah muttered. "And before you ask," she said more loudly, "no, you may have no more—not that there's much left following your raids."

"Raids? I've merely been distributing his lordship's largesse among my neediest parishioners, as is the duty of any vicar."

"Really? I wonder upon whose table the goose and mince pies found themselves last night."

She gave him a glance she made as insulting as she could. He babbled a protest. Her eyes hardened.

"Well, and why not? I have a guest stopping with me." He thrust out his chest. "No reason we shouldn't get some good of his lordship. A vicar is accustomed to such little attentions. Merely remedied an oversight on his part without troubling him about it. Perfectly proper. Now about the rocking horse and—"

"If you wish to ingratiate yourself with Squire Hadley by presenting his grandchildren with playthings, purchase them."

"Totally unnecessary when you've items unsuitable for you, but eminently suited to them—acquired through no effort of your own, may I add?"

Sarah turned on her heel, head high, and started for the kitchen door. Snead grabbed her arm, fingers pinching the flesh of her upper arm through the sodden fabric.

"My friend waits in the lane. Time is wasting."

"No!"

"You retain those items at the peril of your immortal soul."

"If necessary, I suspect my father will speak for me. I also suspect his voice will carry more weight than yours should you happen to be present rather than, ah, *elsewhere.*" She shivered in the bitter cold. "Now, if you'll release me, I'll go inside and change from these wet clothes before I catch my death."

"Better you die before worse happens, or else be brought to consciousness of your depravity through the penance of severe illness." He regarded her, eyes becoming as bland as milk. Then he smiled and eased his grip. "My dear Miss Forte, removing those dreadful objects was done for your good."

"Was it?"

"Common sense tells you that, just as it tells you that you mustn't persist in housing vagrants. It gives you the air of an eccentric."

"Then I shall be called an eccentric all my life."

"As for retaining his lordship's gifts, you risk being labeled a wanton and worse. It's no wonder you remain unwed, rather than being comfortably established with a husband to guide your stumbling steps."

"And who would have a dowerless orphan so long on the shelf she can't remember when she was at her last prayers?" Sarah snapped.

"A sensible man desirous of a well-ordered life and a well-run household. One who requires a frugal wife who knows her place and will keep to it, deferring to him in all things—a solution to the problem you presented your mother she and I often discussed."

Dear God—Mr. Snead meant himself. She could imagine her mother's reaction if there was a word of truth to his hints.

"You did?" she said, eyes wide. "I can't think of anyone in the neighborhood who matches that description. Even if I could, I'd never be the sort of wife such a gentleman would require."

She wrenched free, dashed into the house, slammed the kitchen door and slipped the bolt in place.

"Patsy," she gulped, "bar the front door and don't open it, no matter who knocks. Yes, that includes Mr. Snead and his scrawny guest."

Greatcoat collar turned up against the gusting wind, a scowl that threatened to become permanent furrowing his brow, Edwin Pallister returned to his sister's that night with barely enough time to change for dinner.

At least today the acquisitive vicar and his barely glimpsed crony had quitted the cottage as empty-handed as they had arrived. Of course according to Charlie there wasn't much left. Even the warm shawls intended for the manor's female servants had found their way into the vicar's gig, along with the gloves for the male staff and scarves for tenants and outdoor retainers. Charlie claimed one of the shawls now graced the shoulders of the squire's wife, and both vicar and sacristan were better gloved than ever before. Pallister had no reason to doubt him.

The growl he uttered as he stormed into his apartments would've done justice to a marauding lion. The footman waiting to assist him blanched.

"S'all right, Stephens." Pallister tore off coat and waistcoat as he strode into his bedchamber, then fumbled with his neck-cloth. "Just chilled to the bone and deuced irritated. No, not with you, nor anyone else here. You've everything set out? Good, for there's not much time. Damn and blast—I can't undo this thing. Clumsy as an ox."

"You appear distracted. Permit me, my lord."

"A solid block of ice, more like."

The footman's nimble fingers made quick work of untangling Pallister's neckcloth. Twenty minutes later he checked his reflection in the pier glass and nodded.

"I'll do," he said, still shivering. "No, don't fuss, Stephens. I'm not off to White's, just a pleasant evening in the bosom of my family."

Dinner was interminable, conversation with Monkton desultory at best, the hours spent at whist a bore. Pallister drank too much brandy, trumped his partner's aces, neglected to play high when he could take a trick, and generally behaved as if he'd never sat at a card table before. For a miracle, no one commented, either content to permit him his abstraction or unconcerned his play was less than stellar.

The arrival of the tea tray was a relief. He pretended fascination with Michael's new tooth as described by the rug-crawler's doting grandmama, made appropriate mumbles regarding Monkton's plans for acquiring a Watford hunter, and agreed with Annabelle the weather had been uncommonly cold. As soon as was decent, he made good his escape—or thought he did.

"Edwin?"

He paused at the base of the stairs and took a deep breath. He knew the tone.

"Yes, Mama?"

"I've been hoping for a private chat, but you've been gone before I rise each morning," the viscountess said, a hint of laughter in her voice, "and seeking your pillow at the first opportunity each evening." There was a hush of silken skirts behind him, then a hand on his arm. "It's early yet. Humor an old lady. I haven't been pleased by your air of preoccupation."

"Didn't realize it showed," he muttered.

"Your shopping expeditions haven't been fruitful, have they," she commiserated, guiding him up the stairs. "Indeed, so unfruitful that I find myself wondering if you've been to Chilford at all."

"Oh, I've been there, but only for the length of time it takes to get from one end of the town to the other. There're still four days 'til Christmas. Don't worry—I shan't disappoint the infantry."

His mother propelled him past his apartments, around a corner, and down another corridor to the sitting room of the suite that was her home during the majority of the year. A decanter of brandy sparkled among her favorite cordials. So—she'd been planning this ambuscade for some time.

"Help yourself," she said. "I'll have the raspberry, dear."

Then she sat by the fire and waited. Once he'd taken a seat across from her, the silence grew. And grew. And grew, just as it had when she'd caught him in a *bêtise* as a boy. Her patience, now as then, had in it a touch of the implacable. He shivered despite the warmth of the fire, rose, and began to pace. Finally he faced her and shrugged.

"You've guessed, of course—you always guess everything—though I'm not sure you'll be best pleased with your success this time."

His mother merely smiled.

"I've met the most unaccountable young woman."

"It was that, or you'd lost dreadfully at the tables and taken to the High Toby to regularize your finances. As there hasn't been a whisper regarding highwaymen in the district, I assumed it was the former."

"There hasn't? Well, there should've been," he returned with a bark of laughter. "I suppose you could more correctly say I was borrowed from so another could play Father Christmas, and force me to join in his games. It's discouraging to realize one's character is clear as crystal to clever scoundrels."

"As bad as that?"

"Worse. I was played for a fool, and cooperated from start to finish. The worst of it found me standing in front of a cottage at dawn, ready to thrash the entire household—which happens to consist of a vicar's orphaned daughter, a sickly foundling, and four undersized scraps of humanity the young woman's been sheltering. I won't insult you with my initial assumptions. Suffice it to say they did credit to neither my intelligence nor my powers of observation. Of course, it was devilish cold and devilish early, and I was devilish put out, but that doesn't excuse me.''

''Put out? From the sound of you,'' she chuckled, ''you were a bit more than that.''

''And still am. She hadn't let them touch the food. D'you know what sort of restraint that took? Gruel laced with wind-falls—that's what she tried to force on them. When there was gammon and eggs and pork pie, and heaven knows what all, available. Well, I put a stop to that foolishness. Probably the first decent meal those mites'd eaten in their lives, and that's not the worst of it. Yesterday the vicar walked off with the goose and what I assume were the mince pies, and the day before he—''

''I take it my gown and cape are now in the possession of the vicar's daughter?''

The amusement in his mother's voice had Pallister flushing like a moon calf. He fetched up at the windows overlooking the park and pulled aside the draperies. Moonlight glittered on old snow pocked with footprints, the paths like dark wounds.

''Possibly,'' he growled, ''but it's far more likely the current vicar of Chively has absconded with them unless Patsy had the foresight to hide 'em well.''

''Patsy being the daughter of the former vicar?''

''No, Patsy's the eldest of the infantry. Miss Forte wouldn't think to hide anything, innocent that she is. Here, tell me what you think of these.'' He pulled the notes from William Fitz-morris and ''Father Christmas'' from his coat pocket, strode over and gave them to her.

''The hands are identical,'' she said after a quick glance. ''Come, Edwin—if you're serious, you'd best tell me the whole. Otherwise I shan't be the least use.''

So he told her of the Blue Boar and the Fitzmorrises, his drugged night on the taproom settle, his emptied purse, the purloined gifts, the pilfered larder, the ride down a frozen country lane just before dawn, Sarah Forte and her urchins, Patsy's lecture, and Humphrey Snead. The choked sounds as he described the light-fingered actor and his ginger-haired handmaiden, the sniffs of indignation as the bumptious Snead made his appearance, were all Pallister could've wished. When he detailed Snead's causing the young woman to tumble in the mud that morning, his mother's shocked, if abbreviated, expletive made him smile despite himself.

"Charlie was up the hill on the instant," he confessed, "grabbing me by the ankles so I wouldn't tear down there and make bad worse. Fell full face in what's left of the snow. Deuced unpleasant. Drawing Snead's cork and darkening his daylights wouldn't've lightened Miss Forte's burdens, so Charlie had the right of it."

"Sounds as if you're the one's been planted a facer." She chuckled.

"Given the opportunity, and if I weren't a gentleman, I'd gladly thrash Sarah Forte for what she's putting herself through," he ground out, voice rising. "A prouder, more contrary, more obstinate young woman it's never been my fate to encounter. Or a more warm-hearted or courageous or devoted. But will she listen to reason? Oh, no, not she!"

"Goodness," his mother murmured, "a young woman with the temerity to say you nay? I'm amazed. No wonder you find this one intriguing."

"Intriguing? I don't know about that, but I do know she's deuced uncomfortable. Be warned: I intend to wed her if she'll have me. At least I'll never be bored."

"There's no need to rant. You're in earnest?"

"Never more so. You don't appear shocked. Perhaps you should. While the tale's amusing enough, the reality is that if I'm more fortunate than I deserve, the next Viscountess Pallister will be a congenitally unfashionable near pauper who's been running what amounts to a refuge for homeless children. Her hands're roughened by hard work. She's far too pale and thin. I doubt she has the least sense of style, and her conversation tends to laundry and deadfall, not literature and *on dits*."

"In other words, a young woman of fortitude, determination, and character. Given the light in your eyes when you speak of her, I couldn't ask for more. A good cream will soften roughened hands. Nothing could soften a roughened soul.

"I suspect," his mother continued, brows contracting, "that we'd best have the lot here for Christmas. Otherwise they're certain to have a poor time of it, given what you say of this Mr. Snead. Besides, lurking in the woods is hardly the act of a proper suitor. Someone's sure to notice you. The results could be unpleasant."

"You're serious? You are! I hardly dared suggest it, though of course it's what I want. Anything to get her away from that snake of a vicar. I'll go tomorrow," he said with a sigh of relief, "as soon as I've spoken with Annabelle and Richard."

"Most certainly not. Good heavens, Edwin, *think*. What would be the reaction if a strange gentleman whisked Miss Forte off to parts unknown? What if she refuses you? It could happen, you know. No, I'll issue the invitation. You, my love, shall accompany me as far as Chilford, and run those errands you've been neglecting since your arrival. After all, you've two families to provide for now, not just one."

When Pallister opened his mouth to protest, she raised her hand.

"You've no need to be concerned. I'll be unrelentingly persuasive. If I can't convince your young lady Monkton is preferable to a cramped cottage, then I deserve to be deposited posthaste in the family vault."

It had been another of "those" mornings: Charlie and Patsy vying for position, Tim and Bitsy squabbling, Maria with a worsening cough that had kept them up half the night. By morning the poor mite had barely the strength to swallow a few drops of goat milk, most of which she'd lost. At least the other children had full stomachs, thanks to Patsy's foresight in hiding some of the more practical items from the Blue Boar after Lord Pallister left the first night.

Maria now dozed in her basket by the kitchen fire while

Patsy swept the parlor and supervised Bitsy's dusting. Charlie and Tim were in the woods, supposedly gathering deadfall. Watching for his lordship to make his daily appearance, more like. She hadn't bothered to forbid the exercise. Not only would such an effort have been futile, it would've lent his lordship's spying more significance than it deserved.

Sarah shivered as she retrieved the next piece of charity mending. It was an infant's flannel gown. The temptation to claim it past repair was almost overwhelming. With a shudder she threaded a needle and began to stitch the torn side seam.

He'd soon tire of his games. Not Mr. Snead. Mr. Snead never tired of games. His lordship would. It lacked less than a week to Christmas. Festivities at Monkton would be mandated by generations of nursery parties. A favorite uncle, not in demand? And he would be a great favorite.

No, Charlie's wait in the woods was folly. Lord Pallister had made his last appearance, curiosity satisfied regarding the odd household upon which he'd happened.

She sighed as she set another series of stitches.

"Parlor's clean. We're going to lend Tim and Charlie a hand."

Sarah nodded without bothering to look up. "Mittens and scarves, Patsy. Don't stay too long. It's particularly cold this morning."

"We'll be gone long as it takes. Wood sent over by the squire's gone, but you won't tell him, and you'll be that angry if one of us does, and we can't buy any as you let Mr. Snead pocket most of what his lordship gave us."

She didn't dignify Patsy's reproof with a response, tempting though it was. The girl knew one didn't permit Mr. Snead anything. He appropriated and demanded and commanded. There would be penalties for yesterday's refusal. There were always penalties for flying in the face of what Mr. Snead wanted.

Frigid air blasted through the kitchen door. Maria whimpered and sneezed, then gave a choked cough. Sarah set aside the mending with another sigh as Patsy and Bitsy disappeared outdoors, closing the door behind them. She retrieved the infant from her basket and snuggled her deep within her shawl, much in the manner his lordship had used with the capes of his greatcoat.

"You mustn't become ill," she murmured. "Apothecaries are dear, and a physician's impossible. Why, oh, why won't you take more milk?"

Only a feeble mewl answered her.

A glance out the window revealed Patsy dashing up the hillside, Bitsy stumbling after. The silly child had taken her doll. So much for gathering wood.

She paced the floor, rubbing Maria's back and humming an ancient carol. The courteous knock on the cottage's front door was a welcome distraction. With a determined smile curving her lips, she went to see who it might be. Mrs. Terwilliger loomed on the stoop, Martha just behind her, their carriage waiting in the lane.

"Good heavens," Sarah said, smile broadening, "how wonderful! We've never seen you twice in one year. What's happened?"

"Received word a day beyond Chilford Mrs. Grant'd contracted a putrid sore throat, and we weren't to come," the widow burbled. "Sent a manservant to warn us off. We jaunted a bit, decided to go home, and've only stopped to see how you do, but we can't tarry long. Miles to go, and the sky looks like snow."

Mrs. Terwilliger headed for the chill parlor, Martha tripping after her as she glanced about.

"Perhaps we'd be more comfortable in the kitchen," Sarah said, closing the outer door. "There's a fire in there."

"Handsome toy." Mrs. Terwilliger pointed to the rocking horse. "How'd you come by it? And what are all these puzzles and that globe? I don't remember them, though I know we brought you the slates and chalk."

"It's an odd tale. The morning after you were here a gentleman—"

"Mrs. Terwilliger!" came a chorus of shouts from the back of the house. "Martha!"

"You'll tell me later," the widow said as the children burst into the parlor. "Well, and how are you doing? Haven't quite the same look of starvation you had when we were here before."

"Course we don't," Charlie caroled. "We've been eating ever so well, thanks to his lordship, though the vicar's been eating even better. Took the goose, and the mince pies, and a baron of beef and a brace of ducks, and all the shawls and the snuff—not that we'd any use for the snuff, but Patsy and Miss Sarah could've done with new shawls, and there was enough in one of 'em to make Bitsy a dress, and one for the baby, too. Took a mort of other things, but Patsy hid the ham and sausages the first night so he don't know about those. Now he wants Tim's horse and Bitsy's doll."

"I'd dearly love to draw that rotter's cork," Mrs. Terwilliger muttered, colored up at a stern look from Martha, and added, "if I weren't a fragile female, that is. Charlie, why don't you build up a fire in here—don't worry, Sarah, I'll give you a few shillings for wood—and we can have a comfortable coze. We want to hear about your adventures. It appears you've had 'em in plenty."

The well-kept cottage was just as Edwin had described: commodious enough to house a young woman, an infant, and four children if one wasn't particular regarding privacy. Smoke curled from both chimneys. A nondescript traveling carriage was being walked in the lane. A gig had just drawn up ahead of her, a pair of gentlemen garbed in black beside it on the rutted verge. What on earth?

"Cray?" she called as she descended from Edwin's carriage. "What are you doing here? I thought my son sent you back to London."

Back still to her, the smaller and slighter of the two climbed in the gig and gave the nag the office. Not Cray, then—though she'd have sworn it was. Such mincing steps. Such an air of being above his surroundings. Cray was worse than any fop determined to portray the illusion of refinement. So was this one.

The other was obviously the vicar whose cork Edwin would love to draw. He was presentable enough, she supposed, if one cared for corpulence, thick flaxen hair, hard gray eyes, and a heavy jaw sprouting a brassy stubble.

"Poor girl," she sighed as the man stalked up, chest puffed out beneath his cape.

"What business have you here?" he snapped, blocking the path.

She looked him up and down. "I've not come to relieve Miss Forte of a goose or some mince pies, if that's what concerns you. Now, if you'll be so good as to knock? And don't just walk in as if you own the place. You don't."

She swept around him, every inch a viscountess, strode to the stoop, then waited without bothering to give the insect a second look. It took him longer than she'd have preferred, and lowered him even further in her estimation. Then, when a young girl finally came to the door, the vicar attempted to enter without her. A genuine dolt. Did he think she'd scuttle away merely because her presence inconvenienced him?

"Patsy—how are you, my dear?" she called.

The girl peeped around the vicar, taking in the viscountess and the crested carriage in the lane. With as neat a series of steps as any debutante granted permission to indulge herself with a carefully selected partner at Almack's, she slid around the vicar.

"My lady," she said, dipping a perfect curtsy, "how kind of you to call. Miss Sarah'll be that glad to see you, and we've friends who've stopped by whom I know you'll like to meet. We're about to have tea. Won't you join us?"

This one was every bit as intelligent as Edwin claimed. The look they exchanged was as old as the hills. There was a damsel to protect and vermin to crush. Between them, they would manage it.

"What d'you think you're about," the vicar fumed. "I'm not acquainted with this female."

"It'd be a shocker if you were, Mr. Snead. My lady, may I present our vicar, Mr. Humphrey Snead, what got the living after Miss Sarah's father, what was vicar here afore him and much loved in the region, died?''

"I suppose you must in the interests of expediency," the viscountess murmured, according Snead the slightest of nods. "Mr. Snead, this is Lady Pallister, Viscount Pallister's mother."

He babbled excuses and civilities. She sailed forward, giving every indication she'd pass right through him if he didn't give way, and entered.

She took it all in at a glance: the spotless parlor, the fire that was a motley collection of twigs. A brown-haired lad of about nine—Charlie, from Edwin's descriptions—struggled with a cracked bellows, raising more smoke than flames. The scraps of holly clustered around a pair of pewter candlesticks on the mantel tore at her heart. The lad on Freddy's rocking horse had to be Tim; the carrot-topped moppet with the doll originally intended for Catherine, Bitsy.

The strapping, gray-haired female and her ginger-haired companion cuddling a sleeping infant were a puzzle, however.

"Hello, Tim. I'm Uncle Edwin's mother. Where are you off to, Paris or Rome? Ah—London! Of course—I should've known. One has to cross the Channel to reach the Continent, and then you'd be in a boat." Such sallies delighted her grandchildren. Heaven alone knew if these waifs were acquainted with the world of make-believe. "What a lovely doll, Bitsy," she forged on. "You must be extremely fond of it—almost as fond of it as it is of you."

The children grinned, Tim rocking all the harder, Bitsy bobbing an unsteady curtsy. Good enough.

"Here, you," Snead growled at the boy, "greet her ladyship properly."

"Leave the children be, Mr. Snead," she snapped as a pale young woman with a weary air appeared just outside the parlor, a wooden tray grasped in her reddened hands. "They're fine as they are."

"And what right do you have to be issuing orders in this house?" the vicar complained.

"More to the point, what right have you, Vicar? Oh, dear—how uncivil of me," she gasped, pretending not to notice Miss Forte, "but having been a child yourself, you appreciate one must never be stopped on the road to London. That could cause the worst sort of bad luck."

He turned first pale, then purple. "I'll be taking the horse," he spluttered, attempting to dodge around the viscountess. "Said it would lead to sloth and disrespect, and I was right. Taking the doll, too. Gives the girl a taste for luxuries she'll be unable to acquire in the future except by sinking into the deepest degradation a female can know."

"Good heavens—you can't be serious. Oh, I see you are. Well, Mr. Snead, the rocking horse is my son's. The same is true of the doll. I'm afraid I'll have to summon a constable if you filch a single item. There does seem to be a great deal missing," she said, gazing around the parlor. "I wonder where it can have gotten to?"

That did the trick. Ignoring Snead, still pretending she hadn't seen Sarah Forte, she perched on a stool beside the strangers' settle, her back to the door. "I'm Olivia Pallister. You're friends of Miss Forte's?"

"This is Mrs. Terwilliger, who's a widow, your ladyship," Patsy said, "and Martha. They've come to see us each Christmas for years."

"Try to help out a bit, don't you know, keep an eye on 'em," Mrs. Terwilliger said, clearly flustered. "Janet Forte showed us a real kindness once. That's Sarah's mother, who died last winter. Might've frozen t'death had she not taken us in. Dreadful storm. Middle of the night. Not everyone would've been so charitable. Tried to return the favor ever since."

"I see." The viscountess glanced from the widow's strong features to her large mittened hands, then to her companion's ginger curls. "Good heavens!" And then she laughed. Good heavens, indeed. Mrs. Terwilliger must be wishing her at Jericho. "I suspect in the end it will prove you've been their most excellent friends."

"I'd like to think there's a hope of that."

"I can assure you there is," the viscountess murmured with

a twinkle, "so long as misplaced pride doesn't get in the way. It's my responsibility to see it doesn't, and I've never failed in my responsibilities yet."

"It's always been Mrs. Terwilliger and Martha who've made Christmas happen for us," Patsy chimed in.

"Not like that, though," the widow chortled after exchanging a keen glance with Olivia Pallister. Her broad gesture included the horse and Bitsy's doll. "Practical stuff, most of it. Mittens and stockings, and a few lengths of goods. Not much imagination when it comes to the infantry, never having been blessed myself."

"You really must cease your inappropriate largesse in the future, madam," Mr. Snead snapped from across the room. "It only encourages Miss Forte in behavior of which no right-thinking person can approve."

"And what behavior might that be?" Lady Pallister demanded. "Surely you don't mean offering abandoned waifs a home?"

"Anyone wanting to make donations to my parish in honor of the season should deposit the items at the vicarage. I'll see everything's distributed to those in true need."

"But I don't," Mrs. Terwilliger roared. "What I want is to dr—"

"Hush!" Olivia Pallister grasped the widow's arm as she started to rise. "That wouldn't serve anyone, satisfying though it might be," she murmured too low for any but Mrs. Terwilliger and Martha to hear. "Think of the repercussions for poor Miss Forte."

Mrs. Terwilliger subsided, though the look she cast Mr. Snead from under lowered brows would've had any gentleman less certain of himself quaking. "He's a schoolyard bully," she muttered.

"No, he's a churchyard one. They're far worse."

And now, for the real purpose of her visit.

She rose and faced the young woman hovering speechless just outside the parlor. "Miss Forte?" she said. "I'm Olivia Pallister. My daughter and son-in-law deputized me to invite

you and your band to join us at Monkton for the holidays—
with their children's enthusiastic approval, I might add.''

"My lady,'' Sarah said, managing a curtsy despite the tray
that shook in her hands.

"By all that's wonderful!'' Mrs. Terwilliger murmured as
the children gasped. "Better than we dreamed possible.''

"The aristocracy isn't known for adherence to God's word,''
Snead snarled. "Take the children if you want, and good rid-
dance. Miss Forte remains where she's safe from sinful tempta-
tions.''

"Patsy, perhaps you'd best retrieve that tray before Miss
Forte drops it,'' the viscountess continued smoothly. "You are,
of course, included in the invitation,'' she said, turning to Mrs.
Terwilliger and Martha.

"Most gracious of you, but impossible,'' Mrs. Terwilliger
said, flushing. "It'd be da-deu-idiotish of Sarah not to accept
your invitation, though.''

"No!'' Snead roared. "There'll be riotous living, and punch,
and even the waltz!''

The infant let out a wail. Martha's attempts to comfort it
were as fruitless as they were desperate.

"We can't,'' Miss Forte said as Patsy rescued the tray and
set it on a table, "kind though it is of you to offer. We've no
proper clothes for a Christmas houseparty, and—''

"A family party only. Annabelle asked me to assure you
she can provide anything you or the children lack. As for Maria,
there's a plethora of baby things from which to choose.''

"Like to like,'' Snead thundered. "It isn't seemly! You'll
find yourself roasting in the fires of hell if you so much as
consider it.''

"Toasting before a decent fire for the first time in years,
more like,'' Mrs. Terwilliger muttered.

"Maria's ill and frail, my lady,'' the young woman said,
coming into the room. "While I'm grateful for your generous
offer, I daren't risk her in the cold.''

"We'll bundle her up, and heat some bricks. No problem
there, and Annabelle's nurse is the most skilled I've ever known.
She'll soon make Maria thrive.''

"That settles it," the widow said, rising. "You can't turn down the services of a superior nurse to help you bring the poppet around, Sarah. Your mother'd spin in her grave. No, I won't stand for any more foolishness. A private word with you, my lady, and then we'll be off. Fair distance to go today, you understand."

Three:

Gifts

Sarah huddled against the squabs as the short winter day faded. They had just passed between the stone pillars marking the Monkton property and started up the tree-lined drive, the barren branches stark against a leaden sky. Across from her Lady Pallister looked up and smiled, then returned her attention to Maria, whom she'd appropriated the moment they set off.

It had all happened too quickly: Mrs. Terwilliger's insistence she mustn't refuse the children such a treat or Maria the benefit of expert attention, Martha's more practical request to know if she might help make up their bundles. Still she'd resisted, torn between longing to go and dread of what might eventuate from such a sojourn. Then Mr. Snead had ordered her ladyship, Mrs. Terwilliger, and Martha from the cottage. That had been her undoing.

They were entering the graveled circle in front of the manor now, the team slowing from brisk trot to staid walk.

"Coo-ee!" Charlie whistled.

Coo-ee, indeed. Heavens, but the house was big. Terming it a manor was ludicrous. Palace would be more to the point.

"We've arrived, my dear," Lady Pallister murmured.

"Believe me, you've nothing to dread. Annabelle's the most welcoming of chits, and Richard affability itself."

The carriage wheels crunched to a halt. A groom unlatched the carriage door.

"If you'll hold Maria while I descend?"

And then Lady Pallister was on the gravel, arms outstretched. Sarah clung to the tiny mite for a moment, then handed her down. The children tumbled to the ground, stretching and shouting.

"Let them be," Lady Pallister said as another groom unloaded the rocking horse from the roof, then retrieved their bundles from the boot. "That's how children behave after sitting so long. Certainly you know that?"

Sarah nodded. The front door opened, painting the broad steps with light. Lady Pallister swept up to the portico and across the threshold, Sarah and the children trailing after, the grooms toting luggage such as had never been carried through those august doors before.

There was warmth, spicy aromas, organized bustle, a soaring ceiling, chandeliers whose lusters sparkled like diamonds, the polished marble floor reflecting their light. The immense entry seemed filled with servants.

"But they're my responsibility," Sarah protested as the pleasant-looking, angular governess disappeared with the children. "I'd thought perhaps a room for us in the servants' quarters, and pallets for the children."

"Dear me—is *that* what you comprehended by a visit to Monkton"—Lady Pallister chuckled—"because it certainly isn't what Annabelle intends."

"We aren't your usual sort of visitors."

"Which makes you all the more welcome. No-no, your waifs will be no trouble. Rather the contrary, as they'll entertain Annabelle's older four." She glanced about the entry. "Now, where can Nurse have got to? Ah, there you are."

A mustard pot of a woman bustled up, gown covered by a white apron.

"This is Maria." Lady Pallister's voice softened as she transferred the infant to the nurse's arms, then rearranged coverlet and shawls. "She appears to have a fever, and isn't thriving as one would wish. Miss Forte has been giving her goat's milk. She's just over a week old—isn't that right, Miss Forte?"

"A touch warm, perhaps," Nurse agreed, placing her cheek against Maria's. "We'll soon have that seen to, won't we, lovey?" she crooned. "A nice bath, a fresh napkin, and your supper's what you're needing. You're not to fret, miss," she said, turning to Sarah. "Doubt there's much wrong a cozy nursery and a few extra feedings won't set to rights. Eyes and complexion are clear, though her color's not good."

"You'll send for Dr. Leland?" Lady Pallister said. "His lordship is concerned. She's a dear little thing—such lovely features and perfectly arched brows, and all that dark silken hair—but so frail."

"But I can't afford a—"

"Hush!" Lady Pallister guided Sarah to an immense staircase. "I intend to play godmother to your band. Teething corals and prayer books are fine and well, but what Maria requires now is a physician of sense and a nurse who's seen many infants through these first difficult weeks."

They reached the head of the stairs and turned down a brightly lit corridor running the length of the house.

"We thought you'd be most comfortable across from me," Lady Pallister continued. "The nursery and schoolroom are above. There's a back stair of which I often avail myself. I'll take you up in the morning, but for now it's best both you and the children catch your breaths."

A door opened behind them as they turned into a narrower corridor. Lady Pallister hurried her on as if she hadn't heard the softly spoken, "Mama? Miss Forte?" Then she was opening a door on yet more light and warmth. The dumpling with jet curls and sparkling blue eyes couldn't possibly be Mrs. Monkton—except she had to be.

"So, here you are at last! Let me look at you." The young woman grinned, seizing Sarah's hands and spinning her across the room. "Come into the light."

Sarah had a vague impression of bowls of hothouse flowers, elegant hangings of watered silk, exquisite furnishings, a portrait over the mantel of a young boy more interested in the dogs at his feet than the merry girl at his side.

"And don't tell me I'm being impolite and overbearing, Mama, for I realize it full well," the young woman rattled on. "Miss Forte will forgive me. Everyone always does, for they know I mean nothing unpleasant by it. Quite the contrary."

They fetched up between a pair of ormolu candelabra gracing the mantel.

"Why, you're positively lovely, Miss Forte!" The woman's grin was so infectious that Sarah's lips broke into a trembling curve. "I'd've died for such guinea-gold hair. Why didn't Neddy mention you're a beauty? I expected a dried-up stick, all prunes and prisms and repressive moralizing, and was fully prepared to be intimidated. I'm so relieved!"

"I suppose"—Lady Pallister chuckled—"Edwin considered beauty the least important of Miss Forte's attributes. Miss Forte, my irrepressible daughter, Annabelle Monkton."

"Mrs. Monkton." Sarah attempted a curtsy despite the dimpled hand gripping her chin. She might as well not have bothered.

"What luck! Though our coloring's different with the exception of our eyes," the young woman enthused, turning Sarah's head first this way, then that, "there's not an ensemble I've selected that won't suit you to perfection with the exception of the red. The red isn't that attractive, so it's no great loss.

"Come see what treasures we unearthed. My abigail and I've been at it all day—and a long day it's been. At least we had something with which to occupy ourselves. If you could've seen Neddy once he returned from Chilford!" With the air of a hoydenish schoolgirl rather than a matronly mother of five, Mrs. Monkton grabbed Sarah's hand and pulled her across the sitting room. "A caged lion would've been more pacific, for he despaired of Mama prevailing on you. Nothing Richard said made the least difference," she chattered. "He paced and complained and scowled like the most fearsome beast, and actually growled at Thomas when he suggested a game of lottery tickets would be just the thing to pass the time."

"Forgive her, Miss Forte." Lady Pallister chuckled, following them into the bedchamber. "Easier to stop the wind than my dear daughter when she takes a notion in her head. I should've warned you."

"Look!" Mrs. Monkton threw out her arms. "Didn't we do well, Mama?"

"But—but, I can't!" Sarah gasped.

"Oh, but you'll be doing me the most immense favor. There's not a one I'll be able to wear again, for they're from before Freddy and Michael. Richard's been insisting I do something with them for months. My abigail and I've been in despair as she's even rounder than I am; but they're so pretty, and every one suited to the country, so you must take them. Otherwise I'll receive the most dreadful scold from Richard."

Sarah shook her head, feeling as if she were drowning in waves of kindness. "But, the colors. My mother died only last January."

"And would urge you to do me the favor. After all, Mama would, and I imagine your mother was a woman of sense, too. She was, wasn't she? It's only a few warm gowns, and a cloak and things. Did you know one's feet and hands plump up, too? Well, they do—especially when one is *enceinte*. And of course there'll be Mama's ensemble, so long as that dreadful vicar didn't walk off with it. Neddy wasn't certain about that."

"We've brought it, but Lady Pallister and I settled it's hers, not mine."

"You settled it," Lady Pallister retorted, "as a precondition to coming. I never agreed. Be warned, Annabelle—Miss Forte can be as intransigent as you or I when the mood strikes her."

"Dear me, she can? And you've the air of such a demure little thing." Mrs. Monkton grinned. "I'd never've thought it of you. Well, we'll see who carries the day."

"I'm afraid in this instance it must be I," Sarah said, gazing longingly at the wealth spread before her. "Attempting to turn me into a peacock is hopeless."

"A peacock? Is that what you think I'm about? Because it's not. Say a swan, or perhaps a particularly beautiful lark. Oh, dear, is it because they're made over? I realize that's a dreadful insult, but I so hoped you wouldn't be offended as we hadn't—''

"Offended?" Sarah blushed. "Your thoughtfulness is beyond anything."

"You're certain? You don't hold it against me? Because if you do—''

"How could I?"

"I'm so glad you'll admit that. Just pretend you've been on a long journey, and became separated from your effects. Now, let's see how this does." Annabelle Monkton seized an emerald gown and held it up to Sarah's shoulders. "Christmas Day," she breathed, "with sprigs of holly in your hair, but not for tonight. Oh—I know!" She retrieved a gown of ice blue silk embroidered in silver, held it up. "Yes—this one. Am I not clever, Mama? Miss Forte will appear a positive angel."

"Infinitely clever, but I'm certain Miss Forte is both fatigued and disconcerted by all the strangeness. We'll leave her to the ministrations of whoever you've selected to see to her. There's certain to still be a tuck or two needed," Lady Pallister explained, turning to Sarah, "for Edwin, being a man, could only tell us you were rather like Annabelle when she and Richard were wed. All this was done on a guess."

Sarah had the sensation of tumbling down a very long and very bright tunnel with no notion where the tunnel would lead, or how the journey would end. Lady Pallister patted her cheek, smiled, and sailed out of the bedchamber, ordering Annabelle to follow her within five minutes on penalty of a swift tongue lashing.

Little as Edwin Pallister liked to admit it, Cray had been right. To appear at his best, a gentleman required the services of an expert valet—even at a family party in the country. Perhaps it was his neckcloth? His choice of fobs?

He shrugged. "I'll do, don't you think?" he said to Stephens.

The footman shook his head. "Don't know quite what it is, my lord, but if you'll just let me fetch Gibbons?"

Pallister turned back to the mirror, then laughed. There was nothing wrong with his apparel. Coat of midnight blue, sparkling linen, striped waistcoat—all were perfection. It was just that he had the air of a terrified stripling about to enter his first gaming hell, convinced he'd set a foot wrong no matter how careful he was.

Well, he had every right. What if he'd made a fool of himself, and Miss Forte was less than he'd thought? What if she'd intrigued him merely because of the odd manner in which they had met? Worse yet, what if she disliked him, and hadn't really wanted to come? Annabelle would never let him live it down.

"There's nothing wrong turning the clocks forward or back twenty-four hours wouldn't remedy." He chuckled. "A week might be better."

He let himself into the corridor and paused.

He could go to his mother's apartments and learn her opinion—except he couldn't bear to appear overanxious. Or he could ask his sister—except Annabelle was even more likely to draw the wrong conclusion regarding his having changed for dinner well ahead of time. He merely wanted to be in the drawing room before Miss Forte made her appearance, just as courtesy demanded. Permitting himself the leisure to discard three coats and five waistcoats as unsatisfactory, and making countless attempts at tying his neckcloth before he achieved something passable, had nothing to do with anything.

With a wordless snarl he turned toward the main stairs leading to the entry and the common rooms. No matter what he said or did, it would be misconstrued.

Only Miss Forte and the schoolroom party were missing when he entered the drawing room. Annabelle had the look of a kitten trying to choose between chicken and cream, while his mother's air of unconcern as she chatted with Mr. Whitely was as spurious as his own. He did the pretty with the vicar and his wife, who had been invited for Miss Forte's sake, thankful he hadn't called on the fellow to ask if he knew aught of Humphrey Snead, John Forte, or Forte's daughter. This evening was going to be difficult at best. He didn't need more knowing looks than he was already receiving.

"They've settled in?" he said, drawing his mother aside as soon as he could.

"The children regard it as a great adventure. Miss Forte? Well, you'll see."

"What of Maria? The physician came as I requested?"

"Fading. Dr. Leland couldn't suggest much beyond feeding the poor thing when she cries, and keeping her comfortable. He's given Nurse permission to try anything she wishes. I'll thank you not to tell Miss Forte. If the end is inevitable and near, we don't want her dwelling on it. She's very attached to the mite."

Well, that was an opinion of sorts. His mother's tone was warm. He'd have to be content with that until he could judge for himself how much of a fool he'd been. With luck, they would get through the holiday celebrations without too much discomfort.

He nodded as the schoolroom party streamed in, followed by a slightly harried Miss Breame. Miss Forte's little band had cleaned up well. Patsy, with her air of having become a miniature governess, had him chuckling as his sister did the honors. Monkton swung Catherine up on one shoulder, then—with a trace of assistance—perched Bitsy on his other. Both moppets were giggling as Mr. Whitely joked with the younger boys, and Mrs. Whitely conversed with the older children.

And then Pallister's mother was turning him toward the doors. "Congenitally unfashionable, I believe you said," she murmured, "and incapable of presenting a distinguished appearance?"

"Good Lord! It is she, isn't it?"

"None other. I believe what pleases me most is the inner person caught your attention, not just another pretty face. I hope you're pleased with what we've achieved, however?"

The vision lingering by the door as it gazed about the room made his blood run first hot, then cold. Where had the bedraggled drudge sent into the mud by Chively's vicar only the day before vanished? This wasn't his Sarah Forte. It was a perfect diamond.

"Pleased? Yes, I suppose so. I must be, mustn't I? You're to be commended. She's exquisite."

"Don't let Miss Forte's new air of fashion intimidate you. A silk gown in almost the latest mode, a tissue shawl, and letting her curls run riot are superficials. She remains the same young woman William Fitzmorris was determined you meet, and with the same problems. The poor dear is terrified her hands will snag the silk. We've told her not to concern herself, but she refuses to listen."

"That hasn't changed, at least. She never listens to reason, no matter how delicately one tries to phrase it."

She did look terrified, though he doubted marring the soft silk of one of Annabelle's old evening gowns was the reason. He started over, determined to put the young woman at ease, but his mother pulled him back.

"No, this is Annabelle's task," she said. "For the moment you're merely the fortunate individual responsible for reuniting a pair of old friends. Actually, Annabelle believes she did encounter Miss Forte when on a visit to a school chum whose father had leased Peminster's place while improvements were made to his own. The family attended services at Saint Michael's. It's Miss Forte's golden curls Annabelle remembers, not her features, for Miss Forte couldn't've been more than eight, and Annabelle barely sixteen. Miss Forte remembers Annabelle not at all."

"I see." Not that he did. It seemed the flimsiest of fabrications to him. Sarah Forte was his responsibility. "Is Miss Forte aware of the possible acquaintance?"

"Annabelle mentioned it after I left them, and presumed on childhood friendship to insist they employ given names. It's as good an excuse as any, and will ease things considerably."

Pallister watched as his sister, alerted by a change in the atmosphere, dashed to the door, linked arms with Miss Forte, and led her to the Whitelys and Monkton.

"This," he grumbled, "is going to be the longest evening of my life."

"I suspect you might better say the longest fortnight. I also suspect it will be worth the aggravation, but only if you don't allow yourself to be blinded by what would've been obvious had your heart not become instantly engaged.''

And then Webster was announcing dinner. They paired off under Annabelle's direction as the children were whisked off— Monkton with Mrs. Whitely, his mother with the vicar, he with Annabelle on one arm and Miss Forte on the other. Together they entered purgatory, he blathering the inanities that passed for civility in the polite world, Miss Forte responding to his prattle with monosyllables, his sister smoothing all over with chatter regarding the children, the weather, and any other topics she could conjure to fill the silences his stupidities engendered.

For two pennies he'd bolt for London on the morrow, Pallister decided when the ladies at last quitted the table after a meal during which he'd drunk far too much, eaten far too little, and uttered so much drivel he couldn't remember half of it and wished he could forget the rest.

He pulled the brandy toward him and filled his glass as the vicar and Monkton discussed how best to assist Miss Forte and her waifs. He knew how best to assist 'em, blast it. Unfortunately, he'd just made such an idiot of himself even the most desperate miss would think twice about accepting him as the future father of her children, convinced she might be cursed with a string of lackwits.

He groaned and buried his head in his hands, ignoring the sympathetic glances thrown him by the two older men. What a muddle!

"Miss Forte—but surely I mistake the matter, and a sea nymph has taken residence in my library?''

Sarah glanced up from her book and smiled. At least it was her host—not that Lord Pallister was likely to seek her anywhere, or that she cared if he did. Coming to Monkton Manor had been the single greatest error of her life.

"Good morning, sir,'' she said, rising and dipping a curtsy, skirts of fine seafoam wool spread wide. "I'm sorry to disappoint, but it's a common mortal after all.''

"Not disappointed in the least. Sea nymphs're damp. Sure

to bring on a chill, especially at this season.'' He chuckled, glancing around the oak-paneled library. ''Have you breakfasted?''

''Daisy had a pot of chocolate waiting when I woke.''

''You consider that sufficient? No wonder you've great circles under your eyes—though I'll thank you not to tell my wife I said so. She'd have at me for incivility.''

She smiled again. That seemed easiest.

''Yes, well, family's in the breakfast parlor.'' Mr. Monkton rocked on his heels, hands clasped behind his back. ''Your lot, too. Annabelle sent me to find you and Ned. This is the day we search for the Yule log—which my chief woodsman and I've already positioned so it won't take forever and the children become fractious. One must never ask more patience of the infantry than they can provide—or more sense of a gentleman in a state of confusion. You haven't seen him?''

''Your chief woodsman? I'm afraid we're unacquainted.''

''No.'' He grinned. ''Ned Pallister.''

She blushed and shook her head. The figure she'd seen heading for the stables with the same loose-limbed lope hadn't necessarily been Lord Pallister. Besides, just because he'd spied on her and the children was no excuse for her spying on him, even by accident, when she couldn't sleep.

''Ah well,'' Mr. Monkton said with a mock sigh, ''Annabelle will have to be content with one of you. He's doubtless running errands, though it's an odd hour for it.''

''No doubt,'' she agreed, pretending she was unaware of the sort of errand urgent enough to take a gentleman from his home half the night while snow fell, and well into the next day. His lordship was as disillusioned with her as she was with him— that, or like Mr. Snead, he merely sought a complaisant wife. Well, he'd have to seek elsewhere.

''You'll join us? The children'll be disappointed if you don't, and Lady Pallister is concerned. She says you visited the nursery several times during the small hours.''

He held out his arm, not quite a command, playing courteous host to her punctilious guest.

The morning crept by. The noon hour came, and still no

Lord Pallister. It wasn't until midafternoon that he returned, ruddy-cheeked, and with the air of one infinitely pleased with himself. Nothing would do but they send word to have the pairs put to the sleighs, and the great shire harnessed to drag back the log. The shadows were still short, he insisted. There was more than enough time.

Sarah was quick. Bitsy in her arms, fur rug tucked around them, she was settled behind Mr. Monkton before Lord Pallister realized the figure in the dark green pelisse wasn't his sister. She ignored his scowls, summoned the younger children to join her, and insisted Miss Breame have the honor of sitting beside Mr. Monkton. It was neatly done, she thought. More to the point, it relieved Lord Pallister of her company—and her of his.

They set out, runners cutting the snow, Mr. Monkton's sleigh in the lead. Sarah snuggled her feet against the warm bricks, determined to enjoy her few moments of freedom. The pairs slowed to a walk as they entered the woods, the children pointing and shouting. Sarah could hear Charlie crowing over the wealth of deadfall.

"It's all right." Mr. Monkton grinned when Sarah attempted to apologize. "I've already discussed the matter with my chief woodsman. You're not to give it a thought."

And then Charlie and Thomas were jumping from Lord Pallister's sleigh and dashing ahead. They had spotted it, they shouted—the biggest and best Yule log ever.

"Precisely where it's supposed to be," Mr. Monkton murmured, pulling up and looping the reins around the whip socket. "How fortunate, though hardly fortuitous. I feared the fresh snow might've covered it to the point where we'd have to circle the area ten times before they spotted it. Your Charlie has keen eyes, Miss Forte."

He leaped from the sleigh and waded after the older children. Above them a flock of sparrows scolded at the invasion. Grooms who had been riding behind were at the horses' heads grasping bridles, others assisting the ladies to alight so they could view the great log in its natural setting.

"It's all right," Miss Breame whispered as Sarah held Bitsy

and Catherine back. "This has been as carefully rehearsed as a presentation at Court. There'll be at least two sets of eyes on each, and when it comes time to put the shire to the log you'll see the youngest, even Freddy, riding on the men's shoulders."

The clearing boiled with activity, the children darting about, Lord Pallister and Mr. Monkton everywhere at once.

"It's wonderful—how Neddy and Richard find the perfect log each summer, then have it moved closer to the house to be discovered by the children," Annabelle said softly as Bitsy and Catherine churned through the snow. "This time I do believe they've outdone themselves. I doubt, however, even Neddy could've anticipated the circumstances in which we'd bring it home, for he's found us something of far greater value than the perfect log to brighten our celebrations this year."

Her impish glance had Sarah blushing.

The shire was being backed to the log, the men guiding heavy ropes, chains, and straps rigged to loop around massive branches that were themselves the size of healthy trees. Lord Pallister glanced over and waved.

"I'm a bit chilled," Sarah said. "If you don't mind, I'll return to the sleigh."

Miss Breame smiled down at her. "This time you'll ride with Mr. Monkton, and I'll see to the children. I insist."

"Cleverly done," Annabelle Monkton murmured, "how they harness the shire to the log, I mean. Can you see?"

Sarah nodded without looking. "Very clever, indeed."

Even the most elegant boots weren't proof against snow that crept in at the ankles, melting its way to the toes in an icy trickle. Sarah shivered, climbed into the sleigh, slipped off her damp boots and tucked her stockinged feet among the cooling bricks, then leaned back and closed her eyes. She was so weary—not just from last night, but from all the dispiriting nights and days that preceded it.

There were shouts from the woodsmen and grooms, youthful cheers as the great shire strained against the load, then eased forward, the muffled thud of its hooves more felt than heard. After a bit the sleigh swayed. Then they were gliding through the woods' banded light once more, the flickering annoying against her eyelids.

"Tired?"

"A little," she said.

"Then I'll make this the shorter version of the usual tour."

Sarah's eyes snapped open. "Lord Pallister? B-but where are the others? What do you—"

"We were in accord you should escape the schoolroom party for a bit."

"But the children will want you." She strained for a glimpse of the others. Only a single pair of tracks extended behind them. "There's a special tea planned, and—"

"We'll be back in time: I've barely exchanged two words with you since you arrived if one doesn't count yesterday evening, which must rank high among the great debacles of the century. I don't call that fair. None of them would've met you if not for me."

"Then the person who should be here is Mr. Fitzmorris. Lacking his enterprising spirit, you wouldn't've known us, either."

He ignored her, pointing out the vista across the frozen ornamental water they were circling now that they had come out of the woods. "That's where we'll take the children skating tomorrow," he said. "Have you ever been on skates?"

"Never." She peered at the great house across the lake, catching a glimpse of what might be the others before the track dipped and curved around a bank.

"Then you'll need a chair for support and a stalwart gentleman at your side. I volunteer for the honor."

"Oh, I don't think—"

"You'll do it, and enjoy it. Don't you realize each time you shrink from a new experience you're teaching those protégés of yours to fear all the world has to offer? That's not the mark of a caring guardian."

"Circumspection is their only hope of survival—and mine."

"Bowing to your vicar's every whim isn't circumspection."

"Hardly every whim. I'm here. You know nothing of the matter."

"Oh, but I do. I've had an opportunity to converse at length with Charlie."

"And spied on us from the hill," she blurted.

"Is that what you term it? Say rather I was observing your light-fingered vicar. William Fitzmorris is at least honest in his dishonesty. The same cannot be said for the charming Mr. Snead."

" 'We adore the saints as we know them.' "

"Is that what you do? Adore Snead? And consider him a saint? Good God!"

"Your language, my lord."

"To perdition with my language, Miss Forte. Snead a saint, indeed!"

Lord Pallister guided the pair to a tree-lined track that veered into the woods. Their swift progress, so like flying, should've been exhilarating. Instead she was close to tears.

"There's a riot of wildflowers through here in spring," he commented after they had covered first a mile, and then another, twisting through the sparkling woods.

She pretended he hadn't spoken or she hadn't heard, she wasn't sure which.

"I'm glad to see there are roses in your cheeks—or are they flushed from fury?"

"The shadows have lengthened considerably, my lord. Shouldn't we turn back?"

"Is my company so distasteful," he growled, "or is it the countryside that palls? You treat my family in a friendly enough manner, even give my sister her name. What must I do to have you consider me an ordinary mortal?"

"I doubt that's possible. I've no desire to be despised by all who know me, your family included."

"You're an idiot. That, or you're blind as a bat."

And then it was all happening at once. The lead horse shied, stumbled, and squealed. The other balked and attempted to rear. The sleigh slued on a hidden patch of ice, flinging her against Lord Pallister, then tipped and skidded into a snowbank, dragging the screaming pair with it.

"Good heavens," she breathed as they came to rest.

"My term for it's a bit saltier," his lordship panted. "At least we're nearer the house than you'd think. You're uninjured?"

"A bit breathless is all—and with a faceful of snow." She managed a weak chuckle as she crawled over him into the bank and scrambled to her stockinged feet. "I suspect your condition is much the same, in addition to which I must've crushed you dreadfully. I do apologize. The horses?"

"The leader's fetched up lame unless I misjudge the matter."

He hadn't. They abandoned the sleigh once Sarah donned her boots and he'd unhitched the pair, Sarah leading the lamed gelding, Lord Pallister its now subdued partner, slogging through the woods as the shadows deepened. She laughed off his pleas that she perch on the uninjured horse, insisting if the snow-covered path was as icy and uneven as their accident indicated, she'd fare better on her own. More to the point, so would the horse. No, she told him, she wasn't in the least chilled—other than her feet, which were blocks of ice. His sister's pelisse was keeping her delightfully warm, and her toes would melt once they reached the house.

"You're remarkably uncomplaining," he muttered.

"What good would complaint do, other than to turn a minor inconvenience into a major unpleasantness? You certainly didn't intend this."

"Your faith in my better nature humbles me."

"You may irritate me. You may even anger me on occasion. Well, you do," she said at the look he threw her as they trudged side by side, his hand under her elbow to steady her over the rough spots—an unnecessary precaution she enjoyed too much for comfort or propriety. "You have the most dreadful knack for leaping to unwarranted conclusions."

"So do you, my dear."

She hoped he attributed her fiery blush to the sun's setting glow. "That doesn't mean I have a vested interest in misjudging you at every turn," was all she said.

"Then stop doing it."

They broke out of the woods where the drive curved before

the house. Gilded by the low light, a knot of people clustered around a job carriage. Patsy was there, Mr. Monkton, Webster, even Lady Pallister and Annabelle, and so many grooms and footmen they were impossible to count.

"Good Lord, what now?" Pallister muttered.

A footman turned, spotted them, and pointed. There was no mistaking the squeal of the traveler who broke away from the crowd as they reached the drive. Mr. Monkton grabbed the man's cloak before he could charge them.

"Oh, dear," Sarah murmured. "I fear I'm for it now."

"Leave the rotter to me." Pallister's hand tightened on her elbow as grooms took charge of the pair. "Minor accident, Richard," he said, striding up to the crowd. "My fault entirely. Leader fetched up lame. Sleigh's in the woods north of the lake."

"What," Snead screeched, breaking away from Mr. Monkton, "have you done to my fiancée?"

"Your what?" Sarah, Patsy, and his lordship chorused.

"My fiancée. See here, Miss Forte—Sarah—I won't permit any more nonsense. I've come to take you home."

"We aren't betrothed, nor have we ever been, nor will we ever be."

"But it was decided between your mother and me just before her death. You know it was," the vicar of Chively blustered. "We've only been waiting the requisite year before calling the banns."

"Mother Forte couldn't stand you." Patsy turned to Lady Pallister. "He hadn't been the vicar, she'd never've let him past the door."

"Don't listen to that guttersnipe. Before she died, Mrs. Forte instructed her daughter to obey me in all things, and blessed our union. Now I insist—"

"She did nothing of the sort," Sarah broke in. "Patsy's right—my mother found you beneath contempt, though she hid it as best she could."

"I believe there's some sort of misunderstanding." Mr. Monkton's eyes were twinkling as he turned to Snead. "Miss Forte says you're not betrothed. Patsy agrees. Both insist the only person who could've sanctioned such a betrothal wanted nothing to do with you. Yet, you say you are. I'm puzzled by the inconsistency.''

"They wouldn't know. None of their business.''

"Not Miss Forte's business to know if she's to be wed, and to whom? Chively must have stranger customs than *ultima Thule*. You've come under false pretenses, Vicar. It's just your motive I can't discern. There's nothing of value left at the cottage.''

"Merely ensuring my betrothed's welfare. See here, it's cold. Aren't you going to ask us in?''

"I don't believe so. Can you think of a single reason I should, Mr. ah, Snead?''

Humphrey Snead puffed out his chest. "This isn't settled to my satisfaction. I'll charge Lord Pallister with alienation of affections,'' he threatened.

"Ah—now we come to it,'' Mr. Monkton murmured.

"And who will be your witnesses?'' Pallister demanded, going toe-to-toe with the vicar.

"My own word is all I need.''

"I wonder what Squire Hadley would say to that?''

"What has the squire to say to anything?'' Mr. Snead backed several paces. "Nothing but an interfering sort who encourages Miss Forte to acts of impropriety and rebellion. His wife is even worse.''

"That again? Richard, if you don't chase this blackguard off instanter,'' Lord Pallister snarled, turning to his brother-in-law, "I won't answer for my actions.''

"You want to draw his cork, don't let me stand in your way.'' Mr. Monkton laughed, ignoring his wife's whispers. "He's trespassing. What I'd like to know is why he's got your valet with him. That is Cray over there, isn't it?''

What had been merely mortifying bid fair to turn into a common brawl. Only Lady Pallister's demand for the truth saved things, and then only after she treated the miscreants to a lecture that left their ears burning and Snead fearing for his living, for she claimed to be well-acquainted with the absentee landlord who controlled it. The self-justifications flowed fast and furious then.

It seemed Cray had first followed Lord Pallister to Chively, supposedly to guard him from danger, then called at the vicarage where he was delighted to discover a kindred spirit. Once the best of what was at the cottage was appropriated, the confederates decided his lordship should be made to pay for his interference in the form of a judgment for enticing the innocent girl away from her "natural protector." Who, after all, would doubt the word of a Man of God when he brought charges against a profligate aristocratic libertine whose own valet was prepared to give information against him, and then spread the tale through the *ton?* Snead's claim that the proceeds would've been settled on the poor of his parish—a form of enforced charity—was met with derisive laughter.

After that, only Lady Pallister's snapped "Edwin, do not forget yourself" saved Snead from measuring his length on the drive, and Cray from the horsewhip Pallister acquired during the fracas. Long before vicar and valet made their departures, Annabelle and Patsy had spirited Sarah into the house, Annabelle laughing, Patsy cursing, Sarah white-faced and near tears until Annabelle forced her to see that by so far overreaching himself, Snead had finally lost any power over her and the children. It was really, Annabelle insisted, all quite amusing.

Strangely, the indignant dinner-time conversation regarding the sniveling vicar of Chively's ploys didn't embarrass Sarah beyond the first moments. Indeed, she was laughing as heartily as any by the time the party separated for bed.

"Miss Forte?"

Sarah set aside the miniature holly wreath she'd been fashioning, then rose and curtseyed, smiling over the ache in her heart. It had been a long night and a longer morning, for she'd returned from the skating party the afternoon before only to learn Maria's cough had worsened, her fever risen. Nurse had fetched her in the small hours, then at dawn conferred with Lady Pallister and Annabelle.

"Dr. Leland is here, and wishes to speak with you."

Lady Pallister's expression was all the confirmation she needed. "I never should've come," Sarah murmured. "What a terrible price."

"My dear, don't be foolish."

Lady Pallister opened her arms. After a moment's hesitation, Sarah took refuge there, sobbing as the fire crackled on the family parlor grate. The gay decorations, the clump of ribbon-decked mistletoe suspended from the ceiling, and the gown of deep rose merino were bitterly anachronous.

"You're crying for all of it, aren't you," the viscountess said after a bit, a catch in her voice, as she stroked Sarah's back. "My dear, these things happen. At least God has given you warning."

"Which I didn't heed."

"Maria's best hope lay here. No guilt attaches to you, and no blame."

Sarah shuddered and pulled away, wiping her eyes. "Forgive me," she said. "I won't make a fuss, I promise."

"Don't be foolish, child. There are times one must cry, or turn bitter and old."

Sarah shook her head. "Mr. Snead had the right of it." She sighed. "I consulted my wishes without the regard to what was wisest, and this is the result."

"What would Mrs. Terwilliger say to such idiocy? Something pithy, I don't doubt."

"Dear Mrs. Terwilliger. She means well, but a stranger lady I've never known."

"A strange lady indeed, but one with an excellent heart. Rather clever at achieving her ends, too. Martha's her equal. You'll remember they insisted you come."

"They only said what I wanted to hear." Sarah straightened her shoulders. "I'd best not keep Dr. Leland. This is Christmas Eve. Bad enough he should come on such a sad errand. Inexcusable to detain him longer than necessary."

"I suppose next you'll be blaming yourself for his selecting a profession guaranteed to take him out at all hours. Sarah, you're not Atlas. Besides, if you assume responsibility for everything, what's left for the rest of us?''

Together the two women went up to the nursery where the physician, Annabelle, Nurse, and Lord Pallister waited. Dr. Leland's sympathetic glance almost undid Sarah.

"How long?" she managed as she received Maria from Annabelle's arms.

"She won't see Christmas dawn."

Throat aching, Sarah snuggled the downy head against her neck. "What should I do?"

"Hold her, love her, moisten her lips with water when she frets. Beyond that, her body may be in your arms, but her soul is straining toward God's."

Eyes brimming, Sarah turned to Annabelle. "Will you have Mr. Whitely fetched, if it wouldn't be too much trouble? Maria should be christened."

A strong masculine hand descended on her shoulder, offering support. "I'll fetch him myself," Lord Pallister murmured.

She nodded, glancing about the nursery, then down at her elegant wool gown. Dear heaven, but she hated it. The beautiful thing symbolized everything that had gone wrong over the last days.

"I must find Patsy," she said, turning to Annabelle. "She should be warned. You needn't worry. She'll hold her tongue, but she helped me considerably with Maria, and must have the opportunity to make her farewells if she wishes."

Pallister took the mite from her. "We'll see to Maria until you return. You're not to worry about anything."

"No, I mustn't, must I." Her voice sounded like shattered glass. "That would be the act of a heretic."

Ducking her head, she slipped from the room and descended the back stairs to her apartments only to find word had preceded her. Patsy, Charlie, Tim, and Bitsy were waiting in the sitting room, their cheeks rosy from the outdoors.

"Maria will be spending Christmas with my mother and father," Sarah said. That seemed simplest.

"But, how can she when they're—" Tim began.

"Miss Sarah means she's going to die," Charlie said.

"Oh," Tim shrugged. "We always knew that."

She stared from one to the next.

"You're the only one thought she wouldn't," Bitsy said. "Babies like her don't live. They aren't meant to. Can we go back now? We're having all sorts of fun."

Sarah nodded. There didn't seem to be anything left to say.

As they filed from the sitting room, Patsy paused at the door. "Kindest thing would've been for its mother to've smothered it 'stead of leaving it on your doorstep. That way it wouldn't've had to fight for every breath and die in the end anyway, and you'd still've had Mother Forte's pearls."

Then she came back and put her arms around Sarah. "It's had a better two weeks than it would've saving you. That's what you've got to remember."

"That's why you never called Maria by name, any of you?"

Patsy nodded. "Isn't smart to give something that's going to die a name. You get too attached. Then when it's dead you hurt more'n you should."

And then she was gone.

Sarah pulled the bell rope, went into the dressing room, changed into her old gown and tied on a clean apron. She'd just retrieved the exquisite infant's robe she'd intended for Maria's christening when Daisy bustled in, eyes red-rimmed.

"None of that." Sarah gave the girl a warm hug. "Even the children knew it was bound to happen."

"Still awful sad."

"Yes, it is, but they say those who die on Christmas Eve fly straight to God's side. I want you to bundle up my things. Nothing of Mrs. Monkton's or Lady Pallister's, mind. And the children's, but only what they brought. We'll be leaving when it's over. Turning their home into a house of mourning at Christmas would be the worst sort of thanks I could offer Mr. and Mrs. Monkton after all their kindness."

"No, miss, the worst sort'd be you running off when trouble strikes you."

* * *

When she returned to the nursery Mr. Whitely and his wife had just arrived. She set the delicate infant's gown aside for later and took Maria from the nurse, gave her a gentle kiss, then handed her to Lady Pallister. The service was short, Lord Pallister standing as godfather, Lady Pallister and Annabelle as godmothers, Sarah as sole parent.

"We'll say a special prayer for our newest parishioner tonight," Mrs. Whitely said when her husband was done. "Tradition is each infant receives one of these. I'd like her to have it before she begins her journey." She showed Sarah a tiny cross on a ribbon, then, at her nod, slipped it over Maria's head.

Mr. Monkton told Sarah he'd already seen the estate carpenter, and arranged with Mr. Whitely to conduct the services. "As my wife's goddaughter, Maria will be laid beside the infant daughter we lost between Michael and Freddy," he concluded, "so long as you have no objection?"

Sarah shook her head.

And then Mr. Whitely took the infant from her, bowed his head and said a simple prayer for Maria's soul, using his own words as he entrusted her to God's care and mercy. He murmured the traditional benediction, and returned her to Sarah's arms. The contrast between the foundling's frail whimper and Michael Monkton in the next room, howling lustily at some imagined insult, was striking. Blinded by tears, Sarah sank into a chair by the nursery fire, rocking as the others departed taking Michael with them.

She had no sense of time as the sun climbed to its winter zenith, then began its descent toward night. Over and over she murmured the last words of Mr. Whitely's prayer, "Not according to our will, Oh Lord, but Thine, and trusting in Thy mercy," alternating them with carols she hoped would seem only soft lullabies, but were in truth rebellious pleas that God change His plans just this once. She often sensed Nurse's concerned eyes on her as the gray-haired woman adjusted the fire screen, or brought concoctions she claimed would be more soothing than water to the parched infant.

Lady Pallister came, Annabelle, even Lord Pallister and Mr. Monkton, stayed a bit, and slipped away. She ignored the tray brought her at noon, only sipped the salty broth forced on her by Nurse because that was easier than arguing, dipping her finger in the dregs once it was cool and offering it to Maria because somehow that seemed right.

The sun sank below the horizon. Nurse lit the lamps and pulled the draperies. Eventually Annabelle returned, saying it was time for the evening meal.

"I'll stay with her." She reached for Maria. "If there's the slightest change, I'll have you summoned, but you must get away from this room for a bit."

Sarah shook her head. "I can't. If she must die, then she'll die in my arms."

"But you'll eat if I have a tray sent up?"

"Could you?"

"My dear, this serves nothing." The young matron knelt by Sarah's chair, silken skirts billowing. She ran a gentle hand over the infant's downy head, frowned, then sighed. "You must keep up your strength."

"I'll eat tomorrow, or the next day."

"Neddy will be very angry with me if you don't come. He said you'd refuse, and would have to be forced. He also said I wouldn't find it in me to force you. He has the right of that, at least."

"Lord Pallister's anger will dissipate."

Finally Annabelle left.

Sarah had no notion of the passing hours, nor did she realize Edwin Pallister stood watch with Nurse over her and the infant. The joyful midnight peal of bells in the nearby village was meaningless, so exhausted was she by then. Maria lay in her arms, breathing in labored gasps, skin turning clammy. Occasionally Sarah moistened the infant's lips with one of Nurse's herbal decoctions, but mostly she rocked and tried not to think as she sang carol after carol.

On toward dawn Maria shuddered, sighed, and became still at last as her eyes closed. Sarah clutched the infant to her.

"Dear heaven, how cold she's grown," she gulped, blinded by scalding tears. Gentle hands eased the tiny corpse from her. "No, let me hold her just a bit longer. I haven't said goodbye yet. I don't know how."

Other hands pulled her from the chair in which she'd spent so many hours. Strong arms gathered her close as she sobbed.

"It's over, my dear," Edwin Pallister murmured. "She's at peace, and so must you be. She'd want that, you know, our little guest—for that's all God permitted her to be. You mustn't do this to yourself."

"And what do you know of it?"

"A fair amount. Annabelle lost a seemingly healthy infant a few years ago. At first we feared for her reason. I don't want that to happen to you."

"I'm not thinking," she gulped. "I forgot. I'm sorry. I've ruined it all for you."

"What do you believe you've ruined? Families are intended to stand by each other, not just in the happy times, but in the sad ones. You and your mother stood by each other, didn't you?"

She nodded.

"And the children stood by you when your mother died, and Mrs. Terwilliger's stood by all of you for years, from what you've said. Maria's with God now. There's a new star in the heavens to welcome Christmas morning." He drew her to the nursery window and pulled the draperies aside. "Listen to their singing," he said, still holding her close, though the sound was actually a single determined sparrow greeting the false dawn.

Sarah attempted to smile through her tears, but shook her head.

"I should've done more. There must've been more. Something. Anything. It shouldn't've ended this way."

"Don't be foolish. You sacrificed more for that child than its natural parents did. Yes, I know all about your selling your mother's pearls for goat milk. Patsy told me the morning Father Christmas called. I tried to buy them back from the squire, but he wouldn't take a penny, blast him, and sends you his best wishes. Where do you think I was off to that first morning? Took four hours to get there, and another four to return, because of the snow. At least there were only flurries by the time I left.''

"Oh, my," she whispered. "Oh, dear—I'm so ashamed."

"Because I had a cold ride, or that I woke Squire Hadley at an unreasonable hour?"

"Because of those, too."

She was thankful he didn't press further. Together they watched as the stars began to wink out, first one, then another, his arm firmly around her, her head resting on his shoulder. Gradually the tears that had trickled down her cheeks eased. Behind them Nurse was washing Maria, crooning tenderly as she worked.

"Squire said you were to obey me. Well, listen to me, and not be foolish."

"He did?"

"You're not leaving here—at least not to return to Chively. Neither are your waifs." He gripped her shoulders, and turned her to face him. "Don't you understand why my mother went to fetch you?"

"I thought your family might also have a tradition of taking in outcasts at Christmas. Certainly it's in keeping with the season."

"Oh, my dear girl! No, it's because my mother insisted I court you properly, as you'd been cheated of so much else."

"Court me?"

"I'm dearly hoping in a year's time we'll be welcoming the family to Pallinvale. It's a grand old place, as suited to Christmas frolics as summer revelries. All it's been lacking is a soul. It lost that when my father died. My mother hasn't been able to bear the place since. Neither have I, but now we can hardly wait to return, for I found its new one in Chively. The only way you could ruin our Christmas is to refuse me."

"B-but—"

"My mother agrees. I hope you've come to care for me at least a little," he said, releasing her shoulders and turning to stare out the window, "but if I'm not a sort you find you can abide, we'll make provisions. Chively's out of the question, though—not that Humphrey Snead'll be there long. Peminster owes me a favor or two. Not a bad sort, really, no matter what you believe.

"See here, d'you think you could ever learn to tolerate me? Because, strange as it sounds, I think that's what Fitzmorris expected—that you'd plant me a facer the moment I set eyes on you. Took a bit longer than that, but not much. Within minutes, I'd say, which classes as a *coup de foudre* in anyone's book."

"Yes."

"Yes, what? Yes, it's a *coup de foudre,* or yes, eventually you might not find me totally repugnant?"

"I think we were felled by the same cannonade," she managed, "though we did get off to a rather shaky start."

He whirled to face her, breaking into a grin that bid fair to crack his face in two.

"Yes to everything, then? Including me?"

"Most especially to you. When I consider your kindness, your generosity—"

"I'm no saint."

"Neither am I, as you'll soon learn."

From across the nursery came a strange choking cough. They turned. Nurse was staring at the infant lying before her in disbelief.

"No wonder she seemed cold. Her fever's broken," the woman quavered. "Dear Lord in heaven, I think the wee mite's going to live if only we can find her a wet nurse. Goat's milk don't suit her, I'm sure. Doesn't with some of them. Things started to go better when she didn't have it."

It was the happiest Christmas ever at Monkton Manor. Sarah was joyfully welcomed into the family, and his lordship insisted Maria would become his ward—the first of what he hoped would be their many children. Naturally, he assured Sarah, he'd provide for her other waifs as well. Educations first. Then they would see. Not a one of them, Pallister chuckled, was ever likely to enter into service.

Lord Edwin Pallister and the vicar's daughter were wed by special license on a clear winter morning at the beginning of February, 1819, Sarah's mother's pearls clasped about her neck. Annabelle stood up for Sarah; Monkton for his brother-in-law. Sarah's waifs, unconventionally perhaps, gave Sarah away. Just as Edwin Pallister was lifting his bride's veil, he caught sight of a pair of familiar faces and turned, mouth opening in enraged disbelief. The dowager viscountess stepped in his path.

"Behave yourself, Edwin," she hissed as William Fitzmorris and his better half slipped from their pew. "I promised they'd be safe. I won't have you proving me wrong. For now, suffice it to say you and Sarah aren't the first they've helped while helping themselves. I doubt you'll be the last. They're scoundrels, yes, but scoundrels with good hearts. You can have the particulars later."

"But that was Mrs. Terwilliger's abigail," Sarah gasped. "Whatever was Martha doing with that strange man? And where's Mrs. Terwilliger?"

From beyond the church came merry laughter and the jingle of harness bells.

"Mrs. Terwilliger?" Pallister breathed. "What a dolt I've been! That was Father Christmas—yes, Bitsy, the gentleman does exist, and you've met him. I'll be blessing William Fitzmorris's light fingers and generous spirit all my life, for he gave me the best gift I'll ever receive."

In later years, as Lord and Lady Pallister's children searched for the Yule log and then assisted in lighting it, the story of the year Father Christmas came calling was the happiest of their traditions. The tale, altered to suit circumstances and times, is told by their descendants in London, in Sydney, in Brussels and Montreal and Cape Town, even New York. When the tale is done, children with their eyes aglow creep off to bed and wait for Father Christmas—or Santa Claus, or Saint Nicholas, or Père Noël, or Kris Kringle—to call. He always does.

LADY AMELIA'S CHRISTMAS PARTY

Paula Tanner Girard

One

Amelia Twitchell set her needles to purling and hooking and twisting the yarn into the sweater she was knitting. It was going to be a very special Christmas this year. She could feel it in her bones; she could smell it in the air; she could hear it in her heart.

Outside the house the ground lay bare and winter days were short and crisp, while inside the spacious country kitchen everything was warm and cozy—at least most of the time.

Amelia gave a little shiver. "Germaine," she called from where she sat in her comfortable rocking chair in front of the wide stone hearth. "Do come and rekindle the fire."

In five days' time the villagers of Badger Bend would wend their way through the woods to the manor house to partake of Lady Amelia's Christmas Day feast.

Badger Hall had been used as a hunting box infrequently when the third viscount, Lord Littlefield, acquired it, and none at all when the fourth viscount came into the title at a very tender age. Forty years had passed since then, give or take a year or two. Amelia had lost count.

In fact, Amelia Twitchell had been at Badger Hall so long that her memories tended to get rather muddled. Nonetheless, she never forgot to throw a party on Christmas Day and give everyone, young and old alike, the sweaters which she had been knitting for them all year long. The fact that they were not very well constructed—some could have one long sleeve and one short, or perhaps three sleeves altogether—never deterred the kind and understanding humble folk of Badger Bend from tugging at their forelocks or bobbing a curtsy before saying politely, "Thank you, Lady Amelia."

Amelia could not remember when it was that she had started thinking of herself as the lady of the house. Her recollection was getting a little fuzzy on that point, too. Nor could she remember how long ago it had been since she began to dress in the pretty gowns that the viscountess had left behind in her clothes press. Lovely frocks of embroidered silk and velvet with full skirts and high collars, laces and satin ribbons.

But when Amelia's plain wardrobe began to dwindle away, and since the two women had been about the same size, she did not think herself amiss in borrowing a frock or two. After all, didn't she always wash, clean, and press the garments before she replaced them in the closet?

In reality Amelia was quite rounded, with plump little cheeks and merry blue eyes; and her brown curls, which were not brown anymore but a silvery gray, framed her face quite charmingly. Nonetheless, the important thing was how one felt inside, she told herself, and Amelia felt quite elegant.

Time passed and when neither the viscount nor his viscountess returned to the hunting lodge, Amelia moved into their quarters off the Great Hall. It did seem the sensible thing to do, for then she didn't have to walk so far from the kitchen to keep things tidy.

Neither could she recall the first time the folk of Badger Bend began to refer to her as "Lady Amelia." Perhaps it was when the elders of the village passed away and their children, and their children, and then their children were grown, and couldn't remember anyone other than the dear old lady ever living in the big house in the woods. The title fit quite nicely, Amelia thought.

Germaine was getting along in years, too, but they made

allowances for each other, and Amelia didn't mind cooking for the both of them. After all, they were the only ones left at Badger Hall.

The old butler didn't eat much, and she often found herself finishing up what she had fixed for him as well. He did what he could, and she continued to keep the house up as she had been taught to do when she first arrived at the hunting lodge as a young lass of fourteen years.

"Germaine!" she called once more a little louder. "Oh! Piffle! That man is nowhere around when he is needed," she said, setting aside her knitting and rising from her rocking chair. " 'Tis easier to do it myself than to make myself hoarse. After all, I am not helpless."

Obediah Doo, the woodsman—a great hulk of a good fellow—lived nearby in a small thatched cottage and used the stables to shelter his horse. He stopped by often to make certain Lady Amelia's kindling stayed piled high outside, and that she had an ample supply stacked inside next to the hearth. He chopped the limbs into short little pieces which were light enough for even a child to lift.

Now Amelia threw a stick upon the smoldering cinders, then stepped back and clapped her hands with delight as the dry twigs caught fire, and thousands of sparks popped, spit, and sizzled up the chimney. "Oh, isn't that splendid!" she exclaimed, tossing on another stick, and then another, so that she could enjoy seeing the whole performance repeated over and over. "My, oh my, oh my!" she said, tripping back to her chair where she once again picked up her knitting. "Germaine will be so disappointed that he missed all the fun."

It was not as though no one ever called on Amelia. Mrs. Moss, the postmaster's wife, often made her way through the forest to bring her the necessaries: victuals, tea, yarn, and beeswax to keep the furniture polished and smelling nice. Then when the kind woman would make herself comfortable on one of the high-backed wooden settles, which sat on either side of the hearth, Amelia would serve up a cozy pot of tea and some biscuits while Mrs. Moss filled her in on the goings-on of the village.

"There are now twenty-seven souls in and about Badger Bend," Mrs. Moss told her on her last visit. "The miller's wife had a baby boy a month ago." Amelia had immediately made a mental note to knit a pair of booties for the infant.

Mrs. Moss had added that her brothers would be coming from Kent—she didn't say how many. "A few other folks are expecting visitors for the Holidays as well," she'd said, throwing up her hands. "I can't imagine where we will put them all."

"Do not worry over that!" Amelia had exclaimed. "They are welcome to stay here." However, Mrs. Moss had assured her that she was certain that she would manage.

Now once again Amelia looked at the stack of knitted garments in the basket beside her rocking chair. If she had counted correctly, she would be finished making all the gifts with this last sweater. She always knitted a few additional items: mittens or gloves, scarves, and bed socks, just in case someone brought a guest or—heaven forbid—something didn't fit. However, she was proud to say it had never happened in all the years she had been knitting. Everyone always exclaimed that they did not know how she did it, but Lady Amelia got the sizes right every time.

"What is this entry, Woolcroft?" John Daring, the sixth Viscount Littlefield, pointed to an item on the first page of the huge leather-bound ledger which was opened on the desk before him. Then he flipped a few pages, pointed to another, and flipped a third and a fourth time. He had chosen to call the steward to the library instead of going to the small room attached to the rear of the manor which was used as an office—its only source of heat being a small coal-burning brazier.

Viscount Littlefield wore a fine brown morning coat and tan breeches which were more suitable to the drawing room in Town than the brisk British winter on a country estate in Essex. Three years in the West Indies had spoiled him for warm days kissed by tropical breezes, and he was ill prepared for the snow and sleet he'd been encountering.

He'd not had time to purchase a new wardrobe in the few weeks since his return to England. But Daring thought that was no reason for him to freeze in a back room while his erstwhile friend and traveling companion lounged in the book room toasting comfortably in front of a roaring log fire.

Mr. Turkle Brown, a big blond giant whom the viscount had known since their salad days at Oxford, now sat on a high stool hunkered over a globe which he kept whirling around on its base. He would then stop it with a jab of his finger, give a hoot when he saw where he'd landed, and then twirl it again. Daring only hoped the clumsy jackanapes didn't puncture a hole in it or send it spinning off its stand.

Meanwhile Woolcroft, a stout, bearded, middle-aged man, more suitably dressed in a thick gray woolen sweater, heavy woven breeches, and Wellington boots, leaned over the young viscount's shoulder and squinted to make out the hand-printed words.

Lord Littlefield turned the page again. "I see that each year a stipend has been sent by way of the postmaster of Badger Bend for the caretaker of Badger Hall."

The steward twisted his hat in his hands, looking rather uncomfortable. "The billing was there when I come to work for the fourth viscount, my lord. I assure your lordship that I have paid the fee faithfully as I were instructed."

"I'm sure you have, Woolcroft. I am not questioning your integrity or competency. It is just that I never heard of Badger Hall." It was not the first piece of property to come to Daring's notice in the last couple of weeks of which he had no knowledge. It had been less than four months ago that he'd received a letter in the West Indies informing him that he'd come into the viscountcy.

Woolcroft pulled on his beard, pursed his lips and squinted harder, trying to recall something he'd forgotten. "I believe I heard tell that it were an old manor the third viscount purchased to use as a hunting lodge."

Across the room, Turkle Brown was following the conversation with a great deal of amusement, for Daring had just said that morning that he didn't know what he'd do with all the riches he'd inherited. "So what else will your lordship find to add to your domain?"

Daring thought it best not to laugh in front of his retainer and flipped back to the first page of the ledger. For a poor orphan with little more than a feather to fly with only a few years ago, he wondered himself how many more surprise possessions he would find that he'd acquired with his new title.

Three years ago when he left England he had been plain Mr. John Daring, fourth in line of succession, and a distant cousin to the fifth Viscount Littlefield. He had gambled with the scanty pittance his father had left him to make a life for himself in the New World. Never had he contemplated the remotest chance of ever attaining the peerage—nor had he entertained any desire to return to the land of his birth after his unfortunate acquaintance with a two-faced, ungrateful wench named Miss Marianne De Visme.

The Littlefield and De Visme estates marched along together in Essex, north of London. What he had thought at the time to be a crazy accident which prevented him from attending a summer party at the De Visme country manor had turned out to be a blessing in disguise, and saved him from a loveless marriage. It had also uncovered the duplicity of the termagant whose devious heart was camouflaged by a face prettier than a spring flower. Anger still welled up in him when he thought of what a fool she had made of him.

On the eve of her parents' ball Daring and Marianne had agreed that they would approach her father together and ask permission to marry—or at least that was what he thought they had planned to do. Then he'd met with an unexpected circumstance, which caused him to miss the party. He had arrived at her house the next day rather bizarrely dressed and ready to take a royal scold if need be—but he expected it more likely that he would have to bear her uproarious laughter when she saw his embarrassing predicament. But did he find his intended even concerned over his absence? No! Definitely not!

There in the garden he found her in the arms of another man. Daring's infatuation with the Incomparable Miss Marianne De

Visme had been so complete that had he not seen her betrayal with his own eyes he would not have believed it.

Her lover's face was hidden by the shadows, but Daring did observe that the jackanapes wore the uniform of an officer in His Majesty's service. It was then that Daring realized that he did not have her full affections. Why hadn't he seen the signs? Because he was a stupid, sentimental fool! That was why.

Miss Marianne De Visme was after all the Toast of London Society. No matter how well connected Daring's family had been, they were without means. All he had at that time were his dreams. How could he have thought that he alone had secured the love of one so sought after?

The minute Daring perceived her fickle nature, he left stealthily—the way he had come—through the trees which surrounded the park. He was halfway back to Littlefield when he realized that he still grasped the fistful of pebbles he'd collected in the woods to toss at her window. He threw them down, ground them into the dirt with his heel, and stomped back to his cousin's house. What a nodcock he'd been.

Daring asked himself that if she should reflect so casually upon their own relationship so close to their announcement of their engagement, how would she behave after they were married when he was away much of the time? He did not savor the prospect of being made a cuckold.

Marriage was a commitment Daring held sacred. He did not take it as lightly as Miss De Visme seemed to have done. The memory still stung him deeply, and he had vowed then and there never to allow his heart to be so vulnerable again.

Now fate had dealt him a new hand, and Daring was back in England, titled with more blunt than he ever dreamed he would have. Hah, to Miss Marianne De Visme.

"Where is this hunting lodge, Woolcroft? Do you know?"

"Can't say as I do, my lord."

Daring dug through the box of documents that the steward had brought with him until he found a yellowed sheet of parchment with the inscription *Badger Hall* across the top. The faded writing was in Old English script.

"This looks like a map of the territory south of Littlefield on the edge of Epping Forest. There is a line drawn from Thatchcourne Road—which is the route I plan on taking out of here. It looks like it deadends at a place called Badger Bend. That must be the village mentioned in the ledger. But farther south there is a line going all the way to what I think may be the post road. There is a circle drawn here,'' he said, tapping his finger on a spot located on the second line. ''It says, *Twin Oak* and *Three-armed Witch's Tree.* Sounds sinister,'' he said, laughing. From the startled look he saw in Woolcroft's eyes, Daring surmised the steward didn't find it something to jest about, so he continued more solemnly. ''Arrows zigzag up and around to this point called Badger Hall. That must be the hunting box.''

Woolcroft leaned closer, his eyes widening as he read the notation. ''So it be, my lord. But you cannot mean to go there.''

The viscount nodded his dark head. ''I see no reason why not. It can't be too far off our route. I can stop and have a look-see, then go straight through and still catch the turnpike on the other side.'' Besides, he thought, taking the other route through the forest would allow him to bypass much of the De Visme estate.

Daring threw a cryptic glance at his friend. ''We can still make it back in time to attend Lord and Lady Reuter's ball.'' He planned on spending the next week at Turk's apartment in London. At least Christmas in Town with a fellow bachelor would not be as lonely as in the country all by himself.

''Do you want me to go ahead and dispatch the usual amount at the end of December, my lord?'' Woolcroft asked.

The viscount took a moment to think about that before making his decision. ''It is but a trivial amount, but nonetheless, if this has gone on for as many years as you say, it adds up to a tidy sum. And I for one wish to see where all the Littlefield money has been going all these years. It should be no great inconvenience to take the side road. What say you, Turk? I'm sure it won't put us too much out of our way,'' Daring said.

''No, no bother at all,'' came the jovial reply. ''Don't hurry back on my account. A delay might even help elevate my consequence if the ladies of London have to pine for me another day or two.''

The corners of the viscount's mouth turned upward for the first time that afternoon. "I might even drop by Willoughby Street and surprise Great-aunt Hortense,'' he said, not quite hiding the wicked gleam in his eye. ''Though I doubt she will be that excited upon seeing me after all these years. She was not exactly overjoyed when she was made watchdog over a rather rebellious teenager no one wanted. But what could a spinster lady do when her livelihood depended upon the largess of her brother, the viscount. Poor Lady Hortense,'' Daring said. ''The sanctity of her town house probably never recovered from my stay.''

Turk got up from the stool and made his way to the high-backed wing chair in front of the fire, grabbing a book from a shelf on his way. ''I think she'll be quite impressed when she finds out you're the viscount.''

''I doubt my improved circumstance will impress my great-aunt, Turk.''

Woolcroft cleared his throat. ''So what is it you wish me to do, your lordship?''

The viscount switched his attention back to the steward. ''Don't do anything until I send you a post from London on what I have found out about Badger Hall.''

''Then you plan to stop by to investigate the hunting box, my lord?''

Daring closed the ledger, placed it in the box, and handed it to the steward. ''You are sure you don't object, Turk?'' he called in the direction of the fireplace.

''Not at all,'' came a mumble from the other side of the chair.

''Then we'll do it. We'll leave first thing in the morning. Will you yank the bellpull by the door as you go out, Woolcroft? Keeble and Digsby will need to start packing our belongings.''

TWO

Miss Marianne De Visme was a lovely young lady, in the opinion of much of the *ton*, but whose good humor did not extend to John Daring, the sixth Viscount Littlefield, any more than his did to her. Even if he had now gained a title, as she had heard, it didn't change the fact that he was still a cad and a scoundrel, in her sight, and she hoped never to lay eyes upon him again.

The following day at approximately the same time that Viscount Littlefield and his friend Turkle Brown were planning to set forth on their journey south, our Miss De Visme was preparing to leave London with her brother to return north to her family's country seat in Essex, for the Christmas Holiday.

"I'm glad you agreed to leave a few days early, Marianne," Sir Richard said as they approached their traveling coach. "Our parents were not expecting us just yet, but I don't trust this weather."

"You know Mother has probably had our rooms ready for weeks, Richard. Besides, what is a little snow? I would like to have a white Christmas."

"Let it snow after we get there, but not while we are on the road. You're sure you don't mind missing the Reuters' ball? I

thought you would ring a peal over my head just for suggesting
it.''

"To tell the truth I shall be relieved to leave," Marianne
said.

The young man raised an eyebrow. "Can't make up your
mind between Tasman or Lord Eberly, huh?" he said, trying
to hide what was really on his mind and feeling relieved when
she seemed to accept his teasing.

"Or Mr. Bambrow or Lord Dimwitty . . . You seem to think
I have every eligible bachelor in London in my pocket,
brother," she said, matching him jest for jest.

In looks Miss De Visme made up in originality for what
would be called a lack of classical beauty. Her hair was ginger
brown. She expressed dismay at the freckles which insisted on
marching across her nose when the summer sun blazed in the
heavens, but which she had learned to hide with a little powder
as she grew older; a smile which she thought was a little
crooked, but which seemed to entrance all the young men into
begging her to bestow it upon them; and eyes of an undistin-
guished gray color, except when looking into them. Then they
appeared so deep and caring that they melted the most hardened
cynic.

Marianne gave him that smile now. "You overestimate my
appeal and try to hide your own. I think you are trying to escape
the attentions of Miss Pemberling."

Richard was glad he had coaxed a smile from her. "I have
nothing against the shy Miss Pemberling. 'Tis her dragon of a
mother who is impossible," said the young man, hoping she
accepted that as his reason for wanting to escape the city. "But
tell me, sis, do you look forward, then, to our mother's quizzing
you about when you are going to make your choice of a husband?''

Marianne gave him a sisterly punch on the arm. "Or when
her only son is going to choose a bride?"

"There is that, too," Richard said, "but I prefer her to Mrs.
Pemberly. However, I do think Father goads me more on that
subject than Mother. I'm the one who he says bears the responsibility of producing the next De Visme heir, and he doesn't let

me forget it. Perhaps if we invented mythical sweethearts they would quit hounding us," suggested Richard with a wink.

Marianne giggled. "That will be a Banbury Tale if there ever was one. But they will surely want us to tell all about them, and then we'll give our game away."

"Not necessarily. Not if we painted glowing descriptions from our imaginations of these paragons on whom we've set our sights. These special friends, whom we can't name until we are sure their affections are fixed." Richard could have bitten his tongue off the minute the words were out of his mouth because he knew he'd said the wrong thing.

"Yes," Marianne said, looking down quickly, the light going from her eyes. "Not until we are sure their affections are fixed."

Richard did not miss the catch in his sister's voice. He'd never met Mr. John Daring. He only knew that the blackheart had deserted Marianne and run off to the West Indies on the eve that she thought he was to ask for her hand. Rumors were ripe at White's these past few weeks that Daring was back in England, and Richard was sure his sister had heard them, too. Or why else would she have so readily accepted his suggestion that they leave London early—just before one of the most lavish of Christmas balls?

"Let's do it, sis! It will be fun. You make up your dream prince, and I'll concentrate on inventing some divine creature whom I shall keep nameless, of course. We have the whole trip ahead of us to get our stories straight about these highly presentable people whom we have chosen. That way if I tell our parents that I have been wooing a tall blonde goddess, you won't make the mistake of informing them that I like an exotic dark-haired princess."

Marianne tried to smile for her brother's sake as she let him hand her up the step into the coach. Although she had not seen John Daring at any of the holiday functions which she'd attended so far, she could not count it out that such an encounter wouldn't happen sooner or later. She had heard only the night before that Lady Reuter had sent an invitation to the new Viscount Littlefield. How embarrassing it would be if they should turn up at the same party.

When he was only Mr. John Daring, the charming devil had been accepted and adored by all the Quality for his quick wit and fine dancing skills, not to overlook his good looks and fine appearance. However, it was known among the *ton* that he was a man who would have to enter trade to earn a living, and consequently the mamas told their eligible daughters not to take his advances seriously. Now she heard that he was back in England to become Lord Littlefield.

Marianne had fallen in love with John when he was a mischievous boy, before he was a grown man, before he had money, before he had a title. She had thought he returned her affection. How deceived she had been. Now that he was a lord with several estates and a fine income, all those mamas would undoubtedly do a complete turnabout and throw their daughters at his feet. She did not want to be around to see that happen.

Her abigail, Janet, was already settled inside the carriage when Marianne took her seat. The young girl had only been with her six months, but already Marianne wondered how she'd ever gotten along without her. Sir Richard and his valet, Blume, entered last, and as soon as the footman closed the door, the coachman sprang the horses and they were off.

Leaning her head back on the soft leather squabs, Marianne closed her eyes and tried to think of this imaginary man she would describe to her parents as the hero of her dreams. He certainly *would not* have dark hair or flashing blue eyes. His voice wouldn't sound like gypsy music, or his whistle like a terrible, terrible imitation of a bird he'd called the purple-throated pee-wit. Her hero wouldn't make fun of the freckles on her nose before kissing them, nor would he lie about his affections, or talk nonsense about sailing with her across the high seas to a land of warm sandy beaches and palm trees. He would be proper and predictable . . . and probably very, very boring, she thought, as a tear ran down her cheek.

Richard watched the emotions play across his beloved sister's face and cursed the man who had broken her heart. She deserved the very best. He didn't want to stay in London and take the chance of meeting Daring any more than Marianne did. He was afraid if he should ever confront the man, even if it were to be at one of the grandest parties of the winter season, he would have to call him out for the wrong he had done his sister.

You deserve the very best, my dear, he said to himself. *Don't you think otherwise. But if I ever do meet the blackguard, I'll break his neck.*

Turkle Brown rubbed a circle in the fogged-up glass of the coach window and peered out. "It's a good thing we decided to get back to Town when we did," he said. "The way the snow has been falling we might not have gotten through at all if we'd delayed any longer."

Daring sat with the old map spread out over the fur coach rug laid across his knees, giving little thought to the storm brewing outside. Their valets, Keeble and Digsby, were settled comfortably across from their masters. The Littlefield lands were behind them, and they were now following the Epping Forest to their right. The wind piled up snowdrifts alongside the hedgerows and stone fences that ran parallel to the fields on the left, then capriciously whirled the snow around to form deep hills and hidden valleys to block their way.

"How much longer do you think it will be before we hit the turnoff?"

"Shouldn't be too far from here. According to this map, it's about halfway along the property line of the farm on our left," the viscount said without mentioning any names.

"By the by, who owns all that land?" Turk asked. "Haven't seen any gate or manor yet."

"It belongs to the De Vismes," Daring said curtly.

"Mmm," Turk hummed as if the sound was going to help him conjure up a memory. "Ain't that the name of the gel you squired around London just before you left England? As I remember the bets were on that it was a match. I thought you had a tender for her. But you up and sailed off to the Indies. Shows how wrong the gossipmongers are sometimes."

"Yes, it most certainly does," Daring said. "I suppose she is married and has a couple of children by now?"

"On the contrary," said Turk. "Miss De Visme hasn't been

caught yet—and don't think several haven't tried. I even asked her out once to the theater, but with all those earls and dukes . . . or their sons . . . after her, I didn't have a monkey's chance. She don't seem to want to settle down.''

"You don't say," said Daring, trying not to show his interest. "Wasn't she serious about someone years ago?"

"Well, I for one thought it was you, but if you say it wasn't, then I can't think who else it could have been. If she was setting her cap for someone, he didn't come up to the scratch, or they had a falling out.''

"Knowing her fickle nature she probably played him false," Daring mumbled.

"Oh, I could never believe that of Miss De Visme," Turk said. "She don't seem the type to string a man along."

"Someday you will find out how deceiving some women can be, my friend.''

"Well, I hope not," said the big man. "If I thought I had a chance with an angel like Miss De Visme, I'd jump in with both feet and ask her to marry me.''

"Hah!" Daring barked. He was about to make a not so pleasant comment about that when he saw a split in the road. "I think this is where we turn," he said, and forgetting his quarrel with Miss De Visme for the moment, he thumped on the roof of the coach with his walking stick to signal the driver to stop.

As soon as he climbed out of the coach, Daring mounted the box to sit beside the coachman and told his groom, Checkers, that he could climb inside or take a stand at the back of the coach. He chose the latter. "You tend the cattle, Potter," the viscount said, "while I watch for signs of a fork off the track which may lead us to the hunting lodge.''

The path wove in and among giant oaks and magnificent pollarded hornbeams. The pruning method had been used since ancient times and involved making cuttings seven to ten feet above the ground and then letting them grow back into mature trees. These had not been cut in a long time, and the gnarled old trunks—made more threatening by their undress of summer green—grew their twisted limbs into grotesque shapes, weaving a canopy under the ancient oaks.

"Hark! There ahead, Potter! A double-trunked oak with a pollarded hornbeam under it. I'll be swatched if it doesn't resemble an old witch with three arms. Turn right at the trees and pull up the horses," he said to the coachman. "According to the map, we can't be too far from Badger Hall."

Potter looked with some skepticism at the questionable trail already covered with a heavy blanket of snow, which was still coming down. "The horses ain't goin' t' make it up there with the load they're pulling, yer lordship," he said.

"And if we lightened the load of about one hundred stone— what then?"

"You planning on removing the baggage, m'lord?"

"You might say that," Daring replied, jumping down from the box and opening the coach door. "Out everyone. I think we've found the hunting lodge. Turk, you come with me. We'll go ahead to check it out. The rest of you gentlemen get behind the coach and push."

"Well, will you look at that," said Turk, rubbing snow off an engraved plate he found end-up stuck in the snowdrift at the foot of the tree. An iron hook still sat imbedded in the tree, and he hung the plate back up where it dangled crookedly but above the ground nonetheless. "Badger Hall. You're right, Daring. We're here."

"And we'll probably be here for the night as well. We may have to break in the door, but we can at least build a fire to keep us warm."

Turk pulled his gun from under the seat and stuffed it into his pocket. "There may still be wolves in these woods," he said in way of explanation.

"I think our ancestors did away with wolves long before our time, Turk, but we may need a weapon for other predators," he said, patting his chest to show that he harbored a firearm also. "I never travel without it."

Twenty minutes passed before they saw the walls of the wood and stone structure looming like a three-storied giant peering out at them through a white curtain of snow. Daring

motioned Turk to continue to the back of the house while he
ascended the front steps and made two unsuccessful attempts
to open the heavy front door.

Daring proceeded to the rear of the house and encountered
Turk coming back round. "There is a stable in back with a
horse and feed, and there's a light coming from a room at the
rear of the house."

"Who could be living here? From Woolcroft's record no
one has used the old place for years."

"Well, you said the funds have been going somewhere."

"It could be that it is being used for any number of purposes.
Squatters, do you think? Or thieves?"

"Smugglers?"

"Keep your gun at the ready."

Turk nodded, then pressed against the side of the house and
tried to take a quick look in the window, the hand-blown glass
distorting the inside of the room. "Can't see a thing."

"Stay out of sight," Daring warned as he approached the
back door. "I am going to knock. I've already told the servants
that I don't want my identity known until we see which way
the wind blows. Remember, I'm to remain plain Mr. John
Daring," he said, and raising his fist, he thumped three times
on the door.

Inside the kitchen Amelia was placing a knife and spoon on
either side of a plate rimmed with pink roses and another of
blue violets when she heard pounding. "Lord a mercy! Who
could that be at this hour?" she exclaimed. "Surely not Mrs.
Moss's brothers already."

Whack! Whack! Whack!

There! She heard them again. Three more bangs. Amelia
laid the last spoon on the table and shuffled noiselessly to the
door. "Coming! Coming! COMING!" she called a little louder
each time. She didn't want them—whoever they were—to go
away. Oh, my goodness, no. They would think her a terrible
hostess.

The hinges squeaked, and the heavy door moaned open to
reveal a most remarkable young man shivering in the cold. A
dusting of snow covered him from head to toe. What features

showed above the woolen scarf were comely: a straight nose and firm mouth, ringlets of black curls sticking out from under his high hat, and the most surprising sapphire eyes. Amelia had seen sapphires one time on the viscount, and that was exactly what this young man's eyes resembled. She liked him immediately, but then Amelia had never found anyone yet she did not like.

"Halloo! Halloo!" she said, not believing her good fortune to find such a nice young man upon her stoop, and if this were Mrs. Moss's brother, he was doubly welcome. Amelia had no sooner greeted him than another face appeared over his right shoulder, rounder, and with a fringe of yellow hair showing from under his high beaver. "Well, bless my soul!" she exclaimed. "There are two of you. Come in and warm yourselves before my fire."

Daring, having expected a much taller person, had fixed his gaze at a higher mark only to find himself staring at the most ridiculous peacock feather, its quill bare in spots, its barbules missing and its faded black eye quivering, bowing, and winking at him each time the little lady moved. He lowered his gaze to take in the rest of her.

She was short of stature and either generously proportioned or else the wide skirt and many layers of pleated satins and silks made her seem so. Long sleeves clung to her upper arms, then flared out with pleated laces at the elbows. An abundance of taffeta bows were pinned willy-nilly everywhere like butterflies ready to take flight: at the high neck of her gown, perched upon her shoulders, and one in her smoky coiffeur—which at first glance he had taken to be a powdered wig, but now that his eyes became more accustomed to the light, he found it to be her own hair.

Turk gaped over Daring's shoulder taking in the lady as well as the room. It was a generous country kitchen filled with the aroma of fresh-baked bread. Something bubbled in a large iron pot hanging from a hook over the fire, dried herbs were suspended from pegs along the walls, and the pleasant scent of bayberry wax candles burning on the table added to the plethora of heady fragrances.

One sniff of the stew boiling and bubbling on the hearth brought a low moan from the deep regions of Turk's stomach, followed by a sigh of euphoria. With a hearty shove he urged his friend to step forward.

Daring did.

"I am Lady Amelia," she said with great cheerfulness of spirit. "Welcome to my home, Badger Hall. I am so glad you decided to come and bring your friend. I told Mrs. Moss that I had room for you."

She seemed to be expecting them, but whoever this Mrs. Moss was, Daring hadn't a clue. "Lady Amelia," he said, bowing. "We are indeed in need of shelter for tonight." He could not come right out and challenge her claim to the hunting lodge, now could he? Especially a place he had not been aware existed until a day ago.

He introduced himself as John Daring, and his friend, Turkle Brown. By then the servants had arrived with the coach and four, and a mad scramble ensued to settle the horses in the stables before dark, and to get the baggage and men into the house out of the cold. When the others came into the kitchen, Lady Amelia told them to spread their wraps over the backs of the settle in front of the fire to dry, keeping up a constant chatter as she asked for their names, exclaiming that she was positively in a dither of happiness to have her party start four days early.

"My, what fine-looking brothers you have, John," Amelia said. "Mrs. Moss must be very proud."

Keeble and Digsby, Potter and Checkers stood with their hats in hand and tugged at their forelocks, sniffing the food and smiling from ear to ear.

While Daring was trying to sort out her statement, the little lady picked up a candlestick and—with skirts rustling and feather nodding—scuttled over to a closed door partially hidden behind a large cupboard. She rapped once, twice, thrice. When she received no answer, she opened the door a crack and peeked in. "Germaine is not in his room," she announced with no other explanation. "So if you will just come with me, I shall show you to your rooms. We did not expect you so soon, you see, so you must excuse my butler. He sometimes wanders off. We don't often have company. I hope you won't mind carrying your own baggage."

Everyone looked to the viscount for directions.

Lady Amelia was so accommodating and seemed so genuinely pleased to have them there that Daring picked up one of his own pieces and motioned with his head for the men to follow his lead. Why Lady Amelia persisted in thinking that the servants were his brothers he couldn't fathom, but perhaps it was for the better. He would instruct the men to continue to hide his true identity as the Viscount Littlefield until he got to the bottom of this matter. Right now his most pressing concern was to have them inside before the storm worsened, and from the sound of the wind howling about the old house, it was doing just that.

Holding up the flickering candlestick, Lady Amelia led them into the Great Hall and up the staircase to the first-floor landing. The wind whistled about the great rafters, and the huge chandelier swung—clattering and clanking—from where it hung from a thick rope in the center of the ceiling.

"Choose any room you wish," she said with a generous gesture toward both corridors. "We stand on no ceremony here. First come, first served. You will find kindling and candles aplenty in the kitchen, and if you bring your pitchers, there is rainwater in the barrel by the kitchen door and hot water in the kettle on the grate. When you have finished all your chores just come below to the kitchen and set yourselves down at the table. Germaine's plate is blue and mine is the one with pink roses. Now," she said, "I shall tend to matters in the kitchen and then see if I can find that butler.

"Oh, wait!" Amelia exclaimed, stopping the men just as they poised to make a race for the rooms. "If anybody wants for anything while I am occupied, just call one of my Doxies."

Eyebrows shot up; Potter choked, Digsby frowned, Keeble giggled, and Checkers stared at the ceiling. Daring looked at Turk and Turk at Daring. He was not quite sure he'd heard Lady Amelia correctly. But since the servants were all hungry, and he was sure their interests were more on food than anything else, he decided that he would sort it all out later. Besides, the men had already scattered like rabbits to select their rooms, and he and Turk found themselves left alone in the hallway to carry their own bags.

Three

"I say we continue, Richard," Marianne said as she entered the common room of the Bountiful Inn. With an impish grin and a vigorous shake, she showered snow all over her brother. Only then did she let Janet remove her cloak.

Sir Richard would have been tempted to retaliate had he not been engrossed in asking his man, Blume, to see that they had a private parlor for their repast. "You heard the ostler, Marianne. He said that a huge oak has fallen and is blocking Brambleset Lane. We don't have a chance of getting through to Thatchcourne Road until they've cleared it away. May take a day or two. I shall tell the innkeeper to find us some rooms before they are all spoken for. It is getting nasty out."

Marianne did not acquiesce as easily as her brother hoped she would. "But, Richard, you heard that gentleman in the courtyard who was arriving from the north. He said a worse storm is heading this way. The crossroads will not be passable if we delay our journey. Surely there is another road somewhere around here that we can take before it gets too bad. It isn't dark yet."

"Your safety is my first concern, Marianne. We'd have to

go all the way north to Bauldwick, and even then we don't know if we will be able to reach Thatchcourne Road from there. Now, don't argue with me, sis. I have made my decision and that is final.''

Richard had no sooner begun to look around the room for the proprietor than a peculiar little man in a faded purple coat and green breeches, his hat clasped humbly to his chest, appeared at his elbow blocking his way.

''Excuse me, guv,'' the peculiar fellow squeaked. ''Pip's the name. At yer service. A fellow traveler like yerself. Cudn't help but overhear yer predicament. There is another way to Thatchcourne Road.''

''I'm sorry,'' Sir Richard said, looking down at the stranger beside him. ''We have decided to stay here for the night.''

Marianne was beside them immediately. ''Oh, Richard, do hear him out. We have a fresh team, and if we wait for the storm to be over, we may be delayed ever so long. Where is this shortcut, Mr. Pip?''

''Just a piece up the pike, ma'am. 'Bout a mile past the Collins' mills you get off the high road. Keep goin' until ya come t' the claypits and take the left fork into the forest. They say it once led to an old huntin' box, but now the path's only used by woodsmen and locals to gather firewood. T'ain't difficult to follow. Comes out into Thatchcourne Road.''

Marianne's eyes lit up. ''Let's do it, Richard. Just think how dull it would be to be shut up in a crowded inn with me for several days.''

The twinkle in Marianne's eyes and the excitement in her voice infected Richard as well, for he was not happy in the least to contemplate a boring layover. ''Young maidens are supposed to be given to missish tremors at the mention of adventuring into the unknown,'' he said, laughing. ''All right, we shall press on. You and Janet refresh yourselves, and I'll have Blume request a hamper of food for the coach. Then we'll be on our way.''

''Thank you, Mr. Pip,'' she said, but the little man was already halfway across the common area.

* * *

Pip rubbed his gloved hands together and scurried back to the table in the corner of the room where a much bigger man named Boomer, more tattered than his partner but less serious of countenance, sat heartily banging his large tankard of beer on the small, round wooden table, singing at the top of his lungs. "Who, who, who? Lookee you, you, you! Lookee me, me, me!" He was about to start a second chorus when Pip slapped him across the face.

"Shut up, ya babbling fool! Quit blowin' yer horn in here. Y'wanna draw 'tention to us?"

Boomer stuck out his lower lip. "I was only singin', Pip. Why wun't ya let me sing?"

"Because ya sound like a toad with a bellyache. That's why."

Boomer's pique didn't last long. "Didja do it, Pip? Didja tell the pretty people about the dee-toor? Heh?"

"O'course, Oi did, y'fool. The swells al'ays fall for our shortcut through the forest flimflam. Now wipe thet grin off'n yer platter pan an' listen up."

Boomer placed a finger over his mouth. "Shhhh. They got goodies. Oi seen the pretty lady's necklace when she took off her coat," he rasped hoarsely.

Pip stuck his pointy nose up to Boomer's big one. "The tall nob with her is plump in the pocket, too, Oi betcha. But we wun't get none of hit, ya idjit, iffen we dun't git t' our hidey-hole in the forest afore the dupes pass it. So finish yer swizzle and git the mules."

"Comin'," whooped Boomer, upsetting the table as he rose. The heavy tankard clattered to the floor, rolling and bobbling, spilling what remained of its contents across the room as he happily clumped out after his partner in crime.

"Are we lost?" Marianne asked her brother. "It seems the coach is going slower and slower."

"Of course we are not lost. After all, we are in the forest not on the turnpike."

They had already been two hours on the road, and it had not stopped snowing from the time they had left the Bountiful Inn. A bounce sent Marianne sliding to the right side of the seat. She held on to her hat with one hand and clutched the carriage strap with the other. "Yes . . . but is it the right one?"

Sir Richard was a bit concerned—not for himself, but that he might have misjudged their chances of getting through the forest. "We turned at the claypits, didn't we? Catchpole is being cautious, that's all."

"He's being so cautious that it is already dark outside," she said, peering through the window and seeing nothing but tall, black, shadowy shapes marching alongside of them. Marianne had no sooner stuffed her gloved hands back into her fur muff than the coach pitched again. This time to the left, sending her into her brother's side. She laughed as he set her back in place. Across from them Janet and Blume were trying desperately not to come to a similar pass but without much success. Suddenly one of the rear wheels dipped wickedly, and the coach rocked back and forth and finally came to a complete halt.

There were deep-throated shouts and curses, and neighing of horses, before their footman, James, opened the door and upon ascertaining that no one was hurt helped the occupants out. "We can't go any farther, Sir Richard," he said. "I think one of the wheels is broken. The horses are all right, though. Catchpole has unhitched them."

Sir Richard heaved himself up and out of the leaning carriage and dropped into a drift which came nearly to his knees. "Does he have any idea of where we are?"

"There are faint tracks of horses and carriage up ahead, sir, leading off to the left. The rig must have come from the opposite direction."

Marianne thought back to their encounter at the inn. "Didn't Mr. Pip mention a hunting lodge somewhere here in the forest, Richard?"

Sir Richard took one of the coach lanterns and, after inspecting the broken wheel, retraced the footman's steps.

"There is a sign on the tree ahead that says Badger Hall. I'm afraid that if we don't wish to sleep in the coach, it is our only chance to find shelter for the night."

After a consultation, Sir Richard decided that the party should all go as one to seek out the lodge. Catchpole led the horses in front to trample a path and provide a shield from the wind. "We will just take our overnight bags, and if we find it is not too far, we can ask that their servants come back to help us carry our trunks to the lodge. I hate to leave anything on the coach, but I am just as certain that no sane man or beast will be prowling round the forest on a night like this."

Marianne had a feeling that her brother would have been happier if he did have a villain of some sort to confront. She knew that life in London had been terribly dull for him of late. Richard was used to challenges. "My portmanteau is under the seat, and my jewelry case is in it," she said, handing it over to James. "That is all I will need for the night. Janet has brought a satchel as well."

"Well and good," Richard said, with a lilt in his voice, sounding more cheerful than he should have under such adverse circumstances as he helped the women down into the deep snow. Blume followed. "Then it's off we go. Let us hope we find that our hosts bid us welcome."

It had taken Amelia no time at all for her to add more vegetables and meat to the kettle. The extra loaves of bread which she'd baked that afternoon to make crumbs to scatter to the winter birds went on the table as well, with generous crocks of apple butter and honey, a slab of cheese, and a bowl of apples.

When she was sure that things were as they should be, Amelia set out in search of Germaine. She hoped he was not lost at the front of the house again, but that was where she thought she was most likely to find him. He did so love to look at the stuffed animal heads lining the walls. So it was that she happened to be approaching the front of the Great Hall when she heard the knocks on the door.

The sight of two shivering young ladies standing upon her doorstep was so beyond even Amelia's imaginings that for a moment she just stood with her mouth in a perfect O. On either side of them stood two men, one shorter with direct brown eyes, slapping his arms and sniffing, the other a much taller man with a high beaver hat and a greatcoat with several capes. He was the first to speak.

"Kind lady, I hope we did not frighten you. I am Sir Richard De Visme and this is my sister, Miss Marianne De Visme. We have had the misfortune of losing a wheel on our coach and cannot proceed farther tonight."

"My goodness!" Amelia exclaimed. "Of course you cannot. By all means, come in. I am Lady Amelia and you have come to Badger Hall. There is plenty of room. You poor dears," she said to Marianne and Janet. "You are freezing."

"My men are below with the horses," Richard said, motioning back down the steps.

"They can take them to the stables round back," she said. "The men can come in the kitchen entrance when they are finished."

Marianne stepped into the hall, thankful to be out of the wind. "We were wondering if we could have our trunks brought in from the coach. We don't want to leave them out in the weather if we can help it."

"Of course you don't," Amelia said. "There are plenty of young men here who I'm sure would oblige. Let me show you which way to the bedrooms. Then I'll fetch them straightaway."

"James and I shall start back to the coach," Richard said to Marianne. "Blume, you stay here to assist the women and prepare my room. Both of us need not go, and I am far more used to being out in the inclement weather than you."

Daring stood in the kitchen holding his hands out to the fire. Although he'd seen no servants as yet, he had to admit that however Lady Amelia chose to refer to them, the staff kept everything in tip-top shape.

The beds were made up with clean linens, the woods polished, the fireplaces swept. What did puzzle him was that Lady Amelia seemed to be expecting him and his men. Keeble was elated to have a room to himself as he was sure the other servants were. Daring would not begrudge them their chance to taste a bit of luxury, but he hoped it didn't spoil them to think that it would ever be thus. He had not been that long in the peerage himself to have become accustomed to being waited upon to any great extent.

Keeble had been with him for two years now, Daring having acquired his services in Jamaica when he was just beginning to be able to afford a valet—a former servant in a fine but humble house and capable of making do, which was the sort of man Daring had needed while just beginning to make his fortune. Therefore the man did act a little informal at times.

When the viscount returned to the kitchen he saw neither his hostess nor any servants; but the table now was laid for eight instead of two, an abundance of food had been added, and a fresh bucket of water sat upon the hearth, warming.

"Ahh, there you are, dear John," Lady Amelia said, bustling in with eyes alight with some happiness she had not yet made known to him, but which he knew was forthcoming. When she told him of the stranded travelers needing assistance to bring their trunks in from the coach, Daring immediately volunteered as a gesture of goodwill. Turk, too, came down at that moment for more firewood, and Daring was not hesitant to offer his friend's services as well.

The pair quickly shrugged into their coats, which were now warmed by the fire, and struggled toward the flickering yellow light which danced just beyond them through the trees until they caught up with and joined the two men headed in the direction of the Witch's Tree.

They raised their arms in salute. Conversation was impossible with their faces wrapped with woolen scarves and collars raised high, nor were words necessary as they handed down the chests from the roof of the tilted coach. It wasn't until they had the luggage safely on the ground that they had the opportunity to face one another.

"Is that all you wish taken off, Sir Richard?" James asked.

"Sir Richard?" Daring said, pulling down his scarf and holding out his hand. "I don't believe I know you, sir. I am John Daring and this is my friend, Turkle Brown."

"John Daring? *The* John Daring, Viscount Littlefield?"

Daring was surprised, to say the least, that his identity should be known to a stranger. "Why, yes. I'm afraid you have the advantage of me, sir. I don't believe—" He got no further before a fist smashed into his face, flattened his nose, spun him around, and brought him to his knees.

"Hear! Hear!" shouted Turk, and he would have retaliated in like manner with a resounding facer to the cad if the footman had not dropped the lantern and grabbed him from behind, pinning his arms.

Daring took a deep breath and dove at the fellow who called himself Sir Richard, caught him around his legs, pulled him down, and delivered him a well-deserved pounding. The lantern had by now been kicked twice and rolled into a snowbank where its flame was extinguished, throwing them into an inky blackness. Arms flailed, fists struck out with no true target, legs wrapped around legs and words best forgotten colored the air.

The ruckus would have continued had not Potter and Checkers arrived upon the scene. Not knowing what circumstances had prompted such a roll in the snow, they stood momentarily baffled as to what to do.

Sir Richard—realizing that the odds were now four to two against him and his footman—rose and brushed off his coat and breeches. Then replacing his hat on his head, he swore to Daring behind his gloved hand that he would deal with him later.

"Gad! What happened to you?" choked Potter, holding aloft his lantern.

"An accident," Daring said. "We fell off the coach."

"All of you?" Potter said, unbelieving. "How extraordinary, my lord."

"I wish to hear no more about it. And, Potter, you were told not to refer to me by my title."

"Sorry, my . . . Mr. Daring. Forgot."

Sir Richard caught this exchange, and his eyes narrowed.

"The lady told us to come help you fetch some luggage," Checkers said.

No one was more bewildered by the episode than Daring himself, who a few minutes later limped into the lodge with his nose bleeding and holding his jaw.

"My, oh, my!" exclaimed Amelia as the wounded men came into the hall.

"A slight accident, my lady," Daring said, his eyes throwing daggers at Sir Richard. "Nothing that a little cold water will not take care of. I shall go to my room and tend to it immediately. Pray do not concern yourself."

"Well, you will all feel better after you've eaten. Just leave the chests in the hall. You can carry them up later," Amelia said. "Now all of you go wash your hands and faces and come eat your supper before your victuals are cold."

Daring climbed the stairs with Keeble fussing after him.

"Who is that man, my lord?"

"He's a *what,* not a *who,* Keeble. He's a madman. That's what he is."

"You don't know his name?"

Daring felt his nose gingerly. "His servant called him Sir Richard."

"Sir Richard *what?*"

"I have no idea. Now, do not be a pest Keeble. Go down to the kitchen or else Lady Amelia will make more of this than is necessary. I don't believe it is wise to leave our hostess unguarded with a maniac like that in the house."

"Maniac!"

"He attacked me for no reason at all. Alert Checkers and Potter that there is something havey-cavey about this Sir Richard and his bunch of ruffians. I suspect that he may be hiding under a *nom de plume* for some reason.

Keeble's eyes grew large. "I'll go immediately, my lord. I wouldn't want anything to happen to Lady Amelia. She's too sweet a lady."

"I'll be there as quickly as I can, and—I'm bringing my pistol."

"I think I should tell you, my lord. There are two women on this same corridor."

"The maids, perhaps?"

"No. Lady Amelia gave them rooms. They came when I was building a fire in your fireplace."

"Well, thank you for telling me, Keeble. Do you think there is any connection between them and the madman?"

"I do believe they arrived at the same time, my lord."

"Did they appear odd in any way?"

"I really couldn't say, my lord. I only heard their voices. They are in the kitchen now."

"Well, I'll still feel better if you go belowstairs to watch over matters, Keeble. I will follow shortly."

It took Daring only a few minutes to wash his face and straighten his clothing. He really was quite used to doing for himself. He ran a cloth over his boots. He doubted dinner in the kitchen would be too formal, considering the other guests had only just arrived. Quickly combing his hair, he rushed out into the corridor.

"Oh, John, dear. Do come and meet the rest of our guests," Lady Amelia said, rising from her seat at the head of the table. She now had on a creamy satin dress, with seed pearls sewn here and there, and a white-plumed feather stuck into her snowy hair. Quite out of fashion if she were in London, but on Lady Amelia it somehow looked just right.

Daring stood at the top of the three steps leading down into the kitchen and surveyed the individuals already seated on the benches at either side of the long work table. Facing him and to the left of their hostess were all of his men: Keeble, Turk, Digsby, Checkers, and Potter. He could only see the backs and profiles of those across from them.

"I was just about to go look for Germaine," Lady Amelia said. "I still have not found him, and I do worry when he doesn't turn up for supper."

But Daring was less concerned with his hostess's attire and the whereabouts of her elusive butler than he was in seeking out the tall man who had declared himself his enemy, Sir Richard; and secondly, making note of where his best friend, Turkle Brown, was in case he should need his assistance. Turk was looking at him with a strange expression on his face, one eyebrow cocked. Daring was about to make eye contact with the others of his party when he heard a gasp—a decidedly feminine gasp.

His gaze whipped to the two women seated at the head of the table to the right of their hostess, staring at him: one timidly, one boldly.

"John, dear, this is Miss Marianne De Visme. Isn't she lovely?" Lady Amelia said fondly. "And her young lady, Miss Janet. Of course, you already met Miss De Visme's brother, Sir Richard."

Good Lord! She was the devil's sister. What was she doing here?

Lady Amelia may have said more, but Daring did not hear any of it. He had eyes for only one person. Miss Marianne De Visme.

Four

Marianne was just as lovely as Daring remembered her that first time he'd seen her. They met during his fifteenth summer when his Great-aunt Hortense had sent him to a distant relative's country estate, Littlefield—or more rightly said, farmed him out so that she could travel to Spain with her friends.

John, as he was called then, was left much to his own devices to keep himself occupied. His aunt had convinced the household staff that he did not need much watching after, and he was even given a horse, and the run of the property. As long as he showed up for his meals and was in his bed come nighttime, the staff paid no great attention to him. It had been a lonely beginning, but John was used to being on his own.

While the viscount and viscountess were in residence there was always a round of country parties, dances, and assemblies to attend at Littlefield or at neighboring houses; and although many of the younger children were often brought along with their families, there were few his age.

At first he wished for some other boys to chum around with, but after Miss Marianne De Visme came, John found no necessity that there be more young people.

She had come for the day with her parents, a saucy yellow-haired girl of fourteen, too young as yet to attend the evening dance, and yet too old to play with the children in the nursery. They had paired off immediately and spent the evening outside in the gardens listening to the music and swearing how dumb it all sounded. Oh, yes, Marianne knew a few well-colored phrases that had come from other than polite conversations at an afternoon tea. To John's amusement it only made her more fascinating.

The following week he had attended an afternoon gathering with his cousins at the De Vismes' manor whose lands were only a few miles away. The boundaries of their properties marched together at some points. As before, he and Marianne had commiserated on the dullness of adults and their lack of knowing how to amuse themselves—and those observations had led to their over-imaginative discussions on what constituted fun and what they could do about it.

What began as a lark soon became a habit for him to ride over of an afternoon. John would tether his horse in a copse near a small stream, which ran through her father's game park. He'd sneak through the trees—it was much more adventurous that way—then scout around the hedges in the formal garden to evade the gardener.

Marianne knew just what tricks to pull to escape her watchful governess. Her room was on the second story. They tried to think of a signal he could send her, and she told him to whistle a bird song. He agreed, but since he knew none—and he wanted more than anything to impress her—he invented the purple-throated pee-wit. After all, he reasoned, Marianne was only a female and wouldn't know the difference one way or another. If his whistle ran dry, he pelted her window with pebbles.

She may not have known about the purple-throated pee-wit, but aside from that, Marianne proved not to be at all missish and prissy like he thought girls were supposed to be. Of course, John had to admit that his acquaintance with females was very limited, since he spent most of the year in boys' boarding schools.

Marianne had thought nothing of throwing a leg over the windowsill and climbing down the stout ivy vines which covered the honey-colored stone walls outside her room. They used her father's tackle to fish in the stream, and though she caught most of the fish, she let him carry them back to Littlefield to explain his absence for so much of the day.

She was the first person who was willing to listen to what he wanted to do with his life, or showed any interest in what he had to say. It was too bad that such a sweet-tempered girl had to grow up into such a disagreeable termagant.

Now Daring realized that Lady Amelia was indicating he take a space at the table on her left—directly across from the woman he wished to forget.

"Do be careful to leave room for Germaine, John dear. His is the plate with the blue violets," Amelia said. "Sit down before you starve yourself to death. I will not be responsible for telling Mrs. Moss that I did not feed her brothers."

This puzzling reference once again to Mrs. Moss startled him back to his present obligations. After all, Daring was not devoid of manners. "Miss De Visme," he said, inclining his head. "Miss Janet." He nodded to the others and took his seat. But etiquette did not dictate that he had to look for any length of time at Miss De Visme if he did not care to; and if for the next several minutes Daring seemed to concentrate entirely on partaking of the victuals before him, he was in truth cunningly watching every move made by the man with the swollen eye and bruised cheek next to her, Sir Richard.

John! The name formed on Marianne's lip, but no sound came out. Only minutes before she had watched her brother— looking for all purposes as if he'd been fighting a bear— come into the kitchen without one word of explanation for his atrocious appearance. And now, John Daring, appearing no better off with a cut on his lip and a red nose, sat opposite her. Had it been three years? He was almost near enough for her to touch if she wished . . . and she did wish very much. She thought she was over him, but if that were so, why did her heart pound and the tears fill up behind her eyes?

Marianne had thought he loved her. He had told her so many

times in a number of ways, but evidently a man's word didn't mean that much. Well, she wasn't going to show the renegade that she cared one whit that he ran out on her. She raised her face boldly to his and smiled—a prim, proper, very ladylike smile—only to find that the rakehell wasn't even looking at her. He was glaring at her brother. Out of the corner of her eye she saw Richard's fist tighten on the handle of his knife. Across the table, the man named Mr. Brown was casting a challenge at their footman, James. In fact, it seemed that the assembly was divided into two camps. Everyone on one side of the table was glowering at someone on the other. She and Janet might as well not have been present for all the attention they were getting.

On the other hand, Lady Amelia continued to share her good spirits with one and all alike. "John, I have already introduced your brothers and Mr. Brown to all these nice people, but I just remembered you have not met Mr. Blume and Mr. Catchpole as yet," she said, indicating two men Daring did not know. He surmised they were in the employ of Sir Richard.

Blume was obviously a gentleman's gentleman, and not of a pugilistic bent—therefore of little concern to Daring if he should have to round off with the fellow. But Catchpole was another matter. Albeit he was decidedly past his youth, he had the stout build of a hard worker, with side whiskers that gave him an appearance of a bear, a jaw which looked like a steel trap, and arms the size of tree trunks. The two men glanced first at their master before nodding in Daring's direction.

At least Sir Richard had not given Daring's true identity away to Lady Amelia. He would give him that. However, it may be that he had ulterior motives for not doing so. As long as she did not know that he was a viscount, that would make Sir Richard top of the tree in their hostess's eyes. And yet, it was Daring who was asked to sit beside their hostess. This Mrs. Moss must indeed be a very important person in the community.

Amelia let her gaze sweep the table. She could just feel the excitement crackling in the air. "Isn't this grand?" she exclaimed, clasping her hands to her chest. "I want to thank all of you nice young people for coming to my Christmas party."

Marianne knew her brother was not paying Lady Amelia her due respect as he should and punched him with her elbow. Not only did she think that the men were being very rude in light of the lady's generosity and goodwill, but she was ashamed of herself as well for not making their destination clearer. "Oh, I am sorry, Lady Amelia," she said apologetically. "I'm afraid that you have misunderstood. We planned on being at my parents' house for Christmas. My brother and I will leave as soon as the wheel on our coach is repaired. It can be repaired, can't it, Richard?"

Sir Richard, who had left off a minute from trying to stare down Daring and remembered his manners, smiled amiably toward the ladies. "I do not want to impose upon Lady Amelia any more than you do, my dear, but I am afraid we will have to wait until morning to find out if we can leave as soon as we wished. The snow was almost up to the coach axles when we went for the trunks, and I do not yet know the extent of the damage. If there is no way of repairing the wheel, one of us men will have to ride a carriage horse to get help. It may take another day before we arrive home."

Marianne felt her face flush. She didn't dare look at John. There was no way that she could avoid him if they both were to remain in the same house. But why was he here in the first place? Why was the lady of the manor feeding all of them in the kitchen and not abovestairs? Why were they sitting with the servants? Why were they not addressing John as Viscount Littlefield? All the men at the table *were not* his brothers. John Daring had no brothers. If Richard was not telling her everything he knew, she would wring his neck.

Now he was saying that they might have to wait another day before they could leave for home. Well, if that were so, she would stay in her room to make sure that she did not have to spend one more minute than she had to in the company of John Daring.

*   *   *

Amelia was not the least bit worried that she would lose her guests so soon. She had not seen snow like this in twenty-five years, and that Yule Season of long ago had them snowed in for three weeks.

"We will see. We will see," she said happily, rising from her chair. "I must go look for my butler. He is not used to such goings-on and I am afraid he may be staying away on purpose. If he does not come in time for supper, I shall be very angry with him because then I shall have to put a bowl of stew in his room. And he knows I don't like to do that. Everybody eat and be merry while I am gone. There is plenty for all. Now that everybody is here I want you to bow your heads and give thanks for the food we have received."

After a brief pause, she sang, "Amen!" and hurried off to look for Germaine.

About a mile away from Badger Hall, Pip slipped, slithered, and crawled his way up the icy slope of the dingle. He could see very little of the track through the dark forest from his position at the bottom. "Demme! The coach should've been here hours ago."

Boomer pulled his floppy hat down round his ears, hunched up his shoulders until they met its broad brim, stuck his gloved hands up the sleeves of his oversized greatcoat, and hunkered down as far as he could go without actually sitting on the ground. There he rocked back and forth on his heels trying to warm himself. "I'm cold, Pip."

Pip wedged his large burlap bag behind a bush to keep it from slipping back down the bank, then climbed higher where he could peer between two rocks. "Quit chur complainin', ya dimwit," the smaller man said, his teeth chattering.

"Where are they?" Boomer whimpered.

Pip squinted, trying to see through the thick curtain of snow. "How do Oi know? Never can count on the Swells to be on time."

Two hours had gone by since they had reached their usual hiding place in the rocky ditch paralleling the forest trail, well ahead of their marks. First ankle deep in snow, then knee deep, and now they had all but disappeared in the drift—and still the flakes showered down.

Behind them they heard the snorting of their mules.

"Oi'll go hide with Lem and Dirky in the cave," Boomer said.

"No, ya won't, ya lazy lout. Go git the beasts and bring 'em here."

"We goin' home, Pip? We ain't robbed nobody yet."

"We're going to go back the trail a bit. Just easy like we're out fer a evening ride after supper. When we come across the coach, we'll rob 'em."

The big man's stomach grumbled and churned. "Oi'm hungry, Pip."

"Jest think about the victuals we kin afford after we fence all them pretties," Pip said.

"But if Oi'm ridin' the mule, Oi won't git to jump out o' the ditch. Oi like to jump. It scares ev'rybody."

"No. This time ya git to ride Lem right up to the coach and yell, *'Stand an' deliver,'* like a real Dick Turpin."

That thought made Boomer forget his disappointment. "Oh, that'll be fun, Pip. He's moi fav'rite robber," he said, clambering out of their hole and making for the cave where they left their mounts.

"Oi thought ya wud be pleased. Now hurry with the mules."

Minutes passed and Boomer still wasn't back. Pip called out, "Now whatcha doin', ya idjit?"

Boomer waved his arm in the air; a large object protruded from his fist. "Loadin' m' popper, Pip."

Pip threw himself behind a rock. "Put that gun away, ya fool, afore ya blow yerself up. And quit pointing that thing in my direction."

"Ah, right, Pip," Boomer said, obediently stuffing the pistol down into the large outside pocket of his oversized greatcoat. "Comin'."

The trip back along the trail wasn't as easy as Pip had

imagined. They had waylaid enough coaches to know every tree, bush, and turn, but as familiar as he was with the path through the forest, he had never in his fifteen years of committing mayhem encountered this much snow; and the mules, being much more sensible, and perhaps a bit more stubborn than horses, balked at being forced to plow through the white stuff any faster than they saw fit. Thus when they were confronted by a great object rearing up out of the snow, obstructing the road, the animals stopped and refused to go around it.

"By Jove! It's the Swells' coach," Pip said. He dismounted and looked in the door.

There were no people, no cattle, and only two chests left inside. No amount of pounding by Boomer could break the lids open, and Pip would not let him waste a ball by shooting off the locks.

"Why don't we jest take the trunks with us, Pip?"

"And how do you propose to carry 'em, ya dummy? Our mules don't even want t' carry us. Prob'ly only fancy rags in them anyways. He pressed a finger to his lips and surveyed the area. "Don't suppose they went to the ol' lodge, do ye?"

"Oi thought ya said only an ol' lady lives there."

"I know," said Pip, his eyes lighting up. "All by herself. And if the Fancies had to ask fer shelter, they wud take their jewels with 'em, now wudn't they?"

"We cud jest go take the pretties away from them there," said Boomer, pulling out his gun and waving it around above his head.

"Put that away, ya idjit, afore it goes off. Now Oi'm thinking that we have to have a place to spend the night ourselves—unless ya hanker fer a bed in the snow."

Boomer shook his head vigorously.

"We will just ask the ol' lady if we kin stay the night, too. Then we kin git the lay of the land and decide what's what. That one they called Sir Richard ain't nobody's fool."

"Yer no fool, neither, Pip," Boomer said proudly. "Oi think yer the smartest man Oi ever did know."

The little man straightened his shoulders and stood as tall as he could, which he did quite well for someone barely five feet tall. "Then we'll go to Badger Hall and ask if the ol' lady can spare a bed fer two lost travelers."

When Amelia opened the door and discovered two more bedraggled humans upon her doorstep, she thought her happiness would simply spill over. Her party was growing beyond even her imaginings. "You poor souls!" she exclaimed.

Pip whipped off his hat and summoned up his most humble manner. "Is this Badger Hall?" he squeaked, as pitifully as he could manage.

"It most certainly is."

"Mr. Pip and m'friend Boomer," he said politely. "At yer service, kind lady. Lost travelers in the night lookin' fer shelter and sustenance."

"I am Lady Amelia, the mistress of the house. My goodness, you are shaking all over. Do come in before you catch your death."

The men tumbled over each other to get inside out of the cold. There, sitting in the middle of the hall, were two trunks just waiting to be burgled. Pip's eyes lit up at the sight. He had been right. The Swells had also sought shelter at Badger Hall; and once he had stated their own sad situation, Amelia had, of course, insisted that they must stay the night, too. Ol' ladies were always easy marks.

"Everyone is just sitting down to supper," she said. "Set your bags down beside those chests. You can carry them abovestairs later. The kitchen is warm and cozy, and I am certain you are hungry. Come now, I want you to meet my other guests."

Five

Lud! Those icy blue eyes from across the table were scrutinizing her in the most disturbing way. Storm clouds would be less threatening. Marianne could not imagine why John had taken such a dislike to her, but she was determined to show him that whatever he was thinking made no nevermind to her. Half-hidden from most of the guests by her brother's broad shoulders, she pretended to concentrate on her food while wishing John Daring to perdition.

From the cock and bull stories which were beginning to circulate around the table, it seemed that the men had forgotten that she and Janet were still there. At least that was what she hoped. The meal had started quietly enough, although there was a continual mumbling of unfinished phrases, and half-spoken words of a questionable nature, which were probably better off not interpreted. As each retort became gruffer, and its consequential rebuttal more to the point, she felt Janet tremble.

Marianne gave her abigail a reassuring smile. She had just felt the girl relax when Richard started another ruckus by asking Blume to serve him a particular bun from the bread basket on the other side of the table—when there were plenty right in front of him. She didn't know why he had to kick up another row now. As his servant began to comply with the request, one of John's men—she believed him to be called Keeble—adroitly pierced the designated bun with his knife precisely one second before Blume could reach it—and placed it upon John's plate instead.

"Thank you, brother," Daring said. "Well done."

Keeble grinned knowingly and raised his nose in Blume's direction. Mr. Brown let out a whoop and slapped the table so hard with the palm of his hand that his plate jumped, while Sir Richard clenched his fist and shouted, "That is downright thievery!"

"For heaven's sakes, Richard. Let it be. Fetch yourself another bun."

Marianne did not understand why this battle was being fought between the two sides of the table. She wished she knew what had gone on out at the carriage. Accident? Hah! Not likely from the way they were baiting each other like schoolboys. She would not have been the least bit surprised had she seen the two valets stick out their tongues at one another.

A devilish grin appeared on John's face. The same one that used to set her heart racing—the one that she hoped she'd forgotten—but remembered too well. In an instant all her resolve to remain impassive dissolved.

He took a big bite out of the bun, sighing with contentment, savoring every morsel. The performance was good enough for Drury Lane. Richard looked ready to start a duel. Thank goodness all the men were distracted at that moment by Catchpole. The beefy coachman's long arm—knife in hand—shot out across the table and speared the same sort of bun from Mr. Brown's plate. With a hearty whoop he tossed it to Blume, who passed it on with great relish to Richard.

Richard held up the sadly squashed piece of dough as though it were some great trophy won in battle. Marianne never thought she'd see the day that her pattern-saint brother would act so childishly or in such an uncivilized manner. If it was a male thing, she thought it was disgusting.

The imbroglio was followed by another round of unintelligible words—deep-throated grunts, grumbles, and guffaws—sounds that she could not or would not wish to describe.

It was not as though Marianne was ignorant of how men bantered with each other when they thought women were not in earshot. Heaven forbid! She'd eavesdropped enough upon her brother and his school chums—and yes, even her father and his friends when she was little—and had picked up a few pithy phrases herself. On second thought perhaps it was just as well that she did not try to interpret what they were calling each other.

Thus the two opposing parties were so engrossed in their own machinations that it was only Marianne who noticed that their hostess had returned with two more men, one of whom wore a greatcoat of a particular purple hue which she'd seen only once before in her life—and that not so many hours ago.

"My word! Richard," she said in a hushed tone, "Mr. Pip is here." She may as well have been speaking against the wind for all the good her voice did in gaining the attention of her brother. It took a punch to his arm and a nod toward the kitchen entrance before his head turned.

Amelia was clapping her hands like a school mistress. "Attention everyone!" she said. "We have more visitors."

Mouths popped shut, fists quit striking the air, backs straightened, and proper decorum and respectable behavior replaced mayhem. Keebles even blushed. As well they all should, Marianne thought. She heard Janet let out a sigh of relief.

"This is Mr. Pip and Mr. Boomer who have come to join us," Amelia announced. "Isn't that nice?"

Boomer was already sniffing the air and licking his lips. He would have bolted toward the table if Pip had not stopped him with a stiff crack on the arm. "Wait 'til yer told, ya idjit."

Amelia pointed to the fireplace. "Spread your wraps over the backs of the settles to dry," she said. "Then sit down at the table."

"Can Oi go now?" Boomer asked so loudly that everybody in the room heard him.

Amelia had no sooner gotten the word, "Yes," out of her mouth than Boomer tried to take all three steps in one leap, lost his footing, tripped on his long coat trying to gain his balance, and crashed spread-eagled upon the floor. With a loud thunk his pistol fell from his pocket and bounced end over end, with Boomer crawling, grabbing, and pounding until he managed to smack it to the floor with his fist. There was a loud explosion. *Ding! Bong! Crack!* The ball ricocheted from the copper kettle on the hearth, to a lantern hanging on a nail from a beam, to the crock jar on a shelf, which shattered and leaked jam down the cupboard.

Janet screamed. Every man was on his feet grabbing whatever weapon was available, nearly upending the table. Dishes rattled. A mug of cider tipped over and drenched the table linen. Daring whipped out his pistol from inside his coat. Sir Richard, Turk, and James did likewise. Keeble always had his small handgun tucked somewhere on his person if he could find it. Catchpole kept a rifle tucked under his box on the coach, but now had to be satisfied with a table knife, and Potter raised a huge pewter platter.

Boomer dangled his gun from his fingers and looked sheepishly at Pip.

"You imbecile," hissed Pip. "How many times do Oi have to tell ya not to keep a loaded pistol in yer pocket? Now see what ya done."

"Oi'm sorry, Pip. Oi wanted t' be ready."

"He's sorry," Pip apologized to the other guests. "Iffen it weren't fer the bandits on the road, Oi wouldn't let him carry a pistol."

Boomer blinked, his lower lip quivered. He seemed to be near tears and Amelia could not stand that. "We are just thankful that you did not hurt yourself, Mr. Boomer," she said, giving him a gentle pat on the arm. After all, she had lived most of her life in a hunting box and seen many a foolishness committed by men toying with their hunting guns.

Amelia proceeded to the fireplace where she picked up a large wicker basket with a handle which was sitting near the hearth, then made her way back to the two men. "Now you don't have to worry, Mr. Boomer. We don't have any bandits here at Badger Hall," she said reassuringly. "Put your gun in

the basket. And you, Mr. Pip. I'm sure you have one. Sir
Richard, bring me yours—and Mr. Brown—and John—and
James. I am ashamed of all of you. You could have hurt someone. It is the Christmas Season, after all," she said. "A time
of goodwill. A time to be jolly. I will have no arguing or
disagreements in my house."

Amelia counted the pistols. "When you leave you may have
your guns back, but until then they will remain in the basket.
Now finish your supper while I find a safe place to put them."

The men watched her go before settling back down at the
table.

"Nine chances take ten that she will put them under lock
and key," said Sir Richard as he watched her go.

"I'll wager a shilling it's under the bed or in her closet
behind her dresses," said Turk.

The betting went on well into the night.

The next morning the travelers filed one by two into the
kitchen. The table was laid with a fresh white linen and clean
flatware. The kettle whistled by the fire, and a huge cauldron
of porridge steamed over the hot ashes. Hot breads rose in pans
on top of the ancient wood stove. Already a roast was skewered
on a spit over the fire, and the men gave the crank a turn each
time they came to ladle another portion of porridge into their
bowls. Eggs and a rasher of bacon also sat atop the stove,
sending out an aroma which was proven to attract the male
more readily than the most exotic of French perfumes.

Upstairs Marianne had decided that she would have to face
John sooner or later, and since they would most likely be staying
only one more day, she would not be a coward and stay in her
room. But she had not counted on exiting her room at the same
time as he entered the hallway—or having to walk side by side
with the blackheart all the way down the corridor. Yet that was
what happened, and she could not turn about and retreat into
her room without labeling herself a coward.

However she needn't have worried. He gave her little more
than a nod. Mr. John Daring, alias Viscount Littlefield, seemed

just as disinterested in her as she in him. And although her
curiosity was about to get the better of her, she refused to ask
him why Lady Amelia addressed him as, "John, dear," and
none of his servants said, "My lord."

On the other hand, his companion, Mr. Brown, was not bound
by any restraints to snub her, nor did he seem so inclined. He
bowed low over her hand and said, "What a delight you are
to see first thing in the morning, Miss De Visme." Then he
smiled so charmingly at Janet that the poor girl was brought
to a blush.

Marianne was sure he would have continued his conversation
had not John pulled him away, rather rudely, she thought. And
so they proceeded down the corridor, she keeping up a lively
conversation with Janet—and he with Mr. Brown.

Whether Marianne knew it or not, Daring was very much
aware of her as she walked beside him; just the sight of her,
the cadence of her voice, reminded him of the times they had
had together. And though he didn't think it a good idea to dwell
on it, he wondered if her lips were as kissable as the last time
he'd tasted them. Dangerous thoughts.

He had learned the hard way, but he could see that Turk still
had no sense when it came to women. The good-natured nodcock considered himself a lothario, but he'd meet his match in
Miss Marianne De Visme. You had to watch out for the females
with the sunset in their curls and eyes that promised you Para-
dise. Daring would just have to keep an eye on his eager friend
to make sure he didn't fall under the witch's spell, as he had
done that summer at Littlefield.

When Daring met Marianne in London four years later at
her come-out, they had renewed their acquaintance. John was
delighted to find that although she had learned to deport herself
in a more dignified ladylike way, her eyes sparkled as impishly
and her laughter came just as readily as it had those days in
Essex.

Marianne was courted by many suitors over the next two
years, and John had thought himself quite fortunate to have

gained her attention. She did not make a match that first year, or the second, and hope began to grow in John's heart.

He didn't know exactly when he began to woo her. He was quite ineligible as a suitor, of course. Not because of blood—his was as good as any—but because of circumstances. Her father was wealthy, a member of the landed gentry.

John on the other hand was an orphan, living under the largess of a great-aunt in London. He had a small legacy left to him from his father's estate which was to be his when he came of age, but it had been only a matter of two hundred pounds—enough to back him in some sort of business enterprise. Part of it he invested in an acquaintance's venture in the New World—tobacco and sugar. He even thought of throwing in his lot with his partner and moving to the West Indies, but when he found himself falling in love he decided to delay his trip until after the next Season.

He could not believe his good fortune when Marianne said she returned his affection. When she asked him to come to a country party in Essex, he was reminded of that first summer and eagerly agreed, until he remembered that he had business to attend to in Southampton that same week. She made him promise to at least attend the ball on the final evening. She even encouraged him to approach her father that night to ask for her hand.

Of course Daring had known of other offers of marriage that Marianne had received. It had never occurred to him that she may have solicited all of them as well, then turned down the poor lovesick mooncalves when they made the final plea to her father. It only enhanced a young lady's standing in Polite Society to be sought after by so many.

Now Daring cast Marianne a dark look only to wish he hadn't. She looked just as adorable as ever, and he feared he would cast himself at her feet if she looked his way. Thank goodness she didn't. He hated to make a fool of himself so early in the morning. It usually made for a bad day.

Somehow they managed to traverse the long corridor, descend the stairs, cross the Great Hall, and enter the kitchen side by side without saying a single word to each other.

"Oh, Richard," Marianne called, relieved to see her brother just entering the kitchen from the back courtyard. "Will we be able to leave today?" His answering scowl did nothing to bring her any joy.

Sir Richard stomped the snow from his boots and waited until Blume hurried across the room to help him remove his greatcoat. "I'm sorry, sis. It doesn't look good. The snow is still falling and has already drifted up past the ground-floor windowsills. We shall discuss it in private later. Right now I shall join you for breakfast."

Janet had already gone off to get them some coffee.

Lady Amelia was bustling about fetching a bit of this and a bit of that and shooing the men toward the food. "Help yourselves," she said.

Marianne was surprised to see that Lady Amelia wore the same dress she had worn the night before. In fact, it looked very much like she'd slept in it. But her voice was kind and pleasant to hear. It was a big crowd to care for, and there was no getting around it; Lady Amelia was not young anymore.

The men were not as observant since they were more interested in stuffing their mouths, and therefore less inclined to be paying heed to anything other than satisfying their appetites, thank goodness. At least they weren't playing their silly games. Even her brother seemed more interested in a second and then a third frosted poppyseed cake than in dueling with John Daring.

"John, dear," Amelia said, with a little sigh. "Would you please fetch another pan of sugarcakes from the oven while I put this pitcher of cream on the table? Everybody certainly has an appetite this morning."

"As well they might, my lady. And for that reason I should like to compliment your cook." Daring studied Amelia's face. Something did not seem right. The plume in her hair drooped over one eye, and she kept trying to blow it away. "I have not seen your maids about yet, Lady Amelia. I wanted to compliment them also on how tidy they keep the rooms."

Amelia took great pride in her good housekeeping skills, and she was always pleased when someone noticed. "You mean my Doxies?"

The spoon full of porridge that Marianne was raising to her mouth stopped in midair. "Doxies?"

A profound silence settled over the table.

"Really, Marianne," Sir Richard rasped in low key beside her. "Must you be so outspoken?"

Marianne ignored Richard, put down her spoon, and smiled encouragingly at Amelia while taking the pitcher of cream from her hands.

Amelia's eyes twinkled. She liked Miss Marianne. "I call all my girls Doxie."

Marianne giggled. "All of them are named Doxie?" she asked, ignoring the poke in the ribs her brother gave her.

"No, not really. Oh, dear, no," Amelia chortled. "That is just a little joke I made up. You see, long ago there was a very pretty little maid his lordship brought to Badger Hall on one of his hunting parties, and I overheard him telling a friend that she was his little Doxie—and I thought, *What a pretty name.* Now I call all my girls Doxie."

Marianne deliberately kept her back to her brother and refused to respond to the choking sounds he was making. "That was a very clever idea, Lady Amelia. Many great houses call their coachmen John, so I don't know why they don't call all the maids Doxie. It seems such a practical solution. Especially if you have so many."

"Marianne, that is disgraceful. Now stop it and act like a lady," Richard rasped.

"And you are an old stick-in-the-mud, brother," she whispered back over her shoulder.

Without thinking, Marianne glanced up hoping to share her pun with a pair of blue eyes across the table. John would see the humor. But he was already off to run Lady Amelia's errand. Besides, she didn't want to have anything to do with him anyway.

"Oh, yes. It does simplify things, doesn't it?" Amelia said. "Of course, I never had a coachman or ridden a horse. I have never had need of one here at Badger Hall, you see."

Daring was watching Marianne as he came back to the table to sit down, and something clutched at his heart. The humorous

spirit that he remembered so well was still there in the woman
he had once loved. What had happened that had made her turn
against him? "You say you do not use a horse, Lady Amelia,
and yet there was one in the stables when we brought our own
cattle in. He looks well cared for, and we will expect to pay
you for the feed we have used."

"That would be Stomp 'n fidget," she said. "He belongs
to Obediah Doo, the woodsman. Obediah's cottage is small,
and I have a large empty barn just going to waste. He cuts my
wood, and I let him stable his horse. Everyone is much happier
when you can do for each other, don't you think?"

"Where are your Doxies now?" Marianne asked.

"Can't leave it off, can you, sis?" her brother hissed in her
ear.

Daring grinned, and for an instant Marianne's eyes did meet
his. She looked away quickly. Richard was right. She was
beyond redemption.

"Oh, my goodness!" exclaimed Amelia, putting her hands
to her cheeks.

"What is it, my lady?"

"Of course my Doxies are not about—and now I know why
they did not clean up last night. I always give them permission
to go home to be with their families for the holidays. With all
the excitement I completely forgot."

Marianne gasped. "Oh, my dear lady," she said, rising from
the table. "Do you mean to tell us that you and your butler
did all the work last night? I had no idea."

Amelia took out her handkerchief to wipe her forehead and
sighed. "Not Germaine. He says that washing up after people
is beneath his station," she said.

"Beneath his station? Posh!" Marianne could not believe
what she was hearing. "Why that is terrible, Lady Amelia.
You are the one about to drop. What about this breakfast?"

Amelia shook her head and looked toward the closed door
on the other side of the fireplace. "I am afraid Germaine is
used to sleeping in of a morning."

Marianne was beside herself with remorse. "No wonder you
look tired, kind lady. Oh, I cannot believe that we have imposed

on you in this way. It is unseemly that a lady of your consequence should have waited upon us.''

"But I enjoy doing for others, my dear,'' Lady Amelia said,
patting Marianne's hand. "I don't mind serving you. Really I
don't.'' She reached out and took hold of the edge of the table.
"I'm just a little tired is all.''

Daring was at her side in a minute. "Come. You must sit
down, Lady Amelia. Permit me to help you,'' he said, slipping
his arm around her shoulders to steady her. "Besides, how else
can I have a legitimate excuse to put my arm around a beautiful
lady.''

"Oh, applesauce!'' Amelia said, and with a little sigh of
happiness, she let her head rest against his arm.

Marianne suppressed a giggle. "Let's take her over to her
chair in front of the fire,'' she said, wondering how such a
rogue could be so kind on one hand and so cavalier on another.

One by one the other men stepped aside almost reverently
to make room for them to pass. Catchpole held the rocker
steady, and Marianne and Daring lowered the little lady into
her chair. Janet hurried to fetch the afghan from off the settle
and tucked it carefully in around Lady Amelia's legs.

"Now don't you worry, Janet and I will take care of the
kitchen.''

"You cannot, Miss Marianne. You are my guests,'' Amelia
protested.

"Nonsense,'' Daring said. "There is nothing that says unin-
vited guests cannot be of help to their hostess. That means men
as well as ladies. Now don't you give it another thought. I
know for a certainty that Sir Richard here is an excellent table
scrubber. He will be glad to oblige.''

It took all Marianne could do to keep herself from turning
around to see the expression on her brother's face.

Amelia folded her hands in her lap and rested her head on
the back of the rocker. "My, isn't that nice,'' she said. "Thank
you, Sir Richard.'' Her voice trailed off. She had barely closed
her eyes before she was fast asleep.

Six

Sir Richard's startled smile quickly faded the minute he saw Lady Amelia's eyes close. He swung around to face Daring. "I shall nail you for that, Daring. See if I don't. I will not have my sister washing dishes like hired help. Marianne, I forbid it."

"Fiddlesticks, brother. Would you have our frail hostess, Lady Amelia, clean up after you?"

Sir Richard's face colored. "Of course not. I will tell our servants to do it."

"I don't think Blume will feel any more inclined to cleaning up after the likes of Mr. Boomer than Lady Amelia's butler would. Besides, are you going to let a viscount show you up? If he can scrape a stew pot, you can wipe the table top."

It didn't bother Daring to dirty his hands. It was being waited upon that he was having to get used to. However, his good sense told him that it might be in his best interest to at least keep an arm's length between himself and Sir Richard. Consequently he moved off, urging the others to action. "All right, gentlemen, to your tasks."

"And you, brother," Marianne whispered, thrusting a stiff-bristled brush into his hand. "Let us see if you are as good as your reputation. Fetch a bucket of water from the barrel by the back door and scrub the table.''

Sir Richard held the brush away as though it were a spiny hedgehog. ''The water in the barrel probably is covered with ice.''

''Then get an axe and break it. I don't think it will matter to the table one whit whether it is hot or cold.''

Sir Richard moved off growling under his breath, ''I shall kill that bastard Daring, yet. See if I don't.''

While Amelia dreamed of sugar plums, the table was cleared, the dishes washed, and the pans scoured. Marianne put the china away; Janet swept the kitchen floor; the men rebuilt the fire and refilled the water in the kettle. Sir Richard went after the table top with a vengeance imagining it to be the viscount's hide.

And upstairs. . . ? Upstairs, Pip and Boomer were sneaking from bedchamber to bedchamber helping themselves to all the pretties they could find.

''Looka this,'' Boomer said, holding up an emerald and diamond necklace to his throat and looking at himself in the mirror.

''It'll be the noose around yer neck to hang ya from the gibbet, ya lunkhead, if ya dun't git it in the sack. We has to be out o' here before they come back.''

''Ah, yer no fun, Pip.''

''I said it wud be easy pickin's, not fun. The fun comes later when we spend all that rhino we git when we fence the Swells' trinkets. Now tie up the bag and let's git out of here. We'll hide somewhere below until they come out of the kitchen. Then we'll git the mules.''

''We goin' to collect our guns?''

''No, we ain't. The ol' lady probably counts 'em every hour. Iffen we leaves 'em, nobody will miss us until supper time.''

''Yer real smart, Pip.''

''Jest remember that. Now hustle.''

* * *

When Amelia awakened she wondered if she were dreaming. The kitchen was cleaned, a cozy fire smacked and popped in the fireplace, and the water kettle whistled on the grate. Two candles burned in separate dishes on the table casting shadow puppets on the walls. All was as usual—but she'd had the most pleasant dream. She had served breakfast to a number of young people. Nice, boisterous, lively young people. Badger Hall was all too quiet most of the year.

Then Amelia swore that two of the shadows—one big and one small—darted across the room and out the back door into the kitchen courtyard. Whether they were real or fairy folk made no never mind once they were gone. But the apparition did make Amelia sit up and take notice of the voices coming from abovestairs in the direction of the Great Hall.

"Glory be," she exclaimed, putting aside the afghan. "It was not a dream after all. I must have slept half the day away. My goodness! My goodness! My goodness! I do have company and they are upstairs right now and Christmas is coming and there is so much to do that I dasn't sit here one more minute." Amelia was glad that she was herself again.

"What do you mean, Richard? We can't leave yet."

Marianne and her brother stood apart from the others beneath a rather bedraggled, ramshackle deer head mounted on the wall which looked if mice had already borrowed half the stuffing over the years to line their nests. Sawdust covered its nose; cobwebs swung between its antlers.

Sir Richard watched the other men milling around the huge room. Some of them had already discovered a gaming room with an old billiard table. "Even if the carriage wheel could be fixed, the horses could not make it through the snow with our heavy equipage. We will just have to make the best of it, sis, until it thaws. We cannot make it home in time for Christmas."

"Mother and Father will be so worried."

"They will have received word of the conditions on the byways. De Visme manor is probably snowed in as well. They will know that you are safe as long as you are with me."

Her big brother had always been her protector. "And speaking of protection," she said, the amusement returning to her voice, "did you see the basket by the front door?"

"I did and I'd rather not speak about it."

"How much did you lose on the wager?"

"Nothing. Not one man guessed correctly. Good Lord, Marianne! What sensible, intelligent, reasonable person would suppose that Lady Amelia would put the guns at the front door where anybody is free to take them?"

Marianne wanted to laugh outright, but Richard was still not in the best of moods after having to scrub the table. "Well, I'm sure she had a good reason. And if you wish to find out why she did it, you will soon have your opportunity to ask, because here she comes up from belowstairs now."

Amelia stood for a moment savoring the sight. The Great Hall was full of people once more—just like it used to be when Lord Littlefield and his lady were in attendance.

Marianne and Sir Richard crossed the room to greet her. "I hope you are feeling rested, Lady Amelia."

"I am, dear," Amelia said. "Isn't this room lovely? I never get tired of admiring it."

Marianne glanced up at the chandelier hanging from the high ceiling and pictured the one above her mother's dining room table festooned, as it would be now, with Christmas ribbons and ropes of evergreens.

By now the other guests had come round to inquire as to their lady's health, John among them. Marianne tried not to take notice of him, but it was difficult when he kept making faces at her. So she did the first thing she thought of to draw attention away from herself. "It is a lovely room to have a party in. Why don't you have it in here?" she asked.

Amelia looked at the high beams and the tall windows. "We have not held it in here for ever so long. It certainly would be nice," she said wistfully. She certainly couldn't do everything herself: hanging of the boughs, gathering of the evergreens, braiding and twisting ropes. Tying bows was not so difficult. She could do that well enough—like her knitting. There were candles aplenty, too, in the storeroom, but there was no way that she could lower the chandelier to put them in the holders. Nor did she have the strength to set up the long trestle table.

"There are twenty-seven folks in Badger Bend now, counting the new baby," she said. "They will all be here on Christmas Day. I knit them presents, you know."

"Oh, Richard," Marianne whispered. "Do you think she knows about how deep the snow is?"

"I doubt it," her brother said. "Even a woodsman couldn't get through, let alone women and children."

"She will be so disappointed. I'm glad now that we will be here or else she and her old servant would be all alone for Christmas."

"You have a soft heart," Richard said. "You put most people to shame. I am afraid that I, too, was thinking only of myself."

"We haven't seen your butler yet, Lady Amelia."

"I am afraid Germaine is off sulking somewhere again. I mentioned that since we have all you young people here for our Christmas party that it would be nice to fix up the Great Hall and have the party in here instead of in the kitchen. But Germaine is quite stubborn and said that he was certainly not going to do all that gathering and twining and dragging in logs for the fireplace all by himself."

Everyone turned toward the big stone fireplace which covered half the wall on one side of the hall.

"By George!" said Checkers. "That's big enough to roast an ox in. Too bad we don't have a Yule log."

Marianne grabbed her brother's arm. "We could do it, couldn't we, Richard?"

"Do what?"

"Why, help decorate the Great Hall for Lady Amelia's Christmas party. The dear has her heart set on it," she whispered. "You men can fetch the logs and set up the trestle table."

"And there are ladders in the barn," said Amelia, whose

hearing was just as sharp as anybody's. "You will also find ropes in the barn."

"I saw evergreen trees not too far from the house," James said. "I could trim off some of the lower boughs."

Amelia looked up to the rafters and the bare walls. "I have lots of ribbons and yarns," she said. "Mrs. Moss brings them to me. But, oh dear, we only have one more day before everyone will be here."

"I think I saw a section of a dead tree that has fallen not too far from the house," Checkers said. " 'Twould make a good Yule log."

Daring spoke up. "My men . . . that is, my brothers and I will find your Yule log, Lady Amelia."

Sir Richard bristled. "Why, I was just going to say that my men and I would get it."

"Ruffled your feathers, did I, De Visme?" Daring said in a monotone.

"For heaven's sakes," said Marianne. "Instead of arguing over who is getting what, perhaps you ought to be figuring out how you are going to get a log that size into the house."

"The lady is right," Catchpole said. "All of us together couldn't bring it in. Even I am not as strong as a horse."

Amelia smiled. Things were going quite well considering. Sometimes it was better just to let things work out on their own. "Stomp 'n fidget pulls the logs from the forest for Obediah Doo. I am sure he would not mind if you borrowed his horse to pull the log inside the house. You can bring it right in the front door. It is wide enough."

"I say we give it a try," Daring said. "We'll get the evergreen boughs for the ladies this afternoon and take a look at the tree. If it seems possible, we shall hitch up the horse in the morning and drag the log in. Then we can help wherever we are needed."

"Right," said Turk. "I'm willing." All the others nodded.

"Well, there you are, Lady Amelia," Daring said. "You can tell your man that he need not lift a finger."

"How kind of you," said Amelia. "That is what Christmas

is all about, isn't it? Forgiveness and doing for others. Every year I have a party for my villagers and I give everybody a present. John and his brothers here know that, of course, because they have come this year to celebrate with their sister, Mrs. Moss. Now I shall go find Germaine and give him the happy news that he will not have to lift one finger to get the house ready for the party. Why, with all of you to help, we can hold our feast in style. Oh, my, oh, my, oh, my! I just knew it was going to be a very special Christmas this year."

"By the by," said Potter. "What happened to Mr. Boomer? He could probably lift the log all by himself. Save us the trouble of hitching up the horse."

Unhappily at that moment, Pip and Boomer sat up to their ears in a snowdrift watching their mules head back to the barn with the black bags still attached to the saddles, bouncing and flapping like the wings of huge black birds.

"Dratted boobies,' Pip swore, adding several other pithy epithets.

"Oi don't think Lem and Dirky want to leave, Pip."

"And we're stuck here fer the ol' lady's Christmas party."

"Oi like that," said Boomer with a big toothy grin. "Oi never got to go to a Christmas party before."

"Well, yer goin' to one now." Pip brushed the snow from his coat and started back toward the stableyard.

"What we gonna do, Pip?" Boomer said, lolloping behind.

"Nothin'. That's what. We're stuck like two flies in a honeypot. Even an elephant with a shovel couldn't get through this snow. We're goin' back to the house and act like we been out fer a stroll."

"Kin we keep the pretties?"

"No, demmit! Not if we want to keep our heads. This is what we'll do. Oi'll talk and mingle with the Swells while you hie up to the rooms and put the gewgaws back where we found 'em. Ya got that now?"

"Gotcha, Pip," said Boomer cheerfully.

* * *

Marianne stood back from the window in the Great Hall to study the decorations. The red bows on the swags of pine boughs looked festive, but she needed more greenery. She had thought that if she kept Richard and John busy fetching and carrying for her that they would not have time to quarrel, but she did wish they would hurry. It seemed that they were taking a great deal more time outside than was necessary.

She picked up some ribbon and began to tie another bow. Lady Amelia's unselfish spirit had made her realize that they were all forgetting what Christmas was about. If their hostess could share so joyfully with fourteen total strangers, then Marianne reckoned that she should find a little forgiveness in her heart for John.

Perhaps she had misunderstood his depth of feeling for her. After all, he was young and had very little income three years ago. But she'd told him already that they could live on her dowry, which she remembered had not sat well with him. Had she pressured him to approach her father so much that the only way he could think of to break with her was to run away?

Marianne had just decided to tell Richard that she thought they should call a truce when she heard loud voices approaching the front entrance.

The front door crashed open, and the hall filled with men. Marianne clamped her hand over her mouth. "Lud, John! What have you done to yourself now?"

Five minutes later Daring sat on a stool before the fireplace, his arms still full of greenery, while Marianne blotted with a cloth to try to stem the flow of blood running down his forehead and over one eye. The cut was somewhere above his hairline, and she dabbed with one hand while cradling his head against her side with the other. Daring didn't mind.

"John, you look as if you've been attacked by a wild animal."

"You might say that," Daring stated.

"Oh, no! You, too, Richard?" Marianne exclaimed, looking up to see her brother march into the room, his purple eye now swollen more than ever and a new bruise on his left cheek to match the one on his right. His arms were loaded with logs which he let crash to the hearth before stomping toward her.

"Let me hit him again, sis."

"Richard, you look terrible."

"Then why are you mollycoddling that renegade when your own brother is probably mortally wounded?"

"Stuff and nonsense! I am merely trying to staunch the blood before it gets all over the floor. Besides, you are only bruised. Lady Amelia is right, Richard. This is the time to be charitable. I have decided to forgive John for his misguided behavior, and it might be better, by the looks of you, if you did the same." Marianne eyed both men. "At least for Lady Amelia's sake while we are here."

Daring raised an eyebrow, making him look like a one-eyed owl. They talked as if he weren't even there. He again closed his eyes, trying to imagine what he had done wrong, but grinned immediately when Marianne continued her ministrations.

"Of course," she mused, giving his forehead another dab, "there is no telling how outrageous he may become if we forgive him completely, because then he might think he can get away with anything."

At that moment, Blume approached them. "May I speak with you, Sir Richard?" Richard nodded, then scowled threateningly at Daring.

"For heaven's sakes," Marianne said. "He is not going to attack me, Richard. Besides, his arms are full of prickly sprigs of holly."

"All right, sis, but be careful you don't carry this forgiveness business too far," he said, walking off after his valet.

Daring opened his eyes. "I don't know why I have to be forgiven. He hit me first," he said. "In fact, your brother seems to have taken a distinct dislike to me before we ever met."

"And well he might. Oh, I shouldn't even be talking to you after you ran out on me." She gave his forehead one last swipe with the rag. "There, you are cleaned up."

"Ouch!"

"Serves you right," Marianne said, stalking off with her nose in the air.

Daring thought of chasing her, but that was impossible without spilling his armload of greenery all over the floor. "Wait a minute!" he called. "Don't you think you have that the wrong way round? You're the one who cheated on me." *What in damnation did she mean? Ran out on her.* He looked about for someplace to dump the holly so that he could go after her.

Seven

Daring was restless to talk to Marianne. She had managed to avoid him all last night. If he could make her stand still for two minutes today, perhaps he could ask her what the hell she meant when she accused him of running out on her. But she seemed determined that she would not be alone with him.

Everyone worked feverishly from the moment they rose until late in the afternoon bringing in greenery, stringing garlands around the windows, and the hardest job of all—dragging in the Yule log. As predicted, Stomp 'n fidget was the key. And Boomer, too. The big work horse would perform, it seemed, for no one but his owner, Obediah Doo, until Boomer came banging into the stables, tripped over a barrel, and fell into Stomp 'n fidget's stall. It was love at first sight. The horse followed Boomer around like a dog. So they hitched the horse to the log, sent Boomer up the steps, through the front door of the manor, and the log was as good as in the Great Hall.

In front of the fireplace in the center of the room they set up the long trestle table. However, it needed a covering before they could start setting anything on it.

Lady Amelia sent Marianne upstairs to a large linen closet on the second floor to fetch some white sheets for a tablecloth.

It was a long, dark, narrow room, barely wide enough for one person. She moved up and down the aisle and had just made her selection when a shadow filled the doorway. "John."

Daring had started up to his room when he had seen Marianne, so he followed her in hope of finding her alone. "Don't be afraid," he said. Of course he knew that Marianne had probably never been afraid of anything in her life, certainly not of him, but it was just one of those things that a person says automatically. "Now you are going to tell me what you were talking about when you said I ran out on you three years ago. Hell, Marianne, you were the one who cuckolded me."

Marianne thought that if she pushed hard enough he would give way. After all, she did have her arms full of sheets, and Lady Amelia would be expecting her. Instead he merely let her press against him. It was like trying to move a rock, so she tried the shouting method. "I cuckolded you? How can you say such a thing? We weren't even married."

"Well, if we had been, you would soon have made one of me."

"You were the one who ran out on me. We were to go to my father together. You never showed up."

Daring tapped his finger on the tip of her nose. "Ah, but you are wrong, my sweet. I was there." *Just a day late*, he said to himself.

Marianne looked at him as if he had purple-throated pee-wits coming out of his ears. "What a hum."

"I was never more serious."

She stepped back. There was no sense in shouting at him when their lips were only inches apart. Besides, she suddenly felt surprisingly breathless. "But I waited and waited—you did not turn up. The dance was over and there was no sign of you."

She was so demmed close that Daring would have had sympathy for her if he hadn't previously been treated to a good example of her diabolical here-and-therian nature. "Well, actually I came the day after the ball. You certainly didn't act like you had missed me."

"The . . . the day after? John, I was heartbroken!"

"Well, you had a strange way of showing it."

"It was all I could do to hold my head up. The next day I couldn't even talk to my parents for fear of breaking down in front of them."

He had his own opinion on that. "You certainly found someone to heal your wounds fast enough."

"I refused to see anyone outside the family and servants for a month."

"Hah! Females always fall for a man in regimentals. And I suppose you will say that your officer friend was just doing his duty to protect you. What did he do—run out on you?"

She stared wide-eyed at him. "I have no idea what you are talking about."

"It was true—I was late. Circumstances beyond my control made it difficult—no, impossible—to be at the ball on time. I arrived the next day and thought I could bring you up sweet by pelting your window with pebbles."

"That sounds very romantic," she said sarcastically.

"Well, you once liked it well enough. Anyway, then I came into the garden."

She looked all innocence, like she didn't know what he was talking about. "Yes, then what? Why didn't you signal me?"

Daring was getting angrier. Did she have so many lovers that she could not recall them all? "Because you were too busy hugging and cuddling your new paramour. I didn't want to disturb you."

"My . . . my paramour?" She was beginning to wonder if he always hallucinated. "I didn't—"

"I saw the two of you."

Marianne's hand flew to cover her mouth. "Oh, good Lord! John . . . you nitwit. You cocklebrained idiot. A paramour? In regimentals?" Marianne started laughing. She tried to stop and then started all over again.

He put his face close to hers. "All right, go ahead and laugh at me."

She gave him a shove. He didn't budge. "That was . . . that was Richard . . . my brother. He was on leave from his regiment in India and surprised us by turning up at the ball. He always knew that Mother gave a country party at the end of the summer, and he wanted to surprise us. He was the only one I could confide in. He could only stay a few days. I poured out my heart to him. Later he traced you and found out that you had left within the week on a ship for the West Indies.''

Daring ran his hand up the side of his jaw. ''No wonder he gave me a facer when I told him who I was. And here I thought you were two-timing me before we were even wed. Lord, Marianne, I couldn't face living in England where I would see you but would not be able to have you. So I took my partner's suggestion to leave the country.''

Marianne threw her arms around his neck. The sheets fell to the floor. Neither of them noticed. ''Oh, John. Do you mean that we have been separated these three years for nothing? If you'd only come and told me that you were late.''

There was a pause. The silence pounded in Daring's ears.

''Why were you late, John?''

''I had a little accident.''

Her voice was full of concern. ''Were you hurt? Why didn't you send word to me?'' She drew back so that she could look directly into his eyes. ''Wait a minute. You said you got to our house the next day. What were you doing sneaking through the garden in the first place?''

Daring sighed. He never could lie to her, and he saw that he wasn't going to get her back into his arms until he told her the truth—and perhaps not even then. But he had to chance it.

He commenced to tell her the whole disasterous affair, not the romantic tale of a swashbuckler or courageous knight a girl like Marianne would like to hear.

After his meeting at Southampton, his only thoughts had been to get back to his Marianne, so he'd thrown all caution to the winds and had ridden neck or nothing from the coast to Essex. He was robbed, not by dashing highwaymen, but scoundrels of the lowest sort. Around midnight in a dark forest very much like the one they were in now, he was set upon and knocked unconscious. The jackanapes not only stripped him of his purse, but his clothes as well. When he awakened several hours later he found himself left without horse or weapon, not even his dignity.

Daring knew he was near his destination, so he had run along ditches and behind hedgerows to keep out of sight until he reached the De Visme estate. There on one of her father's tenant farms, he told her, he had turned bandit himself by robbing a scarecrow of his foul-smelling jacket, oversized shirt, and floppy hat.

Marianne tried to control her whimsical nature. She bit her lower lip, pressed her face into his chest, and took several deep breaths. Her heroic efforts to restrain herself did no good. Letting out a whoop, she laughed until the tears ran down her face.

"See, I knew you would laugh. I should have told you a clanker."

Marianne hiccoughed. "You should have stopped and asked for help."

"Good Lord, Marianne, I was stark naked. Even after I got some clothes, anyone seeing me flopping across the fields would as lief shot me on the spot and asked questions later."

This sent Marianne into another fit. Finally she stopped. Somehow she was in his arms again leaning against him. It felt just right. He was not moving or saying anything. He was waiting. Marianne raised her face to his.

"Kiss me, John."

Daring didn't need a second command. In fact, he'd been thinking along the very same lines for several seconds, and his lips were already descending upon hers. He kissed her once, twice. Then he kissed her a third time—longer than the first two put together. He didn't want to let her go, and Marianne seemed inclined to remain where she was, too, with his arms enveloping her.

She rested her cheek against his waistcoat and sighed. "Oh, John, I'm so glad you've come home."

Daring was beyond the point of wanting to say pretty words. Way beyond that. The devil take it! All he could safely do was kiss the top of her head, whirl around, and leave her standing there.

A slightly dazed Marianne finally managed to carry the linens down to the Great Hall where Janet helped her lay them over the trestle table. The maid wondered why spreading a tablecloth should make her mistress hum so merrily.

Daring, himself, was still in a fog and couldn't remember exactly what it was that he'd gone upstairs for in the first place, but as far as he was concerned it really didn't matter. He hurriedly shrugged into his greatcoat and went outside to cool off.

Later that evening, after they had eaten and cleaned the kitchen, they all retired to the Great Hall to admire their handiwork. They carried Lady Amelia's rocking chair up and placed it in front of the fireplace. The Yule log had already been lit and was burning so brightly that it warmed much of the room. Earlier in the day several of the men had lowered the chandelier to be polished and fresh candles installed making it ready for Christmas Day.

Daring came to the conclusion earlier that Sir Richard did not inherit the same sense of humor that his sister had.

"I've never heard such nonsense, Marianne," Sir Richard sputtered. "How can you possibly say that you are in love with the rake after what he did to you?"

Marianne had hoped that her brother would respond favorably to a more heroic version of John's robbery, but it still hadn't swayed him. She also told him how Lady Amelia had somehow mistaken the viscount for a Mrs. Moss's brother, and since their hostess had been so kind to them, he preferred to leave it that he was Mr. John Daring. That only made Sir Richard more skeptical than before, but he reluctantly agreed to go along with his sister's request.

"He'll come round," she said to Daring later, when they had managed to wander away from the others on the pretext of inspecting an evergreen roping she'd put around a window. "It's just that I've always been his baby sister. Since he was a little boy he's had to have a dragon to slay. Now that he has sold out his commission to come home and you have been removed as his number one arch enemy, he will be at sixes and sevens until he finds something or someone else to battle.''

"Well, until then perhaps I'll let him take a punch at me once in awhile to keep him happy."

Marianne couldn't help it. She started giggling.

"It's good to hear you laugh again, my sweet," he said. "I thought that perhaps you had forgotten how."

"Have I been as bad as that?"

"Worse actually. I prefer your brother's more direct approach to your subtle type of torture."

"I'm sure that Richard would have apoplexy if you should tell him that you are the owner of Badger Hall and that he is actually on your property. But I agree with you that until you find out who Lady Amelia is and how she has come to be living here, it is best that the fewer people involved the better it is."

Daring glanced back to the fireplace where an odd motley of men—young and not so young, simple and hardworking, genteelly born and a couple born in the likes of Cabbage Lane—were paying court to a gracious little old lady in a rocking chair. "She seems familiar with everything in the manor. She speaks of the old viscount, and Potter told me that the woodsman, Obediah Doo, referred to her as *Lady Amelia* when he came to feed his horse."

Marianne followed his gaze. "Her clothes are very fine in quality howbeit of another era. She is such a sweet lady and I would hate to see her upset."

"So I cannot come right out and accuse her of trespassing, can I?"

"Of course you cannot. That would be cruel. I agree that this Mrs. Moss seems to be your best bet to unraveling the mystery of how she comes to be here. But that also brings up another matter. There is something which I have not told anyone else yet."

"And that is what?" Daring asked, taking her elbow and steering her toward the center of the hall.

Marianne let out a yip.

Daring put his mouth to her ear. "Shhhh. We are supposed

to be inspecting the decorations remember, and I see Mr. Pip heading this way. If you don't want to have your ear bent out of shape for the next half hour, I suggest we get on with it.''

Marianne agreed wholeheartedly.

"Now what is this matter which disturbs you?"

"John, I am sure Germaine does not exist—except in Lady Amelia's imagination.''

Daring stopped and turned to look at her. "Are you certain? I just took for granted that he was shy. The manor is not that huge compared to one like Littlefield, but still we are just staying in only one half of the house here. There is the whole other side."

"I am quite sure. Lady Amelia had me take a bowl of food into Germaine's room for him tonight. She said she knew that he was not going to come out until everybody was gone. There was the usual bed, clothes press, and chest of drawers. Also an old roll-down desk. It looks as though the room may have been used as an office at one time—a butler or overseer perhaps? The room was tidy, but I could tell that no one has lived in there for years."

Daring weighed that.

Marianne watched John's face for his reaction. "If Lady Amelia has invented Germaine, do you believe she could have made up the party and the villagers?"

"No, the party is true enough. Potter said that Obediah Doo also mentioned that he always comes to Lady Amelia's Christmas party every year. But his cottage is only about a mile away. The village is much farther."

"Oh, dear," she said.

Marianne was thus deep in contemplation when all of a sudden Daring stopped, whirled her around to face him, clasped her face in his hands, and kissed her soundly upon the lips. In fact, he kissed her so soundly that all she could do was stare when he released her, grinning. He pointed upward. "Mistletoe," he said simply. "Couldn't let it go to waste now, could I?"

She shook with silent laughter. Lud! She'd helped make the bough herself that afternoon. Her wits had surely gone begging ever since John Daring had cornered her in the linen closet. "Is this what I'm going to have to put up with for the rest of my life?" she said.

"Possibly," he said.

"Oh, John, do be serious."

"I have never been more serious in my life, my sweet. Haven't I allowed my servants to call me by my Christian name when I am now the viscount—and let your brother's cohorts treat me miserably, stealing food right off my plate. I have scrubbed pots, been called a rake, and had my daylights blackened by a madman."

"Yes, well, under those trying circumstances I would say that you have done quite admirably, my lord. But let us get back to the immediate matters at hand.

"If it is true about what Catchpole told Richard, that the snow is so deep that our team could not even get as far as the road, then how will the villagers possibly get through the forest to come to Badger Hall?"

Daring let out his breath, his expression sobering. "I fear that they cannot get here unless a miracle happens."

"Oh, John, Lady Amelia so has her heart set on a Christmas party for the villagers. Have you seen all the sweaters, and scarves, and mittens that she has knitted? She will be so disappointed if no one comes. She has been in the kitchen all day baking. She said she always makes the pastries for her party. I'm afraid I was not much help, and she shooed me away. She said that I was needed more up here to help with the decorations." Marianne looked around the room. "It does look festive, doesn't it," she said. The scent of pine and wood and beeswax floated everywhere.

"Look at her, John. She can hardly keep her eyes open. I must see that she gets to bed," Marianne said, starting toward the hearth. "It is too bad that she let her maids go, but of course there was no way of her knowing that she would be burdened with fourteen extra people."

Amelia greeted Marianne and John with a twinkle in her eye. "Tomorrow is my party," Amelia said with a weary smile. "My goodness, I am so tired I can't even get up to go to bed."

Marianne brightened for the old lady's sake. "Well, it certainly won't do at all," Marianne said. "What would your guests say tomorrow if they should arrive to find you have slept in your chair all night. Janet and I will gladly assist you."

Marianne helped Amelia into her chambers while Janet ran to the kitchen to get some hot water. Marianne washed the sweet lady's face and hands, and together they helped her into her night rail. Janet turned down the covers. Marianne tucked her into the large four-postered bed.

Amelia asked them to listen to her prayers, and Marianne pulled a chair up beside the bed and told Janet that she would sit with her until she fell asleep. Marianne looked at the two little button eyes, studying her from under a frilly white bed cap, and wondered what the woman could possibly be thinking.

Amelia knew what it was like to be in love. She had been watching John and Miss Marianne. All the signs were there. "John is a very nice young man, dear."

Marianne's lips turned up. "Yes, he is. A very nice young man."

"Take your happiness when you can, dear. True love lasts forever, but not many people find it."

"I shall remember that," Marianne said.

Amelia made little sounds like the chirping of a sparrow. "Oh, I just know it's going to be a very special Christmas this year," she said, wiggling her toes and shifting down farther underneath her warm comforters until just her eyes and nose showed above the sheet. Like a child she soon fell asleep, smiling.

Marianne found John still in front of the hearth. Most of the others had gone up to bed. Richard stood over by the stairway waiting to escort her upstairs.

"Oh, John, we just cannot let Lady Amelia be disappointed."

"And she shall not be," Daring said. "We will harness the horses to logs and plow a path to the village first thing in the morning. I have already talked to the men. They are all willing—even that stiff-rumped brother of yours. Of course he wants to be in charge. Says he knows better than I how to lead men.''

"I'm sure he was a good officer, John. Besides, if he is kept well occupied, he is less likely to hit you.''

Daring contemplated that benefit. ''Yes, there is that. Maybe I'll let him do it.''

Eight

They came in wagons, on horseback, and on foot. They brought food and wine and good cheer. Colonel De Visme led a successful campaign against the elements. He had his soldiers and cattle abroad before the sun was up, dragging logs through the forest to clear a path to Badger Bend. They met halfway with the villagers, who had started their own assault from the other side.

Lady Amelia's Christmas party met all her expectations. Her gifts were accepted with heartfelt gratitude as they were every year, and she even had presents for all of her unexpected guests.

Boomer was especially overwhelmed with his newly knitted gloves which, although they had six fingers on each hand, were far warmer than his old ripped ones.

They all sang Christmas carols, and Boomer got to sing as loud as he wanted without any reprimand. Surprisingly, Mr. Pip was discovered to have a lovely tenor voice, and he volunteered to form the children into a choir and lead them.

Another strange happening occurred before the party even began. It seemed when Keeble was dressing his lordship for the party he discovered a pair of emerald earrings among his cufflinks in his accessory box. This seemed rather unusual because the valet was sure that they had not been in there when he had packed for the journey to London.

At about the same time across the hallway from Lord Littlefield's room, Janet found a ruby stickpin very much like those used in a man's cravat in Miss De Visme's jewelry box. And later, Sir Richard's and Mr. Brown's valets discovered two sets of identical mismatched cufflinks in their boxes—one gold and the other silver. This mystery never was explained unless one believed in mischievous ghosts.

Mrs. Moss brought her two brothers along to the party. Both were married and had their young families with them. Neither of them looked a thing like John Daring.

No matter how discreetly Daring and Marianne asked, they found no one in the village who could shed much light on the mystery of Lady Amelia.

Mrs. Moss said that her husband had been postmaster for twenty years now, and he had just carried on the tradition of the postmaster before him and taken over the duties of overseeing the manor, and the care of the lady of the house.

Even old Mrs. Bentlewood, who was the oldest woman in the village and near to one hundred years old, said that the Quality in the hunting lodge never did have much to do with the villagers until Lady Amelia.

"Do you know how long ago it was when the first postmaster began overseeng the property?" Daring asked.

"The last retainer must have died or left over forty years ago."

"Lady Amelia is a fine lady," Mrs. Moss said. "We watch out after her. I have offered to send my granddaughters to help clean, but she insists she has maids who do just fine."

"What was the last retainer's name, do you remember?"

"No, that was long before my husband and me came to Badger Bend."

"His name was Germaine," stuck in Mrs. Bentlewood. "I remember because he was such a handsome young man—dark hair and coal black eyes. Foreign-looking. French or Gypsy everyone said. All the village maidens watched for him, but he never paid any of them no nevermind. Fetched his supplies and went straight back to the manor.''

Daring thought he might be on to something. ''What happened to him, Mrs. Bentlewood?''

''No one knows. No more than we did about most of the servants who used to come with the lords and ladies when they came to hunt.''

John waited until they were alone before he and Marianne could compare what they had found out.

''Are you going to tell them who you are, John?''

''No, but I will be making two or three changes when we get out of here.''

''You are not going to put Lady Amelia out, are you?''

''No, my sweet—nor will I dismiss Germaine. I doubt that he was a very good overseer in the first place.''

''I believe that Germaine had far better talents in other fields than in butlering,'' she said, then told John what Lady Amelia had told her the night before.

''Well, if that is the situation, I shall leave well enough alone—except that I will have Woolcroft double the yearly stipend for the upkeep of Badger Hall.''

Marianne was curious to know what else he meant to do. ''You said two or three changes.''

''The other,'' said Daring, ''is that the lady of the manor be assigned a visible maid and butler from now on. That way Lady Amelia will not have to do Germaine's work anymore.''

''Oh, John,'' Marianne cried. ''You can make up the most outrageous tarradiddles.''

''Who me?'' he said.

Marianne looked at him fondly. ''Yes, you. You always are telling clankers.''

''I never,'' Daring said, spreading his hand across his chest. ''Cross my heart and hope to die.''

''Admit it, John. There never was a bird called the purple-throated pee-wit.''

''Are you sure?''

''I never saw one and I never found anybody else who has either.''

"Never? Are you sure?" Daring answered innocently. "How extraordinary! They are quite common in the south of England."

Marianne hid her mouth behind her hand.

"You are laughing, my sweet."

"I most certainly am not," she said, her shoulders beginning to shake.

"Then why are you trembling?"

"I am cold—that is all."

"Then come nearer so I can warm you."

"You are just as outrageous as ever."

"Not nearly so, my love. I am afraid I am sadly out of practice," he said, sighing most miserably. So miserably, in fact, that Marianne felt it imperative that she help him find the solution for his melancholy immediately.

"I know where there is another bunch of mistletoe that isn't in the middle of the room."

"Up to your old tricks again, Miss De Visme? Where may this kissing bough be?"

"Right here," Marianne said, pulling out a sprig from inside her sleeve and holding it over his head.

Daring didn't need a second invitation. He pulled her into his arms and kissed her long and hard.

"Happy Christmas, my darling."

BENEATH THE MISTLETOE

Alice Holden

Prologue

Two powerful stallions with hooves flying bore down on a bumping, lurching farm wagon that crawled along on an icy road. Hitched to a red racing curricle driven by a gentleman in a fashionable many-caped coat, the grays galloped over the patches of ice made even more treacherous by a mask of new-fallen snow.

On the wagon, a farmer shivered in a years-old wool coat and nondescript felt hat, which had never been in vogue, and cursed the "damned fool" gaining on him.

When the gentleman whip had closed the distance between his steeds and the rear rail of the wagon to a matter of yards, he shot his horses between the wagon and a deep ditch on the road's verge and veered in front of the plodding mare without slowing.

Unseen by the driver whose fine beaver hat was pulled down to his brow against the bitter cold and blowing snow, a stag raced over a frozen field on a collision course with the curricle. The red deer and the racing vehicle arrived at a bend in the road together. The deer sailed into the air, soared past the horses' noses, landed in the opposite field, and vanished into the brush.

Belatedly, the driver jerked hard on the reins. The curricle, wheels screeching, swerved back and forth across the icy road. In a freakish split, the carriage and stallions separated. The horseless vehicle careened and plunged into the ditch, catapulting the driver from the box. He landed facedown on the hard ground, his tall hat ensnared on the brambles.

The grays, instead of bolting in terror, unaccountably stood docilely in the field as though the animals had been reined in by some divine hand.

The farmer caught up to the site of the disaster and set the wagon brake with a shaking hand. He sprang from the box and crossed the road, his work boots giving him some purchase on the slick surface. He slid down the embankment into the ditch, past the broken curricle with a single red wheel spinning in the cold air, and knelt in the snow beside the inert form. With a sinking stomach he extended his gloved hand toward the whip's shoulder. Just then, the man turned over like someone rolling in his sleep. The farmer tumbled back onto his heels and willed his heartbeat to slow.

"You gave me a fright," the farmer gasped, gazing into the victim's dark, dazed eyes. "I thought you were dead."

The driver raised his head and shoulders from the ground and attempted to sit up. The farmer slipped a stabilizing hand against the injured man's broad back and propped him against the frozen embankment. Blood oozed down one side of his face from a deep abrasion low on his forehead.

Searching for something to stem the flow of blood, the farmer patted his coat pockets and groped inside and outside of his clothes.

"I don't seem to have anything to bind your wound. I'll have to remove your neckcloth," he said.

His fingers were clumsy in his woolen gloves as he unfastened the topmost buttons of the caped coat. But he soon parted the collar and found the white cravat underneath and began to unwind the cloth from around the strong column of neck.

"Who are you?" the whip asked. The farmer was encouraged by the strength in the cultured voice. It was far from the rattle of a dying man.

"Abel Bonner," he answered, the tension dissolving from his keyed up muscles. "I'm a farmer. My holding is a short distance from here."

Abel came to the end of the length of pure white linen, pulled the cravat loose, and rebuttoned the victim's coat. In a matter of seconds, he had the stopgap bandage in place over the injured man's wound and asked in turn, "Who are *you?*"

"Me? I'm . . ." The driver's voice lost its force in bewilderment. He scanned his surrroundings with a blank stare.

"Where the devil am I?" he asked.

"On a country road that leads to York," the farmer said, getting to his feet and brushing the snow from the knees of his stained old tweeds.

"York? In England?"

Abel could see the man's mind was muddled, but the driver was in far better shape than he deserved to be.

"That's right," Abel said. "You don't seem to have any broken bones, but your mind is rather muzzy from the shock of the accident and being battered about."

"There was a deer, I think, at fault."

Abel snorted. "More like an icy road and snow and dangerous speed and a careless driver." In his relief at finding the man alive and in relatively good shape, he could not hold back his need to chastise the whip for his foolhardiness.

The injured man pressed the thumbs of his soft leather, furlined gloves hard against his temples, Abel's scold appearing to have fallen on deaf ears.

The farmer bent forward and placed a hand on the injured man's shoulder. "Head hurt?" he asked.

The man nodded.

"Small wonder, you banged your forehead against the ground which is rock hard. This narrow road is not a raceway for fancy rigs in the best of weather, you know, but it was corkbrained to drive hell bent for leather in ice and snow," he chided in a second mild tirade to his unreceptive audience of one. Giving up on what he was beginning to realize was a futile harangue to pay back the whip in some measure for causing his heart to stop and for filling him with dread, Abel said, "No sense jawing and blaming, I need to get you out of this ditch and under cover.''

Abel looked up the embankment to the road and back down at the injured man. The stranger at six feet or more was at least five or six inches taller than he was.

''You're a big 'un and just might collapse on me if I attempt to move you up to the wagon on my own,'' he said. ''I'm going to need some help.''

He pointed through the denuded trees where the chimney stacks and slate roof of a cottage were visible.

''That's Miss Wyndom's house. She's a kind one and will give you shelter until I can fetch the doctor tomorrow,'' he said. ''My friend Micah works there. I'm going to bring him back down here, so he can help me get you into the wagon. Do you understand?''

The man inclined his head and repeated, ''You are going for help.''

''Right.'' Abel scrambled up the embankment and from the road reassured the injured man, ''I won't be long.''

One

The bedroom contained all of the necessities for an occupant's comfort, but none of those little luxuries, like bowls of colorful flowers, Dresden figurines, and a few small, exquisite paintings that would lead a visitor to exclaim, "How charming!" Abel and Micah had put the injured man to bed and then summoned Megan and left her alone to nurse the accident victim's head wound.

The fire had been built up a short time before against the December cold, but its warmth had not yet filtered into every corner of the room. Megan shuddered, but not from cold. She had stared into the dark eyes of the man in her brother Sam's bed and been shocked to find herself gazing into a handsome face from her past.

But he had no memory of her and groused, "Do I look so ghastly, lass? You're gaping as if you were seeing a ghost."

Her response, whatever it would have been, had remained unspoken. To her immense relief, his eyelids had shut and sleep had overtaken him.

Although her knees no longer threatened to buckle under her, Megan sank into an upholstered armchair which faced the large bed, grateful for the respite that would allow her to calm

her colliding nerves. She turned toward the window where the
plain blue drapes were open to reveal the premature darkness
of the winter afternoon. The snowy landscape beyond was
obscured by the reflection in the glass pane of the dancing
flames in the fireplace behind her.

Five years could play havoc with a recollection, but she had
recognized him at once as the dashing Captain Garrison who
had kissed her beneath the mistletoe when she was an impres-
sionable sixteen-year-old. The marvel of his sensuous mouth
on her untried lips had been a recurring memory each Christmas
when she fastened the mistletoe with a red ribbon to the silver
kissing ball. But in the girlish dreams that she had been spinning
for years, she had embued him with unrealistic romantic quali-
ties to falsely fill in the sketchy facts that she knew of the
army officer who had left Wyndom House the day after the
remarkable kiss to rejoin Wellington's forces on the Peninsula.

Megan's attention was abruptly pulled back to the bed. The
injured man groaned and tossed his head from side to side on
the pillow and cried out. She slid to the edge of the blue chair
cushion and stretched forth a hand, prepared to shake him
gently from his distressing dream. But before she could touch
him, his erratic movements ceased, and she withdrew her hand.
He quieted after a moment, his chest rising and falling in the
steady rhythm of a more peaceful sleep.

Megan watched him close up for a moment. His face was
pale and haggard, but every bit as handsome under the pallor
as it had been a half decade ago. His raven hair flowed over the
white bandage which Abel had fashioned from the gentleman's
cravat. Blood had seeped through the cloth and dried dark.
When he awakened, she would replace the soiled bandage and
clean the wound.

Strange, Megan thought, that his face should be so etched
onto her memory, for their single encounter had been no more
than a vest-pocket moment in time. Chances were excellent
that he would not even remember the brief meeting. She hoped
that was the case, for no decent woman would welcome a
reminder of a lapse in propriety, even if at the time she had
been but a silly schoolgirl.

Megan turned back to the mirrored flames in the window, mesmerized by the red and yellow shimmers on the glass. But suppose he should remember? As a grown woman, she would have to take refuge in humor if confronted with the intimacy, but that possibility, for some reason, seemed unbearable. She would be devastated if the sweet, indelible mark Neal Garrison had left on her secret heart were poked fun at with careless amusement.

Megan looked back toward the bed, and her heart lurched when she caught his keen eyes watching her. She got to her feet and lit the lamp on the bedside table.

The injured man squirmed to a semisitting position on stiff arms and elbows. "The lady I shocked," he said. "Who the blazes are you?"

He heard his own uncalled-for rudeness. Pain always made him irritable and snappish. He knew that through some instinct, but little else about himself.

His brashness further disconcerted Megan, but in as normal a tone as she could muster, she replied, "I'm Megan Wyndom. You are in my house."

"Ah, yes, now I remember. Mr. Bonner mentioned a Miss Wyndom."

He labored up from his elbows into a full sitting position and leaned forward. "Would you adjust the pillow?"

Fortunately, either Abel or Micah had dressed him in a white cotton nightshirt too large to have come from either Micah's or her brother Sam's wardrobes. The garment was open at the neck exposing dark hairs and a portion of muscular skin. She sent a silent prayer heavenward that she was not forced to contend with a huge expanse of bare masculine chest.

She coaxed her feet forward and grasped the goose-down pillow in both hands and held on until his broad back trapped the soft cushion against the oak headboard.

Being forced to speak and move gave Megan back some of her normal aplomb.

"Do you remember the accident?" she asked.

"Yes," he said. "A deer spooked the horses." Regardless

of Bonner's opinion, somehow he knew he was not a cow-handed driver.

Megan's mind was running a parallel course. Abel had a different, less blameless version, she thought, but she had not been there and had no intention of adding fuel to the fire. If he chose to attribute his misfortune solely to the stag, so be it.

"I'm going to clean and treat the head wound you sustained in that encounter," she said, unwinding the makeshift bandage from his forehead and laying the blood-stained cloth next to the lamp on the bedside table.

She walked toward the washstand where she had earlier laid out her medical supplies. His battered valise which must have been strapped to the rear of his curricle was spread out in the corner. The suitcase gave Megan the solution to the appearance of the oversized nightgown and identified her patient as the owner of the garment.

"You really don't have to do this yourself, Miss Wyndom," he said when she moved back to the bed with a towel and a cloth she had soaked in a basin of warm water and began to dab gently at the wound with the wet rag. "You can send a servant to clean the cut," he said.

"I have no servants," she said coolly.

"What about the man who helped Mr. Bonner bring me here? Micah, wasn't it? I heard Mr. Bonner say that Micah worked here."

"Micah lives here, and is, in a manner of speaking, a man-of-all-work, but he is a friend not an employee."

"You mean you live here alone with a man?"

The blunt question had more of the curious than the accusatory about it; but nevertheless, its curtness startled Megan, and she paused in her ministrations.

"I don't live *alone* with him." She emphasized the word and all it implied. "My brother and two sisters reside with me. The children look upon Micah as a sort of foster uncle."

She resumed washing the wound and dried his skin. She walked back to the washstand and rummaged in a small medicine chest, came back to the bed and applied some ointment and a sticking plaster to the cut.

Megan became self-conscious under his overt scrutiny and was certain that like all men of his class, he would not hesitate to think the worst of her because Micah lived under her roof.

"I required someone to do chores around the property but could not offer him a salary," she said, "and Micah needed a place to live. He has a small army pension which covers his personal needs, but is inadequate to pay room and board. Abel Bonner vouched for him, so we made a mutually beneficial trade-off."

"You need not justify your housing arrangements to me, ma'am. How you live is your own business."

Megan fingered her collar and stared at him. "You did ask," she accused.

"I, however, expected a simple yes or no, not a courtroom dissertation," he said dryly. "It never occurred to me that you were in an illict May-December romance with a fortyish, bald handyman."

"Huh," Megan said, equalling his sarcasm. "That you even mention an improper relationship leads me to believe you did consider it." Her blue eyes were defiant as she pushed a strand of golden hair back behind her ear.

"You suffer from an overactive imagination, ma'am," he said. "Look, I have enough on my plate without collecting fodder for the gossip mill. I am trying to remember something of consequence or a significant event from my life, but except for the accident and my current sojourn in your cottage, nothing is coming to me."

Megan gritted her teeth. *Overactive imagination, indeed!* She stepped to the bed. "You have a nasty bump on your head. I suspect that is the source of your amnesia."

"Where?"

He groped at the tender spot and yelped before Megan's "Don't!" reached his ears.

Tongue and temper went out of control with the excruciating self-inflicted pain. He bellowed a lewd word which no true gentleman would utter in the presence of a lady.

Megan went red and bit her lower lip.

He expelled a long breath. "I won't do that again."

"Swear?" she said hopefully.

"What? Oh, well, yes, I shouldn't have said that word, but I meant that I won't touch the blasted spot. Gad, every part of my body aches, but particularly my head," he said, massaging his temples.

"I'll give you something to ease the pain." Megan removed a packet of white granules from her medicine kit and stirred the powder into a glass of water. "Drink this; it will help," she said, putting the glass into his large hand.

He downed the medicine, held out the empty glass to her, and fell back against the pillow. She set the tumbler on the bedside table beside the blood-stained cravat.

"It's deuced inconvenient to have a blank mind," he said, a deep frown line appearing between his eyes. He had an unshakeable feeling that previously little in life had unnerved him, but he was beginning to be alarmed. Suppose his mind remained a blank?

"Don't try to force your memory," Megan advised him over his fears. "It is the worst thing you can do. You need to rest your mind. Your recollections will all come back in time if you just relax and get some sleep."

Megan busied herself cleaning up around the washstand. She piled the used towels on top of the medicine box and returned to his bedside to pick up the soiled cravat to add to her laundry.

"See what you think of this, Miss Wyndom," he said, holding a contemplative finger to his chin. "Before I awoke, just now, I dreamt of a battlefield. Mangled, bleeding soldiers, cannon fire, rifle reports, and soldiers falling. That sort of thing."

"Pain can bring on troublesome dreams," Megan said, recalling how he moaned and tossed his head on the pillow and cried out in his sleep. But she knew that nightmares were not unusual after traumatic experiences.

"Put the unpleasantness from your mind," she advised again. "Really, sir, you are not doing yourself any good by agonizing over your inability to recall your past life."

Lifting the soiled neckcloth from the bedside table, Megan looked at the ruined cravat of especially fine and costly linen.

"What a shame," she said. "I'll never be able to remove the bloodstains and return this to its former pristine state."

"Throw it in the dustbin," he said with a marked lack of interest. "What do you think?"

"Well, as I said, I can't wash the blood out."

"Not that. Don't be so dense," he said without any real reproof in his voice. "If I dreamt so vividly of war, I must be a soldier."

Megan ignored his supposition and fixed on the insult. He was taxing her forebearance. He was proving to be a rather unpleasant man as well as a poor patient. She would leave him now before he pushed her to use the fireplace poker on his head. She picked up the medicine box and the laundry.

"The draft you gave me for my head is not working at all," he complained.

"It takes time," Megan said, forcing her tongue between her teeth and edging toward the door. "But you might need laudanum. I'll bring you some later."

"My brain is dull enough without mind-altering drugs. I wish to regain my faculties, not depress my senses," he grumbled.

With great difficulty, Megan held back the nasty retort that sprang to her lips. "I'm cooking some soup and will bring you a bowl as soon as it is ready."

Ignoring her movement to the door, he said, "You said that your siblings are children? How old?" he asked. Without waiting for her reply, he added, looking around the room, "This is your brother's bedroom, isn't it?"

"Yes, he is called Samuel," she said, turning to face him again.

"From the titles of the books I see on the shelf there," he said, indicating a small bookcase, "I would guess he is in his teen years." The pain in his head was easing, and he realized that the headache powder was working after all.

"Fourteen," Megan said crisply. "Elizabeth is ten, and Rebecca is four."

Suddenly conscious of the time, she said, "I must finish cooking supper. I will bring the laudanum with your soup. You can take it or not as you choose." Her mind was on the girls, who were at a birthday party for Abel Bonner's youngest daughter, but would be back any minute now. Sam had left a while ago to walk them home.

Megan made it to the door and sighed audibly when he called, "Miss Wyndom, wait."

"What is it now?" she asked, not bothering to hide her irritation.

When she looked back over her shoulder, he was sitting a little forward with his hands clasped in front of him and resting on his chest. "Humility, apparently, is not my strong suit," he said. "I seem to be a man who likes plain speaking, but even in my state, I know the difference between frankness and rudeness. I have been rude."

Since the admission, in Megan's opinion, seemed a less than adequate apology, she merely nodded and stepped into the hall where her conscience began to tweak her.

He did seem terribly wretched when he tried to remember. Prolonging someone's physical or mental pain when she had the means to alleviate it was against Megan's basic inclinations. She knew a little of his past. Yet, he was so volatile, who was to say that he would not become more depressed if the facts meant nothing to him? she temporized. Tomorrow Abel would go to the village to ask Dr. Grafton to call. She decided that if the physician deemed that a disclosure was in the best interest of his patient, she would do the decent thing and reveal the circumstances of Captain Garrison's visit to Wyndom House and the bit she recalled of his military connections, but no more.

Two

The boisterous Wyndom children poured from the raw winter cold into the alcove between the outside door and the kitchen. The youngsters with faces pinched with cold talked over each other and stamped the snow from their boots before crossing the threshold into the kitchen proper.

Bean soup simmered in a pot on the iron stove, filling the air with a mouth-watering aroma. Megan put aside the wooden spoon with which she had been stirring the flavorful concoction, greeted her siblings, and began to assist the girls in removing their bulky winter garments.

"Where's the injured man who had the accident, Meggie?" Sam asked, as he unwrapped the brown scarf from around his neck.

"You have heard the news, then. You met Mr. Bonner, I assume, on your way home and he told you," she guessed, tugging Rebecca's woolen mittens from her hands.

Megan heard a chorus of youthful affirmatives in response, followed by a rush of questions.

"Has he remembered his name yet?" Sam asked.

Without waiting for Megan's reply, Elizabeth put in, "Is he from around here?"

"Mr. Bonner said he is a gentleman. Do you know him? Have you seen him before?" came from Sam.

"Sam! Lizzie! Enough," Megan cried, keenly aware that she could not answer her siblings' questions without dissembling.

"Wait until Micah comes inside," she said to put them off and to preserve her integrity. "He was at the scene of the accident and helped Mr. Bonner bring the injured man here. Micah knows more about the accident than I do."

Before the children could overrule her, Megan changed the subject. "Did you enjoy the party?" she asked the girls.

Both Elizabeth and Rebecca nodded enthusiastically. "Mrs. Bonner made a birthday cake with pink icing, and we played blindman's buff," Elizabeth said, pulling her winter bonnet from her golden curls and handing the hat to her brother to place on the high shelf above the coat pegs lining the alcove wall.

Rebecca pulled her arms free from the sleeves of her coat with Megan's help. "Lizzie had two pieces of cake," the youngest child chirped.

Megan kissed the four-year-old's cold cheek and brushed the fine blond hair, several shades lighter than her own, from the child's small brow.

"How many pieces did you have?" she asked, smiling affectionately at the adored little sister whom she had raised from infancy.

"Only one, but it was big," Rebecca said, and climbed into the rocking chair near the stove.

The snow the children had tracked into the kitchen had turned to puddles on the stone floor. Megan wiped up the water with a rag.

"Where *is* the injured man?" Sam asked again. He had seated himself at the large pine table which dominated the cozy room.

"In your bed," Megan said.

Samuel lifted his feet into the air as Megan cleaned the floor beneath his boots. She tossed the wet cloth into a wooden bucket in the corner, rinsed her hands in a basin in the stone sink, and dried them on a dish towel.

"Where am I to sleep?" Sam asked, pushing back the blond hair in dire need of a trimming which threatened to hide his blue eyes.

"You can share with Micah," his sister answered, glancing toward the door of a bedroom directly off the kitchen.

Sam groaned. "He snores like a donkey."

Megan placed a pacifying hand on her brother's thin shoulder. "It's only for one night. Mr. Bonner will fetch the doctor tomorrow."

"The snow has stopped," Sam pointed out.

"I know, but it is almost dark and the roads are unsafe for travel. The doctor wouldn't come tonight even if Abel or Micah took a chance and went for him."

Sam sighed. "Of course, you are right, Meg. Even if Dr. Grafton did come, I'm sure the stranger would not be well enough to go back to town with him. I guess it's me and Micah."

If Samuel had further comments, he kept them to himself, for the door opened and Micah came in, bringing a gust of frigid air and the smell of horses with him.

Rebecca took her thumb from her mouth and cried, "Tell us what happened, Mr. Micah."

The handyman repeated his version of the accident to satisfy the child's curiosity and that of her brother and sister. He answered a spate of questions as best he could and then summed up for his attentive listeners, "Neither the curricle, nor the horses, nor the man, himself, seem to have suffered irreparable damage."

Micah had not removed his coat, and he now said to Sam, "Come and have a look at the gentleman's stallions, Sammy. Mr. Bonner and I put them in our barn."

He reached behind the door for Sam's redingote and handed the coat to the boy. "They're worth a look. You'd have to go all the way to Tattersall's in London to see such splendid horseflesh."

The appealing invitation did not have to be repeated. "Is the curricle there, too?" Sam asked eagerly, shrugging back into his still cold coat.

"No, you and me'll haul that up from the road tomorrow."

When her brother and Micah had departed for the barn, Megan returned to the stove and gave the pot a final stir. She ladled a generous portion of hot soup from the iron kettle into a bowl and cut two thick pieces from the loaf of brown bread on the sideboard and buttered the slices. Placing the food onto a large tray, she added a soup spoon and napkin and moved with her burden to the hall door.

"I'm going to take the driver his supper," she said. Megan noticed that Elizabeth was about to sneak after her. "You girls remain here. Our guest cannot have visitors yet," she warned and added, "and, Lizzie, as soon as you warm up, please bring four apples from the larder and put them in the sink."

"The soup smells delicious," her patient said hungrily when Megan moved the tray under his nose and set it down on his lap. She backed from the bed and sat down in the comfortable armchair to keep him company while he ate.

"Micah is quite taken with your horses," she said to make conversation. "He invited Sam to see them. The two of them are in the barn right now admiring your cattle."

He took up the spoon and tasted the fare. The beans were flavored with generous pieces of ham and chunks of carrots.

"It's good, the soup," he said, and dug in in earnest.

He seemed disinclined to talk as he gave his full attention to his meal, biting off pieces of bread at intervals and obviously relishing the nourishing food.

Megan respected his silence and sat quietly, listening to the clink of the metal spoon against the china bowl until after a while his brows knit together and he said, "You know, Miss Wyndom, don't you, that I haven't the faintest notion how I came to be in possession of those splendid horses or that spanking new curricle?"

While the frantic effort to force memory, which Megan had evidenced earlier, was gone and he seemed more subdued, a faint cloud remained visible in his dark eyes.

"It'll come back to you," Megan said. "Rest is the best medicine, and sleep, itself, can be a great healer."

"So you have said. More than once," he added ungraciously. "Unfortunately, I won't be cured by stale platitudes."

"But you will from bed rest and sleep," she insisted, disregarding his belittling remark, aware that some men had difficulty curbing their biting tongues under stress, although she could not approve of his cynical jibes.

The room was warm with a good fire, and the plain blue drapes had been drawn to seal out the night and the cold. The injured man did not look directly at Megan, but he was aware of her in his peripheral vision. She had taken him under her roof in a humanitarian gesture, but he was proving a burden to her. It was apparent that she had shallow pockets. He sensed that it was not in his nature to take advantage of someone's generosity without making some repayment. He thought of his horses. Sparing a bowl of soup was one thing, but feeding two monstrous stallions was another matter.

"Mr. Bonner had mentioned that Micah would see that the horses were fed and cared for. I assume, then, that you have animals of your own," he said as he swallowed the last bit of broth.

"We keep one mare to pull our small wagon when we go to church or travel to the village for supplies," she said.

He dabbed his mouth with the napkin soft from many washings. He would have liked to have polished off another portion of soup, but since none was offered, he thanked her for the meal and put down the spoon beside the empty bowl.

Megan stood up to clear away the tray. He brushed some bread crumbs from the quilt into his palm and dumped them into the empty bowl. She waited for him to complete the small task before lifting the tray from his lap.

"Look," he said, "I know my beasts are going to put a big dent in your entire winter's supply of fodder. I want you to know that I intend paying you the going rate for your loss."

Megan looked at him. Among the upper classes, it was unheard of for a guest to pay for an animal's rations. Before she thought, she said, "That will not be necessary. I'm sure I can manage to part with a couple days' feed.'' The impact of the inadvertent lie she had just told hit her at once. Winter feed was expensive and her income was meager. Pride could be taken just so far. She did not have the extra money to feed two huge horses.

Megan was about to force herself to repeal her hasty reply when he said, ''Don't be a peagoose. If I were staying at an inn, I would be paying a steep fee for the care of two large stallions.''

On hearing yet another perceived insult, Megan's shoulders straightened, and her good sense was nullified. This arrogant man had had the audacity to call her a peagoose.

''But you are not at an inn,'' she said, tossing away the opportunity to reevaluate her stand and still retain her pride. ''You are a guest in my house. I know the accepted rules of hospitality. And I will thank you not to call me names.''

''Names?'' he said in a genuinely puzzled tone.

''Peagoose?''

''Oh, that.''

She paused a moment to wait for an apology that never came. Well, what did she expect? He was remaining true form.

''Is that laudanum?'' he asked. The green bottle was on the bedside table where she had placed it earlier with a spoon beside the medicine.

''Yes.'' On that terse note, with tray in hand, she showed him her back and swept from the room. *Let him figure out the dosage for himself,* she thought in a fit of pique.

In the kitchen, Elizabeth came from the direction of the larder with a small wicker basket containing four red apples as Megan pushed the door open with her hip.

''How is the injured man?'' Elizabeth asked, putting the basket next to the sink. When she noticed that the soup bowl on the tray was empty and the bread was gone, she noted, ''His appetite seems good.''

''Yes, he is somewhat improved,'' Megan said. She wondered why she could not be more patient with him. Losing one's memory must be a frightening occurrence. From his dreams he had discerned that he had recently been in battle. Under those conditions, he would have been freed from the civilizing presence of decent women. She probably should ignore his careless remarks, but it was not in her nature to remain witless and mute and swallow insults. Besides, he was not demented; he knew when he was behaving like a gentleman and when he was not.

"When can I see him?" Rebecca asked from the rocking chair where she bobbed back and forth.

"Tomorrow," Megan promised, "if he feels better."

"Where do you think the gentleman was going, Meggie?" Elizabeth wondered as she began to set the table for supper. She stepped on a stool to take down the soup bowls from an upper shelf of the cupboard.

"I don't know. Mr. Bonner said he was traveling toward York." Megan poured water from a jug into a pan in the sink and began to wash the apples.

"Maybe he was going to a Christmas party," Rebecca suggested, "like Mary's party, only with a Christmas cake."

"Sam says when Mama and Papa had their Christmas parties, the house was always crawling with people," Elizabeth said, setting the spoons and napkins next to the bowls on the well-scrubbed table.

Megan smiled at Sam's choice of words. "I suppose that is true. But I suspect our brother did not like being relegated to the children's dining room for his meals when Mama and Papa had company. He was nine and home from school. It was quite a letdown to be made to eat in the nursery, Lizzie, even if it was only for a few days."

Elizabeth remembered only a little about the huge house near London that had been filled with laughter and music and happiness at Christmastime. Her memories had been kept vivid through Megan's and Sam's more accurate reminiscences.

"Sam said you purposely used to walk under the kissing ball in the entrance hall, Meg, hoping some young man would catch you. Did anyone ever kiss you?"

Megan raised her brows. "Really, Elizabeth Wyndom! I

would never make such a cake of myself and behave in such a rag-mannered way. I'm going to have to have a word with Samuel.''

Elizabeth convulsed in giggles. ''I bet you were kissed,'' she said. ''That's why you are attempting to fob me off.''

Four-year-old Rebecca joined in the laughter, although she did not understand the humor. ''Well, tell me true, Megan. Were you?'' Lizzie persisted.

''Elizabeth, how you make me blush, but I'll never tell,'' Megan said, sprinkling water from her fingers toward Elizabeth, who lunged out of reach, laughing.

''What's a kissing ball look like?'' Rebecca asked. She had ceased her rocking and had her head tilted like a curious bird.

''You've seen it, Becca. It's the same one we have now,'' Elizabeth explained. ''It's round and silver with red and green stones all over it. Megan ties mistletoe to the bottom of the ball with a red ribbon, and Micah hangs it from a beam in the parlor.''

The children chattered to each other about Christmas. Megan cubed the apples, dumped them into a pot with a little water, and added cinnamon and sugar for a simple stewed apple dessert. She carried the pot to the stove and set it on the fire. Standing there for a moment in the warmth of the stove, she thought again of that last happy Christmas she had spent in her childhood home before her world had shattered. She had stood beneath the mistletoe many times and been the recipient of quick pecks on the cheek, but only once had she been really kissed full on the mouth. Her fingers went to her lips.

For five years, no Christmas had passed without her remembering. If the truth be told, Neal Garrison and the mistletoe memory had become as much a yuletide tradition for her as the pine garlands, the scented candles, and the wassail bowl.

Three

His mind's utterance of his name came on Neal's first waking moment. *Neal Garrison.* The cold fear that his identity had vanished forever was dispelled in a second and supplanted with his normal self-confidence.

He squirmed up erect in the bed, propped the pillow against the headboard, and leaned his back into it. His vexatious disposition improved by bounds, and he felt in charity with the whole universe.

With a faint smile touching his lips, he clasped his hands behind his head. Last night he had taken a small dose of laudanum. The drug had been sufficient to lull him into the healing sleep Miss Wyndom had advocated and for which he had unfairly denigrated her. He was fortunate that she had not given him a rare trimming for his reckless speech. He certainly could not fault her for pinning him with a look after he had cavalierly called her a peagoose. He decided in his newfound benevolence that she richly deserved an apology from him.

Pushing back the quilt, Neal swung his long legs over the side of the bed, stood up, and walked over to the battered valise in the corner that he recognized as the one that had traveled with him from the Spanish Peninsula to Waterloo. He selected a new pair of trousers from among a bunch of recently purchased clothes that bore the labels of some of the most prestigious shops in London. Somewhere down among the soft fabrics in the suitcase he heard the rustle of paper.

Standing where he was, he pulled the pants on under his nightshirt. Curious about the paper, he knelt back down onto the bare wooden planks and rummaged among his costly shirts. His hand touched the source of the noise. He pulled out an official-looking document and perused the letter for a minute before reseating himself on the edge of the bed with his bare feet planted on a colorful rag rug.

The edifying paper opened a window to his mind. Learning that he had been recently separated from the British Army with the rank of major brought forth more slices of his military life, and his spirits lifted with each fragment of recovered memory.

Without leaving his perch on the bed, he verbally answered a firm rap on the door. Miss Wyndom came in with a pitcher of warm water for his morning washup and made for the washstand.

Undaunted by her cool, "Good morning," he returned the greeting with a smile and wasted no time in mending his fences.

"Miss Wyndom, I must make my apologies to you for my lack of conduct yesterday. I can only plead for your understanding when I claim that my pain turned me into a bear."

Megan leaned against the washstand, marveling at his new-found buoyancy and heightened color. Not only had he made a remarkable physical recovery, but his disposition was almost sunny. Given his remarkable reformation and new attitude, she had no desire to remain at daggers drawn with him or to nurse a futile grievance.

"I can be something of a tinderbox myself on occasion," she said, meeting him more than halfway with a less than honest bit of self-deprecation, for she had, in fact, a rather even disposition.

"Truce, then?" he said, extending his hand. His strong fingers grasped her more delicate ones. A ripple of pleasure went straight through Megan from her breast to her toes at his touch.

"Truce," she agreed, disengaging her hand from the large

one that held hers captive and the touch that made jelly of her insides. To hide her dithered emotions, she busied herself positioning the pitcher of water next to the matching blue and white basin, checking the homemade soap, and squaring the white linen towels on the oak rack.

She turned back toward her patient, but his attention was focused on the door. "Hello, there," he said in that direction.

Megan's eyes followed his to where Rebecca stood in the doorway with her thumb in her mouth. Shoeless, her gray woolen stockings peeked from below the calf-length hemline of her paisley dress. The pearl buttons on the bodice were misaligned with the corresponding buttonholes.

Encouraged by the giant man's friendliness, Rebecca skipped into the room and crawled up onto the bed next to him.

"What's your name, poppet?" he asked her.

"Becca," she answered. "I'm four." She proudly held up four small fingers. "Who are you?"

"I'm Neal, a year past thirty, little miss," he said, and bent his head in a bow of obeisance.

Rebecca giggled.

Megan's heart beat a little faster. "You recall your name?" she said, her hand going to her throat.

"Yes," he replied, looking pleased with himself. "Neal Garrison, your servant, ma'am." He dipped his head to her in deference as he had to Rebecca. "My name came to me when I awoke this morning."

His drawing room manners were in marked contrast to his previous barracks' speech.

"That's wonderful, sir," Megan said and meant it, and not solely because it would relieve her of having to make the dreaded confession about their shared past, she told herself. There was that, but she was also sincerely glad that he was free of the mental pain that the loss of memory had caused him. The release had already made him a thousand times more likeable.

Neal still held in his hand the document he had discovered in his valise. He now offered the paper to Megan.

"You might find this interesting," he said. Megan sat down in the armchair and unfolded the official-looking letter.

Rebecca wrapped her arms around her knees and rocked forward to peer over the edge of the bed. "Your feet are really big," she said to Neal. "In fact, they're 'normous."

Neal lifted one large bare foot off the rug and then the other, examining his feet with feigned astonishment.

He shook his head in wonder. "They are enormous. You know, little one, I never noticed."

"You're funny." Rebecca hunched her small shoulders in delight and grinned at him. She leaned in toward him and brought her pert little nose up to his chin. Making a map of her own face, she said, "You have a shadow here and here and here." She guided her small hand over her cheeks, chin, and upper lip.

Neal stroked the bristles on his face. "I guess I need a shave," he said.

Rebecca nodded. "You do. Mr. Micah shaves with a long razor," she said, holding her hands a foot apart. "Sometimes if I'm very quiet, he lets me watch him."

Neal's gaze strayed now and then to his newfound nurse while he bantered with the child. Miss Wyndom's loveliness, the lustrous blond hair and intelligent blue eyes, seemed familiar to him. He had the ridiculous illusion that he and she had shared some intimate moments. But he had never seduced an innocent girl, and when he left England to go to war, she had been a mere schoolroom miss. The dim recesses of his mind had to be playing him false, he decided.

With a tug on his arm, Rebecca switched Neal's attention from Megan back to her. She put a finger to her puckered lips. "Shh," she whispered to him and pulled the cover over her head.

Megan lowered the document and looked up to speak to Neal. She grinned at the twitching covers. "I do declare, it appears that Rebecca has disappeared," she said, playing the game with the child. Muffled giggles came from under the quilt. The adults smiled at one another briefly, but returned immediately to their own concerns.

"You sold out with the rank of major. Were you able to recall that before you read the separation paper?" Megan asked, holding the letter out to Neal.

He took the paper and held it in his hand while he answered her. "No, not before, but it has been coming back to me rather in a rush since. You were right when you said that sleep would prove to be a restorative, Miss Wyndom. For instance, I now know that the dreams I described to you yesterday occurred at Waterloo. I was with Wellington on the Continent in June and remained in France for several months to implement Napoleon's surrender."

Going over to the bed, Megan unearthed Rebecca from beneath the covers and set her on her feet. "You are making excellent progress, sir," she said, kneeling before the child and unfastening the askew buttons and realigning them properly.

"That's better," Megan said, patting Rebecca's chest where she had set to rights the misbuttoned placket. She stood up and with her hand on the little girl's shoulder turned her toward the door. "Run along now, Becca, and put your shoes on. Lizzie will help you hook the buttons."

Rebecca took two steps toward the door, then turned back and looked up at her sister. Her eyes grew round. "Neal is the prince," she said.

Unable to fathom the child's thinking, Megan tilted her head and looked at her quizzically.

With a look children turn on seemingly slow-witted adults, Rebecca repeated, "Neal is the prince."

In one anxiety-filled moment, Megan understood what Rebecca had already begun to elaborate.

"You know, Meggie, in the stories that you tell me, he is always the same." She began an impromptu recitation. " 'His hair was as black as midnight and his eyes as deep and dark as a forest pool. He had a 'ttractive count'nance that set a maiden's heart aflutter.' " She looked at Neal. "That part means he was handsome." She smiled smugly at her own cleverness.

For just a moment Megan wanted to sink from sight. Rebecca had revealed that the recurring prince in the fairy tales she

invented for her little sister was modeled after Neal Garrison.
She came to her senses when she quickly realized he would
never make the connection even if he recalled his Christmas
visit to Wyndom House. He must have kissed a dozen more
desirable and memorable women beneath the mistletoe during
those two days. He would not especially remember her.

Neal's chuckle cut across Megan's reflection. "I daresay,
poppet," he said to Rebecca, "I never saw a prince who fit
that description, but a great many knaves and rogues and rakes
do."

"No." Rebecca wagged her head slowly from side to side.
"Only princes look like that. Megan said so."

"Did she now?" he said and grinned. "I'm afraid your sister
is mistaken. None of the real English princes look at all like
that."

Unconvinced, Rebecca argued, "All princes do. Megan said
so."

Megan got Rebecca through the door and off to find her
shoes without further words between her sister and Major Garrison.
When she turned back into the room, a deep, full-bodied
laugh errupted from Neal's throat.

"Have you ever seen Prinny, Miss Wyndom?"

"Yes, but the Prince Regent in all his corseted corpulence
would never do as a model prince for a fairy tale. The tall,
dark, and handsome cliché works better with children when
one is narrating a fantasy," she claimed with a hint of a smile.

Unexpected spears of pain shot into Neal's temples. He grimaced
and said, "Damn," before he could stop himself.

"Your head is bothering you," Megan said with real concern.

He pressed his fingers against his temples and inclined his
head. "I could use another one of those drafts."

Megan stirred the headache powder into water for him. When
he had downed the potion, she said, "I'll bring your breakfast
tray when the pain subsides."

"The worst seems to be over. I think it was the burst of
immoderate laughter that caused the sudden discomfort. In any
case, I don't want to inconvenience you with toting trays. I'll
eat breakfast with the family if I may."

He had been gallant and charming this morning, much more like her idealized fantasy and the prince in the stories. It is no inconvenience,'' Megan said, ''but of course, you are welcome to take your meals with us in the kitchen.''

He rose from the bed and walked to his valise. ''Give me ten minutes to wash up and put my clothes to rights,'' he requested, and tossed the government decree on top of his folded clothes.

Megan nodded her assent. She looked at the document lying in the open suitcase. ''Micah was in the army until four years ago,'' she said. ''He nearly lost a leg at Albuera before he was pensioned off.''

''I noticed that he had a slight limp,'' Neal said.

''He made a better recovery than expected. At first the doctors feared that he would be crippled for life.''

As Neal washed and dressed after Megan had left him, he ticked off the names of the men he had lost at Waterloo. Barrett, Lovington, Marshall, Coots . . . the list was endless.

The painful memories of war had left an indelible stain on his soul. At one time all he had ever wanted was a commission in the army. He had spent untold years managing crisis after crisis with the lives of his men hanging on his decisions. But now that peace was ensured with the containment of the Corsican Monster, he had left the service with Wellington's thanks and blessing. Henceforth, he vowed as he straightened the collar of his ruffled shirt, he would lead a peaceful existence with no one depending on him.

Children's lighthearted voices could be heard coming from the kitchen when Neal opened the bedroom door and walked down the hall. There was a heartbeat of silence when he entered the kitchen. Micah stood up, held out his hand, and identified himself to the major as a former sergeant while indicating an unoccupied chair at the table set with plain white crockery.

Neal sat down and traded information with Micah about former military postings. During a break in the brief conversation, Megan made Major Garrison known to Samuel and Elizabeth and set a bowl of steaming porridge before him. When the appropriate greetings had been exchanged with the children, Neal sprinkled the cereal with brown sugar, poured on cream, and ate a few spoonfuls. He smiled at the youngsters and to their delight initiated a conversation with them.

Megan listened, amazed, as he enslaved her brother and sisters with lightning speed between mouthfuls of the hearty oatmeal. For a man who could have had little, if anything, to do with children during his military career, he was a natural with youngsters. Megan expected Neal to find her siblings bothersome, especially when all three began to pelt him with questions, but he answered with neither impatience nor condescension, and, in turn, drew them out on small bits of their own lives.

He spoke the cultured speech of Megan's childhood that was free of the country vernacular to which her ears had become accustomed. The sound of his deep mellow voice revived the dreams of a life that she, at times, envisioned for the children, in which Samuel would have a university education, and Elizabeth and Rebecca would make brilliant marriages with fine men of their own class.

Yet in a turmoil of contradictions she mistrusted the Quality, as Micah and the Bonners referred to her peers. She saw the country people who had befriended her as good, honest folk while she did not trust her own class, who had socially ostracized her mother and, with a single exception, had refused to lift a finger to aid Lady Wyndom when her husband died in disgrace.

Neal scraped the last morsel of his second serving of porridge from the bottom of the bowl, laid down his spoon, and sat back, replete. He was content to remain awhile here in this ordinary kitchen where the warmth of genuine love was as palpable as the heat from the big iron stove. He almost envied these people who needed each other, although he, himself, wanted to belong to no one. As appealing as the Wyndoms' life was, he liked being alone. He was his own man, answerable to no one, and he intended to remain his own man with no personal encumbrances ever.

Megan sat across from Neal, holding a coffee cup to her lips with both hands, her blue eyes intent on him. The children and Micah had drifted off, and the two were alone.

"You seem far away," she said, pulling him from his reverie. "More memories?"

"You are an excellent cook," he evaded with an engaging grin that gave her a nice feeling.

She thanked him for the specious compliment. "Your coffee has grown cold," she observed, and picked up his cup, spilled the residue into the stone sink, and poured him fresh coffee from the pot on the stove.

Neal watched her as she moved with a natural grace past the window through which the winter sun was making a brave effort to lighten the room. She had excellent speech and an air of the aristocracy about her.

Megan set the cup of steaming coffee before him, reseated herself, and pushed the sugar bowl to his side of the table.

"I can't help but think that you were born into a higher station than this," he said, mechanically stirring sugar into the hot coffee. "What happened?"

He saw her visibly starch up, her eyes becoming hostile. "You are certainly blunt and direct, sir," she said in a cold voice. "I make no apology for being poor."

"You needn't get your nose out of joint again, Miss Wyndom. What makes you think I expected you to apologize for being poor?" he asked.

With their gazes locked, Megan replied, "The polite world regards poverty as a shame and disgrace. Why should you be any different?"

The major dealt her a quelling look. "Don't lump me in with the views of the *beau monde;* I have never been that elevated in the social scheme. I just recently came into the sort of generous inheritance which would move me to the top of their lists and bring me automatic respect."

"You haven't wasted any time frittering your newfound gold on a frivolous contraption," she muttered. Flustered by her own audacity, her cheeks colored. Abel and Micah had extolled the workmanship in the custom-made curricle and speculated at the stupendous cost of such a magnificent, but ostentatious vehicle.

"Do you honestly think it is your business, Miss Wyndom, where I choose to squander my money?"

Neal recalled purchasing the curricle on a whim. He had never had a top of the line carriage before. At the time, it had felt good to go into the exclusive carriage shop and plop down the cash. But he was no longer certain that the racing curricle had been a wise investment. Yet he did not like anyone pointing out his sins to him. His jaw jutted out, daring her to challenge him further.

Megan was instantly ashamed. He was right, of course. It was none of her affair how he spent his money.

"We are getting nowhere with this bickering, Major. I don't want to argue with you," she said to save face. She went to rise, but his strong hands shot across the table and grabbed her wrists below the lace cuffs of her forest green woolen dress, imprisoning her.

"Really? I never would have guessed. I thought we had agreed to a truce," he said, removing his restraining hands. But Megan did not take advantage of being released. Instead, she eased back down onto the chair. The hot imprint of his fingers was on her skin, and funny things were happening to her insides again.

"You are in the right," she said. "Your affairs are none of my concern."

He smiled then. "I came back from the war and found that my uncle who died during my absence had left me a great deal of money. I suppose I went a little mad, giving my custom to the best shops. You should see the large number of fine shirts piled in my valise. I cannot account for it, for I have never been one to cut a dash. I suppose my excuse is rather a lame one; everyone does something stupid at one time or another."

His confession broke the impasse. Megan gave him a forgivingly radiant smile.

Neal pushed his chair back from the table, stretched his long legs out before him, and folded his arms across his chest.

"Now, tit for tat. Why is someone of your class living in a farmer's cottage?"

Megan gave him a considering look. "It's a story I am sure that you have heard before. My father's downfall started with poor management of his properties and the conviction that he could recoup his loses through gambling."

"Bad choice. Gaming is no viable solution to a financial problem," Neal observed. "More often than not, it merely drags the victim more deeply into debt."

"Yes, that is exactly what occurred," Megan confessed. "Yet, almost to the end, Papa believed he could reverse his slipping fortunes with one more turn of a card. It became an obsession with him. Instead of making headway, his income rapidly diminished into nothing. Then he became ill and died a week later, one step away from debtor's prison. Our house was sold to pay off the mortgage and other accumulated debts." She moved her shoulders in a small shrug. "That is all of it."

"Your father must have left you an income. This isn't a bad house. What it lacks in elegance, it makes up for in comfort."

His eyes settled on her high-necked dark green gown which was ridged with ecru lace at the collar and cuffs. "Your dress is a little prim by London's fashion standards, but perfectly acceptable. Your brother and sisters are not clothed in rags. And neither you nor the children are undernourished."

In spite of their truce, Megan could not suppress a mild spate of sarcasm. "How observant you are, Major," she said, softening her words with a hint of a smile. "You do find it impossible to mince words, don't you?"

"Old habits die hard. But neither are you obliged to answer my questions," he said with an unrepentant shrug. "You can tell me that I can damn well go to the devil."

He was handing her a loophole to escape further questioning, but without too much conscious thought, she decided to answer him. Somehow it felt good to be unburdening herself to him. And, the major did have very broad shoulders.

"The house is not mine," she said. "I pay a small rent to Lord Ames who lives nearby. He knew my parents and has been of some help to me. He lends Sam books from his library so my brother can continue some part of his education which was interrupted when he was nine and Papa was unable to provide further for his tuition at school.''

Megan had never divulged the source of her income to anyone, not the Bonners, not Micah. Only her brother Sam knew how she had come to have the money. Yet she found herself confiding her history to this man whom she did not really know, in spite of their long-ago moment of intimacy.

''My mother had a valuable necklace,'' Megan continued, finding that all her reserve was melting away. ''Mama was increasing with Rebecca and devastated by my father's death and unable to cope. I took control and sold the pearls with the help of a solicitor for a nice sum. Living with my father, my mother had never learned to economize. I knew the money would run through her fingers if I did nothing, so I purchased an annuity to preserve the principal, and we have lived on the yearly interest ever since. It is not much, but managed well, it gives us all our necessities. At least, we shall never be without some money.''

Neal leaned forward, rendered speechless for a moment. When he found his voice, he said in wonder, ''Miss Wyndom, you could have been no more than fifteen or sixteen at the time. Where did you acquire such wisdom at a tender age?''

Gratified by his unexpected open admiration and the unmistakable sincerity in his voice, she flushed with pleasure. ''I must have had an angel on my shoulder,'' she said facetiously.

He shook his head in wonder. ''I have heard of people being born with good sense, but I have never believed it until now. And you have no bitterness toward your errant parent?''

Her smile faded, and for the first time, a sadness touched the corner of her mouth. ''Bitterness destroys people,'' she said with continued candor. ''Papa was simply a product of our times. The gentlemen's code of honor makes it an unpardonable sin to falter on a gambling debt. You must know that.''

Neal had never understood the mentality of those men who bet more than they could afford to lose. In his opinion, her father had belonged to a selfish breed who did not care that their gambling adversely affected the innocent children and spouses that the miscreants were honor bound to protect. But he did not want to destroy the fragile empathy that he and Megan had just shared. A good soldier knew when to retreat.

He rubbed his temples, not wholly in fabrication. "It seems the pain reliever is wearing off again. I do not want to dip into the laudanum. Can you spare another of those headache powders?"

"Of course," she said, and lifted her medicine box down from an upper shelf and handed him a packet. She began to clear the table as he made to leave the kitchen. Stopping with his hand on the door, he turned back toward her. "Do you know if I can hire a carriage in the village?" he asked.

Megan's heart slipped into her shoes.

"Yes, there is a livery, but surely you are not leaving?" In that moment she knew that she did not want him to go. "You must stay until the village doctor examines you."

"I refuse to impose on you any longer. I have decided that if the doctor does not attend me this afternoon, I will move to the village inn for the night and hire a rig in the morning for the journey home. I will send for my curricle later."

"Do you know where you live?" Megan asked inanely.

"I think so." She could hear him chuckling at the absurdity of her question all the way down the hall.

Megan wiped the table top with vigorous strokes. Her spirits plunged and her insides caved into a hollowness. Since her mother's death, her life had been routine and devoid of excitement. Major Garrison made her feel so alive. Never had anyone stimulated her as he did. And now, before she would have an opportunity to discover what that meant, he would be gone.

Neal fell into a natural sleep for some hours. He was awakened by Dr. Grafton's trumpeting voice and took an instant dislike to the short, balding physician with the brusque bedside manner who treated him as if he were an annoying insect.

"Swing your legs over, man, and sit up on the edge of the bed," the doctor demanded in a strident tone. Neal eased his long length up from the mattress and swung his legs over the edge as he had been bid, his eyes filling with resentment.

Lowering his head onto Neal's chest, the doctor listened to the injured man's heart.

"I probably wasted my time coming out here," he groused. "Your heart is robust, to say the least." Standing erect, he reached up and removed the sticking plaster with skilled and surprisingly gentle hands, considering his churlishness.

"Miss Wyndom did a fine job of cleaning the abrasion. No chance of infection there." He probed the lump above the wound and said a gruff, "Sorry," when Neal winced.

For a long moment he stood back, tapping his fingertips together. "You had some memory loss right after the accident?" he said at last.

"Yes," Neal agreed. "I could not remember my past for a short time, but it all came back rather quickly."

"Miss Wyndom informs me," the doctor went on, nodding toward the door where Megan leaned against the doorjamb, listening, "that you want to go home. Where do you live?"

"Verdon Fields," Neal replied, "which is five miles this side of York."

"That's some eighty miles from the village center. Not an insignificant distance. You expect to leave tomorrow?"

"That's right," Neal said. "I plan to put up in the village inn tonight and start off in the morning."

"I would reconsider, Major. My guess is that you have suffered a concussion. You are really not recovered enough to drive that distance."

"I will chance it," Neal said.

The doctor slapped his hand against his thigh. "I knew you were going to be difficult the minute Miss Wyndom said that you were a major in the army. Why are you military types such poor patients? I suspect it is your overblown sense of self-importance. You can give orders, but can't seem to take them."

"Now just a damned minute." Neal thrust his chin out pugnaciously and leaned aggressively toward the bantam doctor.

Unintimidated, the much smaller man held his ground and poked a finger in Neal's chest. "Believe it or not, Major, I do know something of medicine. You have a concussion and risk a fatal hemorrhage if you bounce about in a carriage or prance around on horseback. The last idiot in your condition who ignored my advice tumbled from his horse and was dead before he hit the ground.''

"My presence here is an imposition," Neal said. "I will put up at the inn."

"The inn is no place for a convalescing patient. You will share your room with every random wayfarer and a host of fleas.''

"I have slept in worse places," Neal grumbled.

"What is it with you?'' the doctor said, becoming increasingly contentious. "Here you have clean accommodations, good meals, and a fine nurse."

"I cannot foist myself on Miss Wyndom even one more day. She has been more than generous, but I refuse to become indebted to her further. It is unnecessary."

"On the contrary, my good man, it is very necessary, unless you are bent on committing suicide. I know your conscience bothers you because Miss Wyndom's income is meager."

Megan's quick intake of breath was audible throughout the room.

"Salve your conscience, if you must, by paying her for your lodgings. That should be no hardship since you seem to be extremely deep in the pocketbook."

Megan's cheeks went hot from mortification. "Dr. Grafton," she said in a shaky voice, "Major Garrison is welcome to stay with me as my guest until he is fully recovered. There is no need to speak of payments."

"There you are, Major," the thick-skinned doctor said, winking at Megan, unfazed that she had pokered at his rag-mannered suggestion and was now staring at him with incensed eyes. "Abel Bonner has arranged for your disabled vehicle to be repaired; however, the wheelwright is engaged for two or three days, but will come when he has completed his other commissions. By that time, you should be able to drive without adverse reactions."

Dr. Grafton pulled on his overcoat and fastened the buttons.

"Well, Major, are you to be sensible and live or be stubborn and die?"

"It appears I have no choice," Neal said. "Thank you, Miss Wyndom. I accept your gracious offer."

The doctor sneered. "You sound about as grateful as if you were being sentenced to a prison term in Newgate."

"What is your fee, Dr. Grafton?" Neal asked, very much wanting to be rid of the obnoxious man.

The physician named an excessive sum.

Neal just looked at him.

"I can see you are wondering if I am serious. I am, Major. I expect my well-heeled patients to pay me higher fees so that I can treat my poor patients for nothing. I don't believe any man or woman should go without medical attention because he or she does not have the means, but I am not a wealthy man. I have a wife to support."

Neal reached inside his coat which hung on a chair beside the bed and withdrew his purse.

"Forget the sum I mentioned," the doctor said in an expressionless tone. "Give me whatever you choose."

Neal's countenance was unreadable to either the doctor or Megan, who were both watching him, but he was thinking that the old curmudgeon had at least one redeeming quality. He handed the doctor a sheaf of notes that amounted to more than the doctor had originally requested.

Dr. Grafton stuffed the money into his pocket without counting it. Megan walked down the length of the hall to the front door with him. He retrieved his low-crowned beaver from the hall table and held it before him against his round stomach, grasping the narrow brim in both hands.

"Should Major Garrison have a relapse, send for me, but I think he will do well enough now. He has a vigorous body from soldiering, but also appears to be one of those people who are naturally blessed with excellent health and amazing recuperative powers." He plunked his hat on his head and pulled his leather gloves, which he had taken from his coat pocket, onto his plump hands.

He paused with his hand on the polished doorknob and

bid her a happy Christmas. ". . . For both you and the little Wyndoms," he said.

"And to you, sir, and Mrs. Grafton," Megan reciprocated as he wrenched open the door. The affront she had experienced when he had dared to insinuate that the major should compensate her for her hospitality was forgiven with his insistence that Neal Garrison remain under her roof for a few more days. He had accomplished what was not within her power, but what she had wanted above all things.

Megan had a quick view of the doctor's familiar black gig and the blanketed horse tied to the iron hitching post before she shut the door. She slid the bolt and walked with light steps and a melody in her heart back toward Sam's bedroom.

Four

While setting a tin pan of featherbed rolls on the hearth to rise, Megan turned her head toward Micah, who had just come in from outside and was holding his chilled, chapped hands toward the heat of the stove to warm them.

"The doctor was here, I see," he said as Megan covered the yeast rolls with a clean cloth. "What did he say?"

In a few sentences, Megan repeated the warnings that the doctor had given to the major and told Micah all that had transpired between the patient and Dr. Grafton.

"Verdon Fields?" Micah said as he hung up his coat and scarf. "Is that a town?"

"No, it is the name of the major's ancestral home, I believe," Megan said, wiping the floured board on which she had kneaded the dough with a damp cloth. "The major rather reluctantly agreed to follow the doctor's advice to put off his journey and remain here until his curricle is repaired." She bent over and put away the wooden slab on a low shelf in the cupboard.

"That won't be for a few days yet," Micah said. "The wheelwright has other jobs to complete before he takes on the major's work."

"I know," Megan said with a mischievous smile. "I believe

that is the reason Dr. Grafton used that as a benchmark. Major Garrison is not an easy man to deal with.''

''Not pleased to be hobbled, eh?'' Micah chuckled.

Megan shook her head and laughed. ''Not by half.''

She washed her hands at the sink and replaced her flour-spattered apron with a clean one while Micah drew a tankard of ale from a small wooden barrel and sat down at the table. He looked over his shoulder toward the door to the hall. ''Is he asleep?'' he asked, cradling the pewter tankard in his two hands.

''No, he is shaving,'' Megan said, sitting down across from him. ''I took in a can of hot water a while ago at his request, and he had his brush, razor, and strop laid out.''

''What do you think of him?'' Micah asked, keeping his eyes on the tankard from which he had just taken a generous swallow. ''He has the bearing of a hero, wouldn't you say?'' He gave her a furtive glance from under hooded lashes.

''A hero? Well, I suppose, in his appearance,'' Megan said, thinking of the role she had given Neal Garrison in the fairy tales she spun for Rebecca. ''He is an attractive man and does have an unmistakable presence about him.''

Micah's bent head came slowly erect, a faint grin touching his lips. ''You do like him, then?'' he said smugly. He had not been wrong in thinking that her eyes had been drawn admiringly to the major all through breakfast.

''Like him?'' Megan repeated, not sure what to make of the gleam in Micah's eyes. Those wondrous sensations she felt when the major was near and her almost uncontrollable desire to hum happily when he looked favorably upon her undeniably proved that her emotions were rather firmly engaged.

''Yes, I like him well enough,'' she said a little belatedly in a neutral voice, for she was not about to confide, or even hint at, those true feelings tucked in her secret heart to anyone.

Micah rested his elbows on the table and made a tent of his fingers. ''Megan, I know that you believe in miracles the same as I do.''

His words and demeanor were so completely out of character

for Micah that Megan said, "What?" as though he spoke an alien tongue.

"Miracles," he repeated. "They can happen, you know."

Micah met Megan's stupified expression. Silence reigned between them for several seconds while Megan gathered her thoughts.

"Micah, what is this about? First you ask me if I like Major Garrison," Megan said when she was ready to speak. "Then in a non sequitur you talk of miracles in a hushed, reverent tone. Yet, more than once, in the past, I have heard you say that miracles are a lot of farradiddle."

Micah's chin set mulishly. "If you had asked me a week ago, that's exactly what I would have said. But the accident converted me."

"The accident? What does the major's accident have to do with miracles?"

Micah leaned toward her, and his eyes lit up with a luminescent glow. "The entire incident defies reason," he said in the voice of a happy convert to a new faith. "Just think about what happened and you'll see what I mean. The horses flew past Abel at breakneck speed, parted from the curricle, and yet, without any human hands on the reins, the skittish beasts brought themselves to a complete stop and proceeded to loll about in a field. Horses don't act that way. Never. The rig plunged into a ditch sustaining minor damage, and the major was hurled onto the hard ground with a force which would have killed the average man. However, he emerged with no broken bones, nothing but a sore and muddled head. I never heard of such goings-on, have you?"

"Well, when you put it like that, it does make one think. But, perhaps, it is not all that unusual. Abel might have been traveling so slowly," Megan suggested, "that in contrast, the major appeared to be driving the horses much faster than he actually was."

Micah snorted. "Abel Bonner does not make mountains out of molehills. He described the major's speed as dangerous. The vehicle should have smashed to smithereens, and the major should be dead."

"People survive bad accidents all the time and are sometimes killed in minor mishaps," Megan pointed out sensibly. Yet, oddly, on some level, she wanted to believe Micah, but could not have explained to anyone why that should be.

"Maybe what you say is true," Micah conceded, "but not in this instance. Major Garrison is a cavalry officer and a good one, I bet. Some unseen hand of Providence took over, forced him to act against his instincts, so that he would be put firmly in your path."

"I am almost afraid to ask, Micah. But for what purpose?"

"Marriage, lass, marriage."

Megan looked down at her clasped hands. "Micah, that is fanciful in the extreme. I am not ordained to wed Major Garrison," she said, her voice surprisingly mild in repudiation, for the idea was not at all repugnant to her. An irrational hope rose within Megan that Micah's whimsical interpretation of the accident might somehow be true. Wasn't it almost Christmas? Scolding herself for the absurdity of her fanciful imagination, she quickly put aside her desire to give credence to Micah's notion.

Micah could not draw his eyes from Megan's face. Ever since the accident, some force seemed to have taken over his will and cast him in the unlikely role of matchmaker. Try as he might, he could not unload his mind of the conviction that he was destined to bring Megan and the major together. From the play of emotions on Megan's face, he concluded with satisfaction that she was not going to dismiss his ideas out of hand.

But Megan was preparing to do just that. If she remained mum, she realized that she would be giving her tacit approval for Micah to promote a match between her and the major. She looked toward the door. It would be humiliating in the extreme if Major Garrison overheard their conversation or got wind of Micah's ravings.

"Micah, I cannot give the same construction to the accident as you do. I do not see any celestial hand in Major Garrison's wreck. His misfortune was the result of his own rash behavior as Abel claims."

"I thought you believed at Christmas anything was possible.

I've heard you say so to the children,'' Micah accused her with a disgruntled look. ''Can't you see that the accident has no logical explanation? It is a pure and simple miracle. A Christmas miracle.''

''I don't want to hear any more of this nonsense,'' Megan said forcefully. ''Abel attributes the accident to the major's own carelessness.''

''Abel wouldn't know a miracle if it bit him in the nose. He doesn't even go to church.''

A note of laughter crept into Megan's voice. ''Neither do you,'' she said, bringing a glare to Micah's craggy face.

Megan sighed. ''I forbid you to speak to me of this again. The accident had nothing to do with Christmas miracles or Providence,'' she said. She left her chair, stepped to the sink, and moved a dishcloth agitatedly over the already spotless stone surface.

''You have your opinion; I have mine,'' Micah said stubbornly.

Megan turned her back to the sink and faced her friend. ''Keep your opinion to yourself. You are not to repeat this fustian.''

Before Micah could reply, Neal came through the door, bringing their disagreement to an abrupt close.

Megan's eyes lingered on the major's newly shaven face. He had cleaned up strikingly handsome. When he broke into a smile, she turned away, dropped the dishcloth into the sink, and headed for the hall door in a rush to leave the kitchen.

Neal stepped from her path before she collided with him. She brushed past him and slammed the door shut behind her.

Perplexed, Neal dropped into the chair she had vacated. His smile had gone unanswered while Miss Wyndom had dashed past him, mumbling something about straightening the bedroom. Her moods shifted like desert sands, he thought, and wondered what imagined solecism he had committed now.

''Ale, Major?'' Micah asked, filling a tankard without waiting for Neal's response, and placing the drink at his elbow.

''You're not married, Major,'' Micah said when he sat down again across from Neal.

"No, I'm afraid you see before you a confirmed bachelor," Neal said lightly. He braced his arms on the wooden table, Megan's strange behavior passing from his head. The kitchen was warm and comfortable and redolent with the yeasty aroma of rising dough. He drank a deep measure of the home-brewed ale with pleasure and gave his table companion a faint smile which was ignored.

"Not a *confirmed* bachelor?" Micah protested with furrowed brows, already setting aside Megan's admonition not to promote a match.

Neal's smile faded. He fixed his eyes on the older man, not understanding his intensely serious outburst. "Definitely confirmed," he said, his chin set at an obstinate angle.

"But, but," Micah sputtered, "you own property and should be seeking a wife and securing the estate to your own issue."

Neal looked askance at the highly personal remark. "It's no concern of yours, Sergeant," he said, giving the grizzled veteran's rank an ominous ring. "But if you must know, I don't care a fig if I have an heir or not. Some distant, unknown relative will creep from the woodwork at my demise, I'm sure. But I trust that event is some time off in the distant future."

Micah stared into his ale with a woebegone expression, embarrassed by his own bungling. He had taken a great liberty and should have known better than to confront a former officer head on. But he was not certain that wrapping his speech in clean linen would have been any more palatable to the major. He should have listened to Megan and not brought up the subject at all.

Neal was fairly skilled at reading a man's emotions. But he was very unsure why his own bachelor's state should send Micah into a blue funk and what caused him in the first place to audaciously claim that he, himself, needed a wife and heir unless. . . .

"Does this have something to do with Miss Wyndom?" he asked with sudden inspiration.

The major was too quick by far, Micah thought, but he found himself saying, "As I see it, you need a wife, and Megan needs a husband; you'd be perfect for each other." The words had found their way to his lips without his directing them to go there.

For a moment, Neal was completely taken aback at the blatant pairing of himself and Miss Wyndom by this man whom he had just met. "Miss Wyndom might need a husband, but I'm damned certain that I don't need a wife. Does she know you are matchmaking?"

"Megan would never cast out lures for a man," Micah said, averting a straight reply with a show of indignation. "This is my own idea," he hedged. Megan would skin him alive if she suspected that he had approached the major to encourage him to make a declaration for her.

Neal stared at Micah. He did not know whether to be angry or amused. The former sergeant was as improbable a matchmaker as one could imagine. Moreover, although Miss Wyndom was virtually penniless, she had looks and potential and a friend in Lord Ames who could put eligible suitors in her path, if that were her wont. Certainly she was not so desperate that she needed a handyman's assistance to find a husband.

"Why me?" Neal asked. His curiosity overrode his inclination to rip up at the former sergeant and give him a colorful setdown.

"It's divine Providence," Micah muttered. He was unable to meet the major's dark, penetrating eyes. He was making a huge mistake, but that unseen force had a hold of him, and he did not seem to be able to shake himself loose.

Neal was dumfounded. "Providence?"

Micah swallowed hard. His confidence was slipping badly. Even in civilian attire the man across from him was very much a commanding figure.

"Explain yourself." The major's succinct command shook Micah. He was back in the army and on the carpet.

He went through his premise about the accident with far less verve than he had done with Megan. His listener's face was expressionless until Micah came to the end of his tale.

Then, Neal screwed up his eyes in utter disbelief.

"Are you trying to gammon me?" he said, arching a dubious eyebrow.

Micah traced circles with a calloused finger on the table in the condensation that had dropped from the pewter mug, his long face speaking volumes.

"You *are* serious," Neal said. He had to admit that the accident had strange aspects to it, but when his head cleared he would solve the aberrations. Everything had a rational solution. *Divine Providence! Fustian!*

"There was no magic at work on that icy road," Neal said severely. "I erred in judgment, got lucky, and managed to emerge with my skin intact." He would be a candidate for Bedlam if he believed Micah. As for his being the answer to Miss Wyndom's prayer, that was pure stuff and nonsense. Heaven would have to be running amok for some godly figure to select him as the fulfillment of any woman's dream.

Micah looked so miserable that Neal went uncharacteristically soft. Yet, the former soldier's officious interference, however well-meaning, was a disservice to both Miss Wyndom and himself and could not be completely brushed off.

"Look, Sergeant, I am not a do-gooder," Neal said, keeping his voice even. "You are making a grave miscalculation if you see me as the key to Miss Wyndom's problems. I would make her the worst kind of husband. I like being alone and want no encumbrances of that sort in my life."

The old soldier still refused to meet Neal's eyes. "I thought you both needed a little assistance," he mumbled into his ale in one final attempt at justification.

Neal's voice took on a hard edge. "We don't. I don't. You are poking your nose where it shouldn't be. Do not intrude in my life again. Now or ever, understand?"

Micah shuffled from the kitchen to the barn, feeling as abysmally low as he had when the military doctors said that he might be crippled for life. Megan had never scolded him before, and now the major had dressed him down as well. All because he had paid attention to the nonsense that came unbidden into his head after the accident. It had been as if angels were whispering directives into his ear to secure Megan's happiness. Well, he had no intention of listening further. He put his gloved hands over his ears in a symbolic gesture. Considering how he had landed in the soup with both Megan and the major, it was more likely he had been hearing devils than angels anyway.

Megan sailed through the minor cleaning chores around the washbasin and straightened the quilt on Sam's bed. Not wanting to rejoin the men in the kitchen just yet, she sought the comfort of the armchair and sank down onto the soft cushion for a coze with herself.

Her hoydenish behavior had been inexcusable just now. She had ludicrously believed that the major had smiled at her because he had read in her eyes that she found him appealing. Her argument with Micah had colored her perceptions and caused her to act irrationally. She must get a hold on her emotions and not see a hidden meaning in Neal Garrison's every grin and frown, or he would think that she was a little mad.

Megan rested her head against the back cushion of the chair. She looked toward the ceiling where her little sisters' indistinct young voices and their light footfalls could be heard in their bedroom directly above her, which, like hers, was reached by the narrow staircase at the end of the hall.

Megan sighed. For five years she had been trapped between two worlds and had been unable to leach from her inner self all vestiges of longing for her former life. She had found contentment living among country people here in the north far from London. Yet, her dreams of the man who had first set her heart on fire had never vanished, the image remaining starkly vivid since their long-ago brief encounter.

The banister had been festooned in pine garlands and decorated with red satin ribbons that December evening in 1810 when she had stood in the center of the entry hall, mesmerized by the approach of the dashing captain, awesome in his uniform of scarlet, navy, and gold. He descended the staircase which she should have been ascending to the schoolroom at the top of the large house where Elizabeth and Samuel waited for her. But her legs refused to move. Her eyes locked on his as he walked to her side, tall and smiling. He pointed to the mistletoe high above their heads. The green sprig dangled on a red ribbon from the magnificent crystal chandelier lit with twenty-four candles.

Captain Garrison lowered his sensual lips full onto hers. The whisper of a kiss was a firebrand that had reached deep inside Megan and ignited a bonfire of pleasurable sensations and previously unimagined desires.

"Someday, little one, you are going to break hearts," he said, his voice smooth as warm honey. But his legacy of awakened love was denied its fulfillment. Her father's death thrust her into a world without eligible suitors. Captain Garrison's prediction turned out to be a sterile promise. She had broken no hearts.

The sound of her sisters' light footsteps coming down the stairs penetrated Megan's consciousness. Elizabeth and Rebecca stepped into Sam's bedroom and stood just inside the door.

"Did you want this, Meg?" Elizabeth asked, holding out a feather duster to her. "I cleaned both upstairs bedrooms."

"Hang it in the kitchen," Megan said. "And thank you, Lizzie. Where are you going now?"

"To play with the cats in the barn," Rebecca chirped, looking around the room. "Where is Neal?"

"In the kitchen with Mr. Micah," she said, frowning. "You should not call Major Garrison by his given name, Becca."

"Neal does not mind," Elizabeth put in, her small chin raised defensively. "He has never taken offense. He even told Rebecca that was his name, so he must have wanted her to call him Neal."

The major could turn the children up sweet without half trying, Megan thought. But she knew she was being unfair. It was her own fault that the children called him Neal. She should have corrected Rebecca when her baby sister first used the major's given name, instead of sanctioning the improper behavior with her silence. At the time she had been more concerned with concealing her own former fraternization with Neal Garrison to pay attention to Becca's social blunder. Lizzie and Sam had followed Rebecca's example, and she had failed to intercede because her own mind was always on the major, not on the children's gaffe.

"I suppose it is all right," she reluctantly conceded, not wanting to penalize the children for her own lapse.

"We are going, then," Elizabeth said, running after Rebecca, who was already skipping down the hall.

"Dress warmly," Megan called after them.

Rising from the chair, she glimpsed her face in Neal's shaving mirror. She was not beautiful, but neither was she a complete dowd. Her skin was smooth, and her color was good. She might even turn a few heads at a society ball if her blond hair were fashionably dressed instead of being pulled back into an uninteresting bun and her plain gown were silk or satin and designed by a London modiste.

Did God really send angels to take a hand in people's lives? she wondered. Could she and Major Garrison be destined for each other as Micah claimed? It would be wonderful to be gathered into the major's strong arms and to be held. She gave herself a mental shake. There was no profit in yearning for things she could never have. Walking leisurely, she made her way back to the kitchen.

The major was alone, staring at the pewter tankard he was rotating indifferently round and round the table in front of him.

Megan crossed to the hearth, lifted the cloth from the feather-bed rolls, and then replaced it. She wondered if in his close concentration he was reconstructing more of the lost pieces of his former life.

Glancing at him with hooded eyes, her cheeks colored when she remembered that she had made a cake of herself when she had dashed past him like a varietal hoyden. He smiled lazily, and she realized he was looking at her. Her heart flipped and her blush deepened.

But his smile proved to have nothing to do with her former conduct. "Lizzie and Becca are delightful conversationalists for such young children," he said with a warmth she had not until now heard in his voice. "You have raised exceptional children, Miss Wyndom." His praise sent good feelings for him coursing through her and caused Megan to forget her former embarrassment.

Neal drained his goblet and set it aside and refused her offer to draw another mug of ale for him. She sat down across from him. Whatever had upset Miss Wyndom earlier, he found, she had hidden away. Her elbows were propped on the table with her rounded chin resting on her folded hands, her demeanor relaxed and friendly.

Megan had made up her mind that she would have a companionable visit with him. After all, she and the major were not quarreling children, but civilized adults. Yet there was no sense in taking a chance on their butting heads again, so she searched her mind for some neutral common ground to open their conversation.

"Christmas is almost here, Major," she said, pleased with herself for hitting on a timely, yet noncontroversial subject.

"Christmas?" he replied as though he had forgotten the holiday existed. "Next week, is it?"

"Yes, you will be home in time to celebrate," Megan said. On a small laugh, she added, "I can see that your recent trauma has temporarily pushed the holiday from your mind."

Neal ran a finger around the rim of the tankard. "Christmas has no meaning for me. It is a holiday for families."

"Oh." Megan was taken aback. "You don't have any family?"

"I suppose I must have some kin somewhere, but my recently deceased uncle who was my guardian after my parents died in an influenza epidemic when I was seven was somewhat of a recluse."

"I see, now you won't have him to celebrate Christmas with you." She pictured the major sitting alone in brooding silence over his loss on a day that should be festive.

Her compassion must have shown in her face, for when she raised her eyes to him, his face was not sad. In fact, he looked vastly amused. "My dear Miss Wyndom, I can see your eager breast welling up with misplaced sympathy. My uncle did not encourage close associations with either friends or relatives. My own parents were not much different. My mother was a demanding invalid; my father, a cold, remote man. There were never any yuletide celebrations at Verdon Fields, and there won't be any now.''

"You have no one at all with whom you can keep Christmas?''

"Correction, I choose *not* to celebrate Christmas with anyone. The holiday was never more than a respite from school during my youth. While my uncle did not deprive me of material things while I grew to manhood, he was indifferent to me otherwise. By mutual agreement he and I kept from each other's sight as much as possible until the new year's school term began again. Once I was at university, I seldom went home. Then the army became my home.''

"I'm sorry,'' Megan said.

"Good Lord, ma'am, that all happened ages ago. While I am touched by your solicitude,'' he said dryly, "your pity is misplaced. Since December 25th is significant in your life, Miss Wyndom, you view those of us who find no importance in the holiday to be sad creatures. Being alone is not necessarily being lonely, you know. My cold relative's apathetic care helped me to become self-reliant at an early age, and the lesson has served me well. I don't need anyone's company to remain content.''

Unable to meet his eyes, Megan looked down at her idle hands, resting on the table top. So much for a safe topic. She pushed herself back from the table and went to slip the rolls into the oven.

Major Garrison was right. Christmas was not an "alone'' day. It mattered only to those who cared for someone other than themselves. It was obvious that he did not need or want anyone, certainly not her. Any wild thoughts in that direction must be squashed before she began to take them seriously.

The heaping platters of roast goose and stacks of meat pies and gravy and jellies and sweet butter that had graced the yuletide table at Wyndom House were gone. The plump hen she bought from Abel Bonner and the plum pudding ripening in the cupboard were modest by comparison, but it was not the rich food that was important, rather the family together.

The uneven ticking of the little clock on the sideboard caught Megan's attention, and she glanced at the hour.

"It is almost teatime. I must fetch Micah and the children from the barn," she said, reaching for a shawl. Her talk with the major had depressed her more than she wanted to admit even to herself.

"Permit me to run the errand for you," Neal said. He pushed back his chair and rose. "I would like to have a look at my horses and to see the damage I have done to my curricle. I just need to get my coat."

Neal saw Miss Wyndom's deflation. He had cut up her peace again. Christmas meant something to her, and his naysaying had demeaned the holiday. No two people could be as ill suited, Neal thought, remembering Micah's ludicrous matchmaking. He opened his mouth to apologize and decided he would only make matters worse.

Megan rehung the shawl on its hook and reached for the teacups on the cupboard shelf as the major's footsteps receded down the passage. She was foolish to remain strongly attracted to him. He was cynical and brash and reclusive, but, oh, with so much charm. His flaws did not seem to matter. For five years he had lived in her mind. Maybe he was just a bad habit, but she wanted to know the kind of love that existed between a man and a woman. And she wanted to know it with a man like him. If Neal Garrison beckoned, she would willingly fall into his arms.

Five

The featherbed rolls, hot and delicious, were served at tea with a choice of sweet butter, wild strawberry jam, or honey.

Neal was beginning to feel a real contentment whenever he sat down to a meal with the family in the cozy kitchen.

Sitting across from him with a Friday face, Micah ate his rolls with honey in silence and kept his eyes averted from Neal's. The old soldier had been standoffish when Neal had gone to examine his curricle and the horses in the barn. It was obvious to Neal that Micah bore a grudge over their earlier dust up. But Neal was not about to give ground and agree to anything as foolish as a belief that celestial beings interfered in the affairs of men.

"Will you, Neal?" Rebecca's small voice dented his consciousness.

"Sorry poppet," he said. "What was that about going to the woods?"

"You are woolgathering," Elizabeth put in with a mischievous grin. "Becca invited you to come with us tomorrow to gather Christmas greens to decorate the house."

Neal looked suitably contrite. "You caught me out, Lizzie.

But I do remember hearing that the outing was to be to Lord Ames's woods, wasn't it?''

The girls nodded in unison.

''I would be delighted,'' Neal assured them, pointing out that he had always enjoyed trekking over the fields and through the woods on his Verdon Fields estate.

''What is your house like, Neal?'' Sam asked, leaning forward with his elbows on the table.

''Oh, yes, please tell us about Verdon Fields,'' Elizabeth seconded.

Neal thought a minute, wondering how to describe the hundred-year-old house of gray stone covered with ivy. He gave them that detail, but before he could add more, Samuel asked, ''Who lives there now?''

''A caretaker and his wife,'' Neal answered, ''although I imagine that most of the rooms are closed off. There are too many for two people to care for. It is a very large house; why, if every one of us here at the table took one of the bedrooms for our own, there would still be a dozen or more leftover.''

''You must have a great deal of land, then,'' Sam said. Megan had been listening with as much interest as her siblings, but she now chided her brother for asking too many personal questions.

Neal, who sat next to her, put a hand on her arm. ''It's all right, Megan.'' The two had settled on using first names, agreeing that it was silly for them to remain wedded to formal appellations when the children already called him Neal. Unoffended by Sam's blatant curiosity, Neal continued his litany. ''In addition to the house, stable, and gardens, there is a forest for hunting, a home farm which supplies a considerable portion of the food for the manor house table, and extensive park lands for walking and riding.''

However, the edifying conversation was soon aborted when Elizabeth blurted out, ''Oh, Neal, you must be frightfully rich!''

Neal threw his head back and laughed, but Megan reprimanded her little sister for her impertinence and sent the girls off to their room to work on some lessons that she had prepared for them. With pouting lips but not a spoken word, the girls went off, and tea came to an abrupt close.

The next morning Neal pulled aside the unadorned blue drapes and flooded the bedroom with bright sunshine. The brunt of his bruises no longer plagued him. His headaches had vanished, and he had slept through the night without a boost from drugs or medicine. To escape Micah's snoring, Sam had been allowed to move a cot into the bedroom with Neal; but the lad had risen earlier, and Neal had the room to himself.

Standing at the window, Neal looked out onto the dormant garden where a flock of small winter birds were pecking at the seeds on the withered flowers. He had noticed yesterday at teatime that Megan was not comfortable with talk of his afflu-ence. She had asked no questions when the children quizzed him about Verdon Fields and had cut off their queries and pokered up when his wealth became apparent. She had this strange notion that her peers looked down on her because of her reduced circumstances. He was not at all certain that she did not tar him with the same brush.

Yet last night long after supper when the girls had been tucked in and Sam and Micah had retired, the two of them had talked over a cup of hot chocolate. Neal had told Megan a great deal more about himself than he had meant to. And she, too, had spoken of things that Neal was certain she had never discussed with anyone before.

He had loved watching her move with unconscious grace between the stove and the table in the comfortable kitchen, fulfilling the menial task of preparing their hot drinks which once would have been beneath a Wyndom daughter. Nothing in her early life had prepared her to become the head of a household or to live on meager funds. Neal admired her courage and determination. What he did not like was the faint stirrings of a too deep affection for her that posed a danger to the path he had set for his life.

The birds swooped into the air in a flock as if reacting to

some silent signal, and Neal moved from the vicinity of the window to the fireplace.

Ridiculous! he thought. His odd feelings were no more than an unaccustomed sympathy for someone in distress.

Neal leaned a hand on the mantel and stared into the crackling fire. But there was no doubt that he felt protective of her. It was something he had never felt for a woman before.

He had danced attendance on fashionable ladies in London's drawing rooms and lusted after lightskirts, but that was the sum total of his congress with females. He was familiar with kissing hands and warming beds, but not this desire to protect and cherish.

Moreover, he had never before mixed in the personal affairs of someone who had fallen on hard times. He had at hand the means to alleviate Megan's financial straits with the stroke of a pen, and he wanted to. But with stiff-necked pride, she had even rejected his legitimate overture to pay for the feed and care of his horses. He would be setting himself up for a put down if he offered additional assistance. The thunderous look on her face when Dr. Grafton had suggested that Neal pay Megan for stopping under her roof was imprinted on his mind. He was certain that she would rather starve in the gutter than accept his money.

At the rap on the door, he called, "Enter."

The door opened and Elizabeth walked in. Neal had moved his hand from the mantel, but he stood before the fire looking out of place. Lizzie gave him an odd glance.

"Neal, you are woolgathering again," she said with her little fists pressed to her waist.

"I'm afraid so, Elizabeth," he said, summoning up a smile which she returned promptly.

"Well, you have to come to breakfast now," she said in a voice that suggested that he had no business standing around doing nothing. "Meggie says we can leave for the woods to get the Christmas greens right after you eat."

"All right, Lizzie, give me a minute to collect my things," he said, chuckling at her managing ways.

* * *

A long-ago ancestor of the present Lord Ames had planted spruce and pine trees among the native oaks, breams and beeches to create a small forest. On the tips of the evergreen branches, bits of frozen snow glittered like diamonds in the bright winter sun. The air was crisp and invigorating. The last leaves had blown from the deciduous trees, and filtered sunlight made patterns of light and shadow on the forest floor.

Megan and Neal sat on tree stumps a foot apart, exchanging bits of conversation and watching the children gather pinecones and stow them into one corner of the handbarrow which was piled high with the greens cut earlier.

Megan was so physically aware of Neal that every nerve ending in her body seemed to prickle. He was large and strong and masculine. Several times he had put a gloved hand on her coat sleeve when he made a point. The nearness of his smiling, handsome face and the scent of his shaving soap when he bent toward her made her skin tingle. He was the prince incarnate from the fairy tales with which she had filled Rebecca's susceptible little head.

Elizabeth came running over to them, interrupting some desultory talk. "Neal, I need you," she cried. "There's a holly branch real high up where I can't reach it. Please cut it down for me."

"Lizzie, we have all the greens we need," Megan said. "I don't think the barrow will hold much more."

"But this is special," the child pleaded. "The berries are the reddest, densest clusters I have ever seen."

Neal got up and said, "Come on, poppet. Show me where." He winked at Megan and followed the little girl down the narrow forest path.

Megan watched Neal's broad back disappear among the trees. She was so much in love with him. The thought sprang suddenly into her mind from where it had lingered in a small dark corner for some time. He was really quite wonderful. He might be blunt and plain-spoken, but he was also kind and had a gentle side. Still, it was futile to love someone who would not love in return. He valued his independence and had no desire to take on a wife, and, in her case, a whole family, for the children came with her. Yet if she could have had him, her life would have been complete, for he was the fulfillment of her fondest dreams. If only Micah's notions about a Christmas miracle were true. *Stop it!* she rebuked herself. To become mired in pitiful wishes and bootless discontent would spoil a near perfect day.

"Don't drop me, Neal! Don't drop me!" Rebecca's squeal came from the distance. Megan stood up and walked down the path and peered through the trees to see Neal hoisting Rebecca high above his head, his large, competent hands completely encircling her tiny waist. Her little sister was pulling at a vine which, as she moved closer, Megan identified as mistletoe.

Neal was laughing as were Sam and Elizabeth, who stood watching their wriggling sister tug the parasite from around a branch of an oak tree. Megan left the path and walked to Neal's side. She placed her hand on his back. "Don't drop her," she echoed Rebecca, sounding a little concerned.

"Your chick is perfectly safe," Neal said, smiling down at Megan as he set Rebecca on the ground.

"That was fun!" the child cried. "Do it again, Neal."

"I don't think so," he said. "You are a wiggle wart."

"I won't wiggle next time," she promised, but Neal just smiled and shook his head and handed the mistletoe to Megan. She laid the parasite on top of the greens in the barrow.

"It's pleasant here," Neal said. "Shall we take a stroll?" He offered Megan his arm. She hooked her own through his and set off, quite happy just to walk beside him.

The children ran ahead of them, the girls coming and going back and forth to reveal some childish confidences to the grown-ups.

To Megan's delight, Neal took her hand in his, in a more intimate manner. Hand in hand, the two walked on, laughing together over the girls' antics and sharing tales of their own childhood misadventures.

It had been a long time since Megan had felt so happy. In the back of her mind, she was conscious that this pleasant outing would eventually join the mistletoe kiss as just a memory. But she wanted to capture this moment permanently to take with her through the long, unremarkable years ahead of her. She savored the feeling of her hand firmly clasped in Neal's and pretended that they were lovers.

A breeze rustled the dead leaves and whirled them around on the forest floor. The scent of woodsmoke came from a brick chimney on a house that could be seen through the leafless trees.

"We can't go any farther," Megan said, looking up at Neal. "The rear gate to Ames Manor is just ahead."

Neal looked with interest through the grillwork at the imposing brick Georgian manor. Lord Ames was a long-standing Wyndom family friend, yet his lordship had been sorely remiss in providing meaningful assistance to Megan. Giving her the use of the cottage was no sacrifice. She paid rent like any tenant farmer and could not be accused of picking his lordship's pockets. What she needed was an entry back into society. Had Lord Ames done his duty, Megan would have been invited to dances and dinner parties where she could have met eligible gentlemen of her own class. But, illogically, Neal doubted that among Lord Ames's spineless, aristocratic acquaintances there was even one who was discerning enough to see Megan's true worth or had the backbone to set aside her lack of dowry and offer for her on her own exceptional merits.

Neal had dropped Megan's hand when he had stepped to the gate to get a better view of the mansion. Megan now tapped his coat sleeve to regain his attention. "We must start back, Neal."

Sadness enveloped her as she realized she might never hold his hand again.

Taking Rebecca's hand, Megan led the others down the path cushioned with pine needles to the holly tree where they had parked the barrow. Sam took charge of the vehicle and made himself the leader for the trek from the woods. Neal came last with Megan and the girls between him and Sam.

Megan had been so carefree during their time in the woods, and now as if a spell had been broken, she felt extremely

melancholy. She looked over her shoulder and forced a weak
smile in answer to Neal's grin. She pushed her mopes aside
and was in a better frame of mind by the time she stepped after
Sam from the forest to the edge of the frozen field they had
tramped over earlier to get from the house to the woods.

Rebecca went on tiptoe and lifted her arms to Neal. He took
up the child, who wrapped her arms around his neck and clung
like a burr. Neal felt a tender emotion unlike anything he had
ever known. He patted Rebecca's small back and hugged her
to him before he fell in beside Sam, his stride long and easy.

The children were tired and subdued. The outbound trip had
been filled with tomfoolery and laughter. Neal slowed to allow
Megan to catch up to him. Rebecca had eased her head onto
Neal's shoulder and was still, but not asleep.

"She must be heavy," Megan said.

"I'm not," Rebecca piped up.

Megan and Neal laughed together. "She is fine," Neal said.
"I was wondering what is going on behind your quiet face."

Megan had been thinking how much she loved him, but that
would be the last thing she told him. "Just that we had a lovely
time in the woods," she said instead.

"It was nice," he agreed. "I never collected greens for
Christmas before."

They lapsed into a silence, but it was not stiff or uncomfortable.

When the house and grounds came into view, Samuel was
the first to notice the strange wagon parked near the barn.

"The wheelwright has come to repair your curricle, Neal,"
the boy said.

"That was quick," Neal observed, lowering Rebecca to the
ground. Megan imagined she heard a hint of regret in his voice.
Did he rue the wheelwright's premature appearance? Probably
not. Neal had wanted to return to Verdon Fields since the first
day of his convalescence. It was her own desires, not his, that
she heard reflected in his voice. She was the one who wanted
him to remain with her forever.

Male voices came from the barn where Neal had gone to
discuss the repairs to his curricle. Megan stared straight ahead

to hide the sheen of tears which clouded her sight. After tomorrow she would never see Neal again.

"Is Neal going home?" Elizabeth asked, her pretty blue eyes touched with sadness.

"Yes," Megan answered in a controlled voice, determined not to let her own desolation infect the children. "Come, it is time to set luncheon on the table." With those final words, she headed inside.

Six

While the heart of the Wyndom cottage was the kitchen, Christmas was celebrated in the parlor. The room had been closed off for the past three months to conserve fuel. Now the kindling that Samuel had brought in from the shed had been fired, and Neal had added oak logs that had caught into a good blaze. With the parlor warmed up and the chill dissipated, the greens were carried inside, and the decorating began.

Earlier, when Neal had come in from the barn, Megan's worst fears had been confirmed. The curricle would be repaired by late afternoon, and Neal planned to leave tomorrow at first light.

Megan hid her fractured heart as she and the children began putting the trappings of Christmas in place. It would not do for Neal to notice her lowish spirits and guess the reason for them. He had made no move to actively participate in adorning the parlor, but at least he was present and watching her efforts. She was grateful for anything that kept him near to her during his remaining moments in this house.

The loveseat from which Neal observed was covered with a green-and-yellow-striped shawl to shroud the threadbare upholstery. The tables and chairs in the room were of a different era, but were not exquisite enough to be considered antiques. Megan kept the old wood polished to a high sheen, and the jade velour drapes dust-free, giving the room the illusion of being grander than it was.

The papier-mâché box, the size of a small chest, that Sam had brought down from the attic, sat in the center of the faded faux oriental rug. Megan removed and set aside the flowered decoupage cover of the storage chest and lifted out red satin bows and gold stars fashioned of stiff gilded paper. Rebecca and Elizabeth lined up the ribbons and glittering stars into neat rows, handling the decorations as if the common fripperies were priceless objects.

Neal's eyes surveyed Megan admiringly, approving her quiet beauty and indomitable spirit. Her unfeigned enthusiasm for Christmas was contagious. As the room hummed with happy voices, she almost had him believing that he might somehow find joy in the holiday.

As she handed around decorations for the children to place, she spoke of yuletides past, keeping alive good memories of their parents for the children while the room became increasingly more festive in green and red and gold. The children were high-spirited, and Megan would join in their laughter, her more subdued giggles reminding Neal of tinkling Christmas bells.

Spruce and pine boughs were laid on the white mantel of the fireplace and adorned with red bows. Elizabeth pointed to perfect spots for the pinecones, delegating an eager-to-please Rebecca to fetch and carry and place at her sister's direction.

Neal volunteered a suggestion now and then about the placement of scented candles and holly boughs, but mostly he sat quietly in wonderment that he had lived for over three decades and had never before watched a room being decorated for Christmas.

After a time, Elizabeth came and sat beside Neal on the small sofa. She shivered and snuggled against him.

"Are you cold, Lizzie?" he asked, drawing her into the full circle of his arm. "Why don't you move nearer the fire? There is a chill in this part of the room."

Elizabeth shook her head. "I want to sit with you, Neal." He was flattered that she had sought his company. Until a few days ago, his discourse with minors during his adult life had been almost nonexistent. He could not have guessed that he would be a favorite with the Wyndom children, nor that their good opinion would have mattered to him. But it pleased him that the youngsters liked him. He would miss them nearly as much as he would miss their sister.

"A penny for your thoughts, Elizabeth," he said with a smile. "I wager it has to do with Christmas."

She grinned, thinking that he was very wise to have read her mind. "Did you get lots of toys from Father Christmas when you were little?" she asked.

"No, my parents died during an influenza epidemic when I was seven, and my uncle who raised me did not keep Christmas. To me, the holidays meant nothing more than going home from school for a few weeks." He chuckled. "I don't think I even learned that there was a Father Christmas until I was nine or ten."

"Truly?" Elizabeth's blue eyes got big. "That is horrible."

It did not seem horrible to him, but to a child raised in a loving family where Father Christmas was a familiar concept his isolated childhood would indeed seem horrible.

Neal did not attempt to explain away his young years to her. His isolation would be incomprehensible to her. He inclined his head and said, "It's true. I knew nothing of Father Christmas when I was little."

Elizabeth seemed to consider this for a moment. Sounding grown-up, she said in a whispery voice, "Of course, I know that Father Christmas is a symbol, but Becca believes. She doesn't know that Megan buys each of us a small gift each year. You see, Sam and I remember all the toys we got at Christmas when our mama and papa were alive, but, of course, Becca doesn't because she was born here. Since Mary Bonner and them only get one present, too, she thinks that is all Father Christmas ever brings anyone."

Rebecca sat cross-legged in the corner watching Megan and Sam arranging spruce branches in a tall red vase. Looking furtively toward the others, Elizabeth said in the same lowered voice, "When I say a small gift, I don't want you to think that Meg is cheese-paring, Neal. She would be generous to a fault if she were able, but the things Sam and I would want are beyond her means. We are not rich, you know."

Such a display of understanding in a ten-year-old child had to be rare. Neal was touched, and he felt suddenly bereft because he had never given anyone a Christmas present.

He lowered his head and tailored his tone to Elizabeth's. "Lizzie," he said, an idea taking hold, "suppose you could ask Father Christmas for a gift, any gift, what would it be?"

"That's simple," Elizabeth answered without even considering, "a doll with a china head and long silk hair and a beautiful silver and gold dress. It is what I have wanted every Christmas since I was six years old." Her piquant face became wistful. "I suppose soon I shall be too old for dolls."

"Is that all you want, just a doll?" he asked. It was such a modest gift. Children her age must have a list as long as his arm.

"Yes, for myself, but if I had some shillings, I would buy Sam an atlas," she said. "An atlas is a book of maps. There is a big one in the village bookshop which Sam would like to have." Elizabeth lowered her voice into another whisper. "He wants to find all the places he will go when he becomes a soldier. Did you know that the king's army once fought in America? You have to cross a big ocean to get there. When Sam gets his atlas, he is going to show me where America is."

"What about Rebecca?" Neal asked. He found himself making a mental list of the two items. Later he would write down a description of the doll and the atlas. He was going to play Father Christmas to the Wyndom children, although he would be an absent one. Certainly Megan could have no objection to a few gifts in keeping with the generosity of the season.

"I don't know what Becca would want. But I do know that she likes animals. Perhaps I would buy her a toy dog made of real fur. I know what I would get Megan, a gold lady's watch that she could pin on the front of her dress."

Neal added the new items to his mental list and began to

make plans. When he arrived home, he would send a servant to York . . . no, he would go himself and do the thing right . . . and buy the presents Elizabeth had mentioned, wrap them in tissue paper, tie the packages with red and green ribbons, and send them to the Wyndoms. He would add a couple yards of blue watered silk the color of Megan's eyes for her to sew into a pretty Sunday dress for herself.

The prospect of giving presents was beginning to excite him. It was completely the reverse of all he believed, but, what the deuce, he owed this family a small measure of happiness. If he was not here, Megan could not fling the gifts back into his face. He smiled smugly. Besides, she was really too tender-hearted to force the children to send back Christmas presents.

Megan's announcement that the decorating was done brought Neal back from his pleasant musings.

With her hands on her slim hips, Megan admired the room with a small smile of satisfaction at the corner of her lips.

"Wait, Meg, you forgot the kissing ball," Sam reminded her, reaching into the box which had held the decorations.

"Leave it," Megan said, stepping toward her brother to stop him from removing the bauble from the chest. "We need a step ladder to hang it. Micah will put it up tomorrow."

"Neal can reach that high," Elizabeth said from the sofa. "Can't you, Neal? The beam is lower than the holly branches were."

Megan grew frantic. Under no circumstance did she want Neal to get a look at the kissing ball. "We will hang it tomorrow," she said sharply. "Let's clean up now."

But it was too late. Sam held the silver ball decorated with red and green stones aloft. Megan watched Neal's expression go from interest to bafflement to dawning to full recognition. And then, she cried craven and refused to look at him. Would he be angry because she had withheld their previous meeting from him? Or would he pretend as she had that he had never met her and had no memory of the kiss?

"We need to fasten the sprig of mistletoe to the bottom of the ball before Neal hangs it," Sam reminded Megan.

With an inner sigh of resignation, she picked up the scissors, cut a piece of mistletoe, and fastened the sprig with a red ribbon to the round screw in the bottom of the ornament with quivering fingers, the muscles in her stomach tightening.

"Do you see the hook in that beam, Neal?" she said, pointing to a small round screw above her head. She was relieved that her voice did not tremble.

"Yes, I see it," Neal said in a husky tone from across the room.

"That's where it goes," Megan said. She did not watch him put Elizabeth from him and rise from the sofa, but she heard the tread of his boots on the thin rug as he moved to her side.

He took the kissing ball from her without touching her hand and examined the hook embedded in the top of the silver ball.

He raised up on his toes and lifted the ball high into the air on his large palm and clipped the hook unerringly onto the companion eye. The children cheered. The red ribbon with mistletoe attached dropped down, and the ball bobbled for a split second, catching the firelight and causing the red and green jewels to shimmer.

Megan broke into a storm of activity, sweeping up pine needles from the rug with a straw broom into a dustpan. The needles were added to the crackling fire, filling the room with the smell of pine.

Neal tilted his head up toward the ornament. The elusive memory of the younger Megan had shoved itself onto the periphery of his conscious mind ever since the accident, but whenever he grabbed at the edges, he would doubt his own impressions. Now there was no mistake. He had kissed Megan beneath the mistletoe the Christmas season he had gone to Wyndom House at her father's invitation for a high stakes card game.

She had been a vision of young loveliness, standing in the center of the vacant hall in a green velvet dress, her blond hair threaded with matching ribbons, staring up at him as he descended the garland-draped staircase.

Her blue eyes had been wide with wonder when he reached her side and pointed to the mistletoe above their heads and smiled at her. With his hands behind his back, Neal had lowered his lips full onto hers. The sweetness that flowed from her kiss had left him aching for more. But she had been an innocent who was not even out, and he, a man of considerable experience. To this day, he could not explain what had possessed him to kiss her. A half dozen women with one or two Seasons to their credit had stood with him beneath the kissing ball that day. He had done no more than salute each one with a chaste kiss on the cheek. Yet he had tasted that young girl's innocent lips and found them heady.

"The parlor looks nice," Micah said, appearing at the door and looking around the room. "There's hot chocolate and sweet biscuits waiting in the kitchen if you are finished."

The children swarmed toward the door, clamoring that they were famished after all the work.

"Major, your curricle is fixed," Micah informed Neal over the children's voices. "The wheelwright had another appointment down the road and asked that you stop at his place tomorrow and settle the bill on your way home."

Micah thought the major looked bemused standing under the mistletoe. Had he heard him?

Now that the major was leaving, Micah had decided to forgive the former officer for flying up into the boughs. He tried again. "Or you could leave the money with me, and I'll see that he gets it."

"Yes, thank you, Micah; that would be fine," Neal said, his mind elsewhere. "Megan, may I please speak with you for a moment . . . alone."

Micah followed the children, who had preceded him into the hall. He turned around and gave Megan and the major a knowing look. Seemed Providence was taking a hand after all, he thought, as he reached back and pulled the door closed.

"You remember, don't you?" Megan said, running a finger over the edge of a table where she stood a few steps from Neal.

"Yes, Wyndom House near London the Christmas of 1810. How old were you?"

"Sixteen," she said.

"Gad, I was twenty-six. Had your father come upon us, he would have horsewhipped me, and deservedly so."

"You did not do anything so grievous as to warrant such a harsh punishment," Megan said. "Besides, I enjoyed it."

Their eyes met and held. Megan could hear his quickened breath, joining her own. He still stood directly beneath the mistletoe with a strange light in his dark eyes, moistening his lips with his tongue in a provocative manner.

Megan sensed that he wanted to kiss her. And she wanted to kiss him more than she had ever wanted anything. She stepped to his side, lifted her head, and offered her mouth to him.

Neal caressed her flushed cheeks with his fingertips. The curve of her cherry lips was deliciously sensual. This was not the wide-eyed schoolgirl of their first meeting, but a desirable woman.

He cupped her face in his hands and brought his lips over hers. She melted against him and responded to the heat of his mouth on hers. Her mouth opened to his own, and her hands ran through the thick hair that curled at his coat collar. The simmering passion intensified, and for a long time, neither could stop kissing the other. Neal's hands began to wander to the soft swell of her breasts when the children's pervasive squeals and laughter came from the direction of the kitchen, followed by Micah's chiding voice.

Neal muttered, "This blasted house is too small." His faint grin softened his crabbed complaint. In truth, he welcomed the intrusion. He had been maddeningly out of control for a few seconds, and he did not want that. It scared him more than a little to be drawn into a maelstrom of passion that could leave him without options.

Megan released him with a nervous titter. He stood with his hands on her shoulders, looking down into her eyes with a serious expression.

"What do you know about my presence at Wyndom House?" he asked.

"Very little. I caught glimpses of you now and then, but you were gone by Christmas Day, which was reserved for close friends. I suppose you were there just for the gambling."

"You know full well that was why I was there. Sir Cyril

had never met me before. From some idle conversation between two of my fellow officers, your father made the mistake of concluding I was any easy mark and invited me to Wyndom House. Megan, I am not a hardened gambler. I never wager more than I can afford to lose. I think I won something in the vicinity of twenty pounds from your father that day.''

Megan wound her arms around his waist and looked up into his concerned face. ''Oh, Neal, don't think I blame you for Papa's affliction. No one forced him to gamble. If you had not come to Wyndom House, someone else would have been there in your place. You played no part in the days and months and years before that houseparty which led to his ruin.''

''Did you have no friends or relatives to step in and stop him?''

''None. But you know yourself, gaming is tolerated by everyone. If someone is a member of the *ton*, he can live on the tick for years. But eventually even the richest families can lose their fortunes.'' She paused a moment.

''The hardest part was that my father's passing tore the heart from my mother. People who had been our friends turned from us. Oh, not everyone at once, but we had to sell the house to settle Papa's pile of debts, and eventually, even those who were kind at first dropped away. Mama felt humiliated. She could not bear to stay in the city. She decided to take us as far from London as possible, so she swallowed her pride and appealed to Lord Ames, an old friend, for she knew he had extensive properties here in the north, far from London.''

Neal disengaged himself from Megan's arms, took her hand, and led her to the small sofa. When they were seated beside each other, her hand still in his, he said, ''My dear, I am surprised that Lord Ames has not done better by you, at least socially.''

Her smile saddened. ''Mama, I think, expected he would, but I have never been invited to Ames Manor for social occasions, and Lady Ames never comes to call. After a life of wealth, Mama found the world she had been cast into through no fault of her own unbearable. She hung on for a time, I think for Rebecca's sake, but then she went into a steady decline, finally dying from an undiagnosed illness. It hurts, Neal, to be shunned simply because one is poor.''

"You need not worry anymore," Neal said impulsively. ''My uncle left me with more money than I can spend in a lifetime. You and the children shall have the best of everything from now on. I will always be here to protect you.''

Happiness surged through Megan as she anticipated his proposal. She smiled at him, her eyes filled with love.

Neal released her hand, stood up, and began to pace. ''And don't be concerned about your good name.'' Dismayed by his own traitorous tongue, he hated the words pouring unbidden from his mouth, but could not stop himself. ''No one need ever know where you got the money. All I ask is that this time, you do not dismiss my offer out of hand, for I want to help you.''

Megan's stomach dropped. Neal could not be saying what she was hearing. Yet there was no ambiguity in his unprepared little speech. It was apparent that he was not on the verge of making a declaration. Nothing had changed. He was offering her money, not marriage.

Her newfound joy exploded into shattered fragments. His kisses were counterfeit. How foolish she had been to expose her heart to him before he had honorably committed himself to her.

''Accepting money from a bachelor implies a *carte blanche* in society's eyes.''

Neal stopped his pacing and stood tall over her. Megan's truism had caught him unawares, but he was quick to reassure her. ''Gad, my dear, no, no. This is not an indecent proposal. I am genuinely fond of the children and hold you in the highest regard. I offer my assistance from a sense of . . . ah . . . the deepest gratitude for taking me in after the accident.'' He sounded like a pompous fool and knew it. His words were hollow and patronizing. But he could not retrieve them, for he had spoken the truth. Her sweet face which a moment before had shone with a dreamlike expression had faded to a look of hopeless despair.

Megan struggled for self-command and gained enough to

say with quiet dignity, ''You owe me nothing. Money is not the answer to everything, Neal.''

''I know, but . . . ,'' he got out before she held up her hand and silenced him with, ''Please, don't say another word.''

Her look of contempt pierced Neal's heart. It would have been easier on him if she had ripped up at him. He walked to the window and looked out at the frozen field which was as cold as the indictment in her frosty blue eyes. He kicked himself for having botched the well-meant overture.

Megan remained on the small sofa, her hands clasped before her, unable to move. Her lips still burned with his kiss. But her heart was numb.

''I must leave tomorrow,'' Neal said, turning back to the room. ''Since my uncle's death the house has been in the hands of caretakers. I have no idea what I will find or how long it will take me to put things to rights.''

''Of course, you must do what you must do.'' His ambiguous words seemed to hold out a promise of an eventual return. Yet the indecision in his voice and the wariness in his dark eyes crumbled all hope of a new beginning. He had offered her money in lieu of love. In his arms the future had been fraught with promise. Now his hard words had dashed her hopes into dust. She would never see Neal again. This was the end. He would leave, and after a month or two a letter would come expressing his regret at having been indiscreet and ask her forgiveness. But there would be no offer of marriage.

''Micah and the children must be wondering what has become of us,'' she said, finding the room suddenly confining. Her spine was rigid as she rose from the sofa and walked toward the door without looking at him.

Feeling abysmally low, Neal followed her, but excused himself before they reached the kitchen. He slipped into Sam's bedroom and dropped into the armchair, his elbows on his knees, his head buried in his hands.

He had insulted her with an offer of money when she had wanted so much more from him. His own response to her kisses had been far from benign. He had longed to sweep her into his arms and carry her off to bed, but his strong attraction to her had to be a passing thing born of his overlong abstinence. Gad, he had not made love to a woman for nearly a year. And he had never had marriage in mind when he kissed Megan. It would be unconscionable, even cruel, for him to compound his bad judgment by making false promises and expressing intentions that he knew he would regret when he was back at Verdon Fields. He knew from the military that one quick blow in the long run was the kindest, but he took no comfort from the thought.

Seven

The bedroom was in semidarkness, illuminated by a single candle in a small lamp on the mantel. The fire had died down into embers and added little light. Neal scanned the dim room for overlooked belongings. Satisfied that he was leaving nothing behind, he fastened the strap on the leather case.

Samuel stirred on the cot against the wall and raised himself up on one elbow. "You're going already, Neal," he said drowsily.

"Yes," Neal said. "Go back to sleep."

"I was going to talk with you some more about the army last night, but you were already asleep when I came to bed," Sam said, sitting up and flinging his legs over the side of the cot, his flannel nightshirt riding up to his knees.

"I turned in early in anticipation of today's long journey," Neal said with a half truth. He had been awake when Sam whispered his name last night, but he had been in no fit mood to make small talk with anyone.

The severe strain of sitting across from a woman whom he knew he had wronged, pretending nothing was amiss between them, had caused the former idyllic kitchen to become cramped, overheated, and stifling at suppertime. Robbed of his own appetite, Neal had found it painful to watch Megan, too, moving her food around on her plate with a fork. He had finally bolted down a little of the savory-smelling stew which tasted like straw and left the supper table before anyone else.

Back in the bedroom he had selected a book chronicling England's greatest naval battle from Sam's bookcase. His scheme to liberate himself from thoughts of Megan by reading had failed after one coherent paragraph, when the words on the page had begun to swim into an incomprehensible jumble. When Megan's image had appeared to superimpose itself onto mental visions of Drake firing on the Spanish Armada, he had given up the pretense of reading, doused the light, and assuaged his guilt by berating himself until he fell asleep.

This morning Neal felt like the monster he was sure Megan must believe him to be. He bemoaned his blunder of kissing her with such passion when he had no intention of proposing to her, but remained stubbornly firm in his resolve that he would make a poor husband and that matrimony was not for him.

"Would you build up the fire?" Sam requested. He pulled the quilt from his bed, moved to the soft chair, and cocooned himself in the warm cover. "It's freezing in here."

Neal crossed to the hearth, threw a log on the fire, and picked up the bellows and blew the embers into a decent blaze. After the log caught, he stood with his back to the fireplace and withdrew his watch from his waistcoat pocket and snapped open the lid.

"Will you get home before dark tonight?" Sam asked.

Neal pushed the timepiece back into his vest pocket. "If I can leave now before the household comes alive."

The bright stars he had seen through the window when he awoke were set in a cloudless blue-black sky which promised a sunny day and good weather for fast traveling.

"Meg and the girls are going to be disappointed that you aren't staying for breakfast," Sam said rather wistfully.

Neal felt a pang of guilt and a twitch of irritation, but ignored the lament. "Sam, would you please see that Mr. Abel Bonner gets the letter I left there on the mantelpiece. I did not have the opportunity to thank him properly in person for his help the day of the accident.''

Sam nodded, looking at the letter propped against an unused candlestick.

Neal picked up his valise and walked to the door. ''Take care, lad.''

''Godspeed, Neal,'' Sam answered, heading back to bed, dragging the quilt after him. ''We are going to miss you.''

A lump formed in Neal's throat. He lifted a hand, waved, and stepped into the hall where his heart lurched when he saw a light under the kitchen door. He had planned to avoid Megan and the girls by decamping while it was still dark. Maybe she was less of a coward than he was. He could not bear to face her after what had passed between them. But when he opened the door to the kitchen, Megan was not there. Micah was stoking the iron stove.

''Morning, Major,'' he said cheerfully. ''I thought you might need some assistance harnessing your team.''

''Kind of you, Micah,'' Neal said, and waited for the older man to don his coat, grateful for the unexpected help.

In her upstairs bedroom, Megan sat in a chair next to the window wrapped in a woolen shawl. The morning sky was just beginning to lighten.

For the last half hour her ears had been attuned to catch Neal's movements belowstairs. When she heard the outer door close, her spirits slumped. Her wits must have gone begging for her to think that he might not leave.

Last night she had fallen into an exhausted sleep, the emotional turns from hope to despair having taken their toll. What a ninny she was. Like a small child she had looked for a Christmas miracle, expecting Neal to rap on her door, enfold her in his loving arms, and confess that he adored her.

From her vantage point, Megan had an unobstructed view of the drive. With a sinking heart, she watched the curricle roll past the house. The magnificent grays stepped high in the brisk winter air. Neal was bundled in his greatcoat, but his head was bare, his black hair blowing in the wind, his profile heart-stoppingly handsome.

Megan leapt up, her shawl falling from her back. Ignoring the chill, she laid her palms and forehead against the cold glass. He was really going! How was she to face all the years ahead without him now that she had fully tasted his kisses?

Megan felt her temples begin to throb. For one wild second, she thought she should fling the window open and shout to him not to leave her. The curricle veered into the drive that ran down to the road. She stared at the back of Neal's head until the horses turned from the lane and headed toward the village. She had one last glimpse of him and then he was gone.

Megan fell back into the chair with a choked sob and rewrapped herself into the woolen shawl. Her fingers ran over her lips. The kisses she had shared with him should have sealed a promise of eternal love and been followed by a proper proposal. That was the way of her class.

Slowly, anger born of hurt rose in Megan's breast. Neal had taken advantage of her because she had no father to protect her from being used like a lightskirt. Her birth was as good as his if not better. How dare the rake trample on her heart? She should have known that he was a man of dubious character. Hadn't he very nearly sullied her reputation by taking liberties with her when she had been nothing but an innocent schoolgirl? She bristled with indignation at his insulting behavior. What a fool she had been to throw herself into his arms. Everyone knew that unlike women, men were notoriously unreliable and did not kiss only where they loved.

The tears came, and when they were spent and her eyes dried, she claimed that Neal Garrison was not worth a moment's remorse. In a weak moment, she might feel a trace of sadness for what might have been, but never would Micah or the children see that she had suffered a broken heart.

Still, good intentions sometimes do not take hold when emotions run deep and love won't die and tears threaten to spill from one's eyes again and again.

Micah read Megan accurately and saw how badly she hurt. Although she worked to put on a good front before the children, much of her speech was reduced to uttering monosyllables. To make matters worse, the two little girls were crushed that Neal had not said a proper goodbye to them. Their conversations were fraught with complaints.

Megan sat darning stockings in the rocking chair in the kitchen late on the afternoon of Neal's departure when Rebecca said with a pout, "Neal should have stayed for Christmas." She left the table where she had been helping Micah to fold freshly laundered towels and stood beside her sister's chair, her small hands on the arm of the rocker.

"Meggie, you could pen him a note inviting him back for the holiday," Elizabeth suggested. She sat on a kitchen chair next to Megan, rolling the mended stockings into matched pairs. "Neal doesn't live so far that he wouldn't get a letter in time."

"Write to him," Rebecca demanded. "I want Neal here for Christmas."

"No!" Megan's refusal was sharp and bitter. "Both of you, stop your blabber mouthing. Rebecca, I don't think it much matters what you or Lizzie want!"

Rebecca's heart-shaped lips worked, and her small chin trembled. Two large tears rolled down her cheek. "Why is Megan so cross?" she whimpered to Micah.

He interceded with a gentle, "Come away, now," and swept the four-year-old into his arms and motioned Elizabeth to follow. He left Megan alone to deal with her pain.

An hour later Megan went up to her room and sat thinking. She was furious with Neal, for giving her one brief moment of bliss. She was not entirely blameless, for she had thrown herself quite openly at his head, willingly waltzed into his arms, and offered him her lips. But he had snatched back her rapture and replaced ecstasy with hopelessness. Her resentment was against him, but she was unfairly venting her wrath on the children. Even if her heart was in pieces, she must not spoil the children's Christmas by wallowing in self-pity. She made a vow not to let her temper get the better of her again. She would be hurting herself and the children, not getting back at Neal, with such self-indulgent behavior.

* * *

On Friday, three days before Christmas, the Bonners were invited to the cottage for a Christmas party.

Abel and Micah had cut a Yule log that was set ablaze with proper ceremony in the parlor fireplace from a charred piece saved especially for the purpose from last year's log as custom demanded.

Plates stacked with slices of mince pie and gingerbread were placed on the refreshment table with bowls of nuts and platters of sweet biscuits cut in various holiday shapes.

The adults gathered around the wassail bowl. The roasted apples bobbed up and down as Megan dipped the ladle into the spicy ale and filled the crystal cups.

"To our health, happiness, and prosperity in the coming year," Abel toasted when everyone had been served.

"Hear, hear," the others chorused.

Joseph Bonner, Abel and Hester's oldest at thirteen, pushed his blushing mother under the mistletoe. "Kiss her, Da," he urged his father.

"Kiss her! Kiss her!" The nine-year-old Bonner twin girls took up the chant as did little Mary and the Wyndom children.

Abel grinned widely and set his puckered lips upon his flushed wife's mouth. Megan envied the love shining from the couple's eyes. If only the breathtaking kisses she had shared with Neal had contained the same kind of commitment from him. Whenever she thought of him the ache in her heart seemed to revive. And she thought about him more than she would have liked. She had given Abel the letter from Neal, and he had stepped aside to read it. Megan was glad to see genuine pleasure on the farmer's honest face as he slipped the message into his pocket. At least, she thought wryly, Neal had done right by Abel.

The children made a game of running under the mistletoe without being caught until they tired of the sport. The older girls settled down to play spillikin on the floor while Sam and Joseph moved two chairs to a corner where they could talk without being overheard.

The bayberry aroma of the candles mixed with the fragrance of pine gave the room a holiday aura. Micah and Abel sat in front of the fire, imbibing mulled cider, indulging in neighborhood gossip, and discussing farming matters while Megan and Hester conversed on the sofa with Rebecca and Mary on the rug at their feet playing with rag dolls. Thus the afternoon passed pleasantly in an atmosphere of holiday good will and cheer.

Standing on the porch, Megan, the children, and Micah waved to the Bonners huddled together for warmth in the old wagon. Cries of "Happy Christmas," and shouts for a safe trip to York, where the Bonner family was going to spend Christmas Eve and the day itself with Hester's parents, echoed through the icy air.

As Megan cleaned up the remains of the party, she paused and stared at the kissing ball. Her hand went to her lips, for she could not help but be reminded of Neal's warm mouth on hers whenever she looked at the silver ball with the mistletoe dangling from the red ribbon. It would always be so. Just as the bauble had reminded her of him in the past, so it would in the future. The difference was that now the memories would be painful ones. In time the ache in her heart would diminish, but the hurt would never be permanently erased. For now, her pigheaded emotions refused to obey her command not to love him. But that would change. The world was populated with thousands of more worthy gentlemen than Neal Garrison. Her dilemma was that should she line up those superior specimens from one end of the earth to the other, fool that she was, she would still choose Neal.

Sunday, which was also Christmas Eve, the sky was gray, weighed down with impending snow. Micah came in from the barn to the kitchen where Megan and the children, dressed for the morning service, had waited while he hitched Sunbeam, their old mare, to the wagon.

"I think we're in for a blizzard," he said. "Do you want me to drive you to church?"

"No, that will not be necessary," Megan answered, shepherding the children toward the back door. The cold dampness struck her as she stepped over the sill into the yard. "We shall be back before the snow starts," she said confidently to Micah.

But by the time Megan stood up to sing the last hymn, the drifting snowflakes that she had noticed during the sermon had thickened.

"It's coming down hard," Sam whispered, looking through the church window. She nodded, picked up the line in the music and sang along on the last verse, glad the service was ending.

The fields surrounding the stone church were white when Sam removed the horse blanket from Sunbeam's back and shook off the snow. He folded back the canvas which covered the wagon's floorboards, exposed the dry floor, and helped the girls into the wagon. He hopped onto the box next to Megan, who drove the old horse from the churchyard at a snail's pace, the snow blowing around the wagon's wheels and sweeping over the road.

The wind would have seared their faces had Megan and the children not wrapped their bright-hued mufflers over their mouths and chins. But Sunbeam plodded on surefooted and steady with her head bowed, and a half an hour later, Megan brought the reliable mare to a stop in front of the barn.

Micah came from the house where he had been pacing back and forth and casting worried glances through the window, cursing the inclement weather.

But the snow pleased the children. Sam and Elizabeth jumped from the wagon and squealed and hollered and ignored the cold that reddened their exposed faces. Micah lifted Rebecca to the ground to join in the enthusiastic shenanigans.

Sam and Elizabeth scooped up balls of snow and hurled the snowballs at the side of the barn. Megan smiled, watching them and remembering what fun it was to be a child playing in the snow. Sam began to roll a huge ball for the start of a snowman. Megan sighed softly and walked to the house.

By late afternoon tree branches, bare and brown the previous day, were heavy with snow, and on Christmas morning a thick blanket of white covered the walks and driveway, making it impossible to know where the paths began and the dormant gardens ended.

"The snow has let up some," Samuel said as he came into the kitchen where Megan was preparing a hot breakfast.

"It took Micah fifteen minutes to shovel a path to the barn to check on Sunbeam and the cats," Megan said. As Samuel reached for his coat, she added, "There's no need for you to go out. I am sure Micah has everything in hand."

Samuel hooked his coat back onto the peg. "All right," he said, and leaned over and kissed his sister's cheek. "Happy Christmas, Meg."

"And to you, Sam." She gave him a warm hug. "Put some more logs into the stove, please. The kitchen was like ice when I came down."

Sam went to the wood box and removed two split logs and lifted the grate and pushed the wood into the birthing fire. The back door opened and closed in a rush as Micah came in, stamping snow from his boots and slapping his hat against his side.

"The whole countryside is under snow," he said. "It's everywhere. I haven't seen an accumulation like this in years."

Micah and Samuel exchanged Christmas greetings. "Shall I awaken the girls?" Sam asked, starting toward the hall door.

"Let them sleep," Megan said. "It is going to be a long day. I'm afraid we are going to be confined to the house. The drifts have already covered the snowman you made yesterday."

"I'll go build up the fire in the parlor," Micah said, and headed in that direction. As he opened the hall door, Elizabeth and Rebecca in plaid woolen dresses walked through to the kitchen, crying, "Happy Christmas!"

"Can I open my present now?" Elizabeth asked.

The gifts were laid out near the hearth in the parlor.

"Micah is just going to see to the fire. Let's wait until the front room warms up. We will eat breakfast first," Megan said, giving each of her sisters a hug and pushing a mug of hot chocolate into their hands.

* * *

Later Megan's laugh was light as she gave the children their presents and handed a gaily wrapped package to Micah. She seemed a shade happier, he thought, than he had seen her any time since the major had left. But, then, she wasn't one to let anything keep her down for long. Neal Garrison might be a right one in handling military matters, but he sure didn't have a lick of sense where women were concerned.

Thank yous and hugs and kisses were much in evidence, and in the end, Elizabeth was delighted with the box of watercolors, brushes, and drawing pad, Samuel with a small illustrated book of regimental uniforms, and Rebecca with the farmyard of painted wooden animals and fences which could be hooked together to form pens. Micah gave Megan and the children new mittens and gloves and a tin of chocolates. He promised that he would smoke the cigars he received only outside or in the barn. Megan was duly impressed with the pen wipers and the hand-made calendar which the children had painstakingly copied from one borrowed from Lord Ames and decorated for her. The wrappings were thrown into the fire, but the ribbons were rolled up and saved.

"It's time I started dinner," Megan said when the excitement had abated. "I need to get the chicken stuffed and into the oven if we are to eat on time."

Elizabeth and Micah came to the kitchen with Megan to share in the preparation. Sam remained with Rebecca and helped her set up her miniature farm.

Megan was grateful that the children had not spoken of Neal all day. He had not been mentioned when the presents were dispersed, nor was he allowed to intrude on the Christmas dinner. Clearing up afterward, neither Sam nor Elizabeth evoked his name. Megan knew she had Micah to thank for the reprieve. But she, herself, had not been able to keep from wondering how Neal was spending the holiday. She pictured him in his large, empty house, sitting happily alone in a big, comfortable chair near the fire, content in his selfish isolation, never giving a moment's thought to either her or the children.

Megan hung up her apron. The best china had been put away, and the kitchen floor was swept clean. She was to join the children and Micah in the parlor for the remainder of the afternoon, but she wanted a few minutes of solitude.

She rubbed a clear patch into the whorled pattern of frost on the windowpane. The snow had stopped. She contemplated the frozen landscape for a while, thinking that the pristine white countryside where nothing moved looked incredibly beautiful. Under the window two small brown birds pecked at the bread crumbs the children had tossed onto a snowdrift for them.

Megan began to turn back toward the room when in the distance she glimpsed a movement near the buried road. She wondered if it was a deer, for the dark shape was rather large. She watched with interest until the indistinct form slowly penetrated her consciousness and showed itself to be tall and male. Megan bit her lip, and her heart began a slow race. It was not him, she told herself. It looked like him because that was who she wanted it to be.

The man trudged forward in the knee-deep snow, drawing nearer and nearer as Megan's heart beat faster and faster. She laughed aloud when she could no longer deny that the man coming toward her was Neal, drawing behind him a child's sled with his old valise and a large sack tied to the sleigh bed with a hemp rope. His breath came in labored puffs of white mist. Megan's crossed arms pressed against her breasts where a hundred scattered emotions fluttered in her body.

Neal was only yards from the house when she finally moved. She ran to the door, laughing and sobbing at once, and hurled herself into his arms when he reached the walk that Micah had swept earlier.

Neal's teeth chattered as he crushed her to him and grumbled, "W . . . woman, after this, you w . . . would be the v . . . veriest birdbrain if y . . . you questioned my love for y . . . you."

His backhanded declaration was composed of the sweetest words that Megan had ever hoped to hear.

In the warm kitchen, Neal placed on the stone floor the sack and leather case he had unlashed from the sled, crossed to the warmth of the stove, and removed his outerwear. He beat his arms against his chest, continuing to shiver uncontrollably as if he were a mass of loose bones.

Standing apart at first, their eyes met at last in perfect understanding. Nothing of what had passed between them before mattered.

Megan moved into his strong arms. Neal gathered her close and knew he was home at last. For the longest time they clung and kissed and clung again.

At last the two sat down in kitchen chairs facing one another, so close that their knees touched. Neal held both of her hands in his. Waves of love shot through him. He leaned forward and touched his forehead to hers.

"How did you ever manage to get here?" Megan asked.

He leaned back, sighed, and shook his head from side to side in wonder. "It was not easy," he said. "Yesterday, under gray skies, I set out from Verdon Fields in my curricle, determined to spend Christmas with you. I had been on the road for two hours when it started to snow."

After a time his spent horses had begun to slip on the road, forcing him to stop and put up for the night at an inn.

"This morning the deep snow forced me to hire a horse and sleigh, but when I reached your village, the snow had become too deep for the horse. If I were to see you today, and I was determined to spend Christmas with you, shank's mare was all that was left me. I tied my belongings and the sack to the sled the stableman's son sold me and set out and here I am."

"Oh, Neal." Megan was too overcome to say more. While she had pictured him sitting uncaring before a warm fire, he had been braving the blizzard to reach her.

"I love you, Meg," he said, and felt a dull ache in his chest. Several times he had stumbled in the deep snow and feared that he would fall and be unable to get up. Although he had wrapped himself tightly against the freezing weather, the biting cold had penetrated his clothes and gone straight to the bone. He did not fear death, which had been a ubiquitous presence during his military campaigns, but he dreaded that he might die without Megan ever knowing how much he loved her.

"I love you, too, Neal," she replied. It was then he realized that he might have died without ever hearing those same sweet words from her lips. Never before had he cared if anyone said "I love you" to him, but he did now. He wanted Megan's I love yous for the rest of his life.

"Megan, I want you to be my wife, if you will have me."

She set her hand against his face. "Can you doubt it?"

He caught her hand in his and kissed her palm, his mood lightening. "Is that yes? I never proposed to anyone before."

"Idiot," she said with affection. Smiles passed between them for a moment before Megan turned in her chair.

"What is in there?" she asked, pointing to the bundle he had set on the floor.

Neal gave her a cocksure grin.

"A Christmas goose," he said, his grin widening. "I know it is too late to cook the bird today, but we can feast on it tomorrow. There is a hamper of holiday goodies, too, and gifts from Father Christmas for the children. An atlas, a china doll, although the dress is pink, not silver and gold, and a large velvet dog. I don't think anyone manufactures fur dogs."

Megan furrowed her brow. "What?"

"I will explain later," he said with a chuckle. "There are other things, too, for a special lady." He winked and touched the tip of her nose with his finger. "Incidentally, where are the children?"

"In the parlor."

Megan began to rise, but Neal said, "Wait," and she settled back into the chair.

Neal began to speak fast; his words came in a rush, all running together. "When the girls are old enough we will take them to London for a Season and arrange parties and balls in their honor. Sam shall have the best private tutor we can find to prepare him for university; if after that he still has his heart set on the military, I will buy him colors in the regiment of his choice. Micah can come and live with us, too. The house is wonderful, Megan. I know you will love it. My uncle made all sorts of improvements. I was amazed. I'm rambling," he said, cutting himself off abruptly as he noticed her amused half smile.

"No, Neal. I was just wondering if anyone, anywhere, is as happy as I am this minute."

Neal's fingers caressed her cheeks. "I was such a fool, darling. When I awoke the first morning after I left you, I was astonished to find that I was lonely. I, who had always believed I needed no one. I realized then it was you I missed, and that I loved you with all my heart and never wanted to be alone again."

Megan thought of the link between the kissing ball and the accident. Micah had been right. She and Neal had been destined to love each other. She was convinced that Providence had taken a hand in their lives from that first long-ago kiss beneath the mistletoe to the crash that had brought Neal back to her. But he would laugh at her conviction.

Or so she thought, until he said, "Sweetheart, I don't know what happened the day of the accident, nor do I plan to examine any of it too closely. But Micah had this crazy notion that a divine force had brought us together. Angels? I don't know. Let's just say, though, that I have come to believe that such miracles are indeed possible, and I will be well pleased to tell Micah so."

ROMANCE FROM JO BEVERLY

DANGEROUS JOY   (0-8217-5129-8, $5.99)

FORBIDDEN   (0-8217-4488-7, $4.99)

THE SHATTERED ROSE   (0-8217-5310-X, $5.99)

TEMPTING FORTUNE   (0-8217-4858-0, $4.99)